EFTIAM LEGACY

A Novel by

Rustyna Lynne

CCB Publishing
British Columbia, Canada

Eftiam Legacy

Copyright ©2022 by Rustyna Lynne
ISBN-13 978-1-77143-533-8
First Edition

Library and Archives Canada Cataloguing in Publication
Lynne, Rustyna, author
Eftiam legacy / by Rustyna Lynne. -- First edition.
Issued in print and electronic formats.
ISBN 978-1-77143-533-8 (pbk.).--ISBN 978-1-77143-534-5 (pdf)
Additional cataloguing data available from Library and Archives Canada

Cover artwork courtesy of Pixabay.

Special Note: This novel contains intentionally misspelled words and uses incorrect grammar to capture the dialect, slang, slurring, etc. of the person(s) speaking.

Order this book online at:
Amazon.com, BarnesandNoble.com, or CCBPublishing.com

Publisher: CCB Publishing
              British Columbia, Canada
              www.ccbpublishing.com

DEDICATION

Pop and Ron—your words came through,
guiding me every step of the way in this endeavor.

Acknowledgements

Elaine, who edits out all my horrible habits and makes my words blend.

Mary L, Ernie, Roberta, Beth, Vanessa, Mickey, Jen, Mike, Cee, Pam; for having the patience to read *Eftiam Legacy* and offering suggestions along the way.

Clarence—my love—for your patience and understanding.

Books by Rustyna Lynne

Women's Fiction:
    Pepper and Salt
    Chemically Insoluble—Sequel

Science Fiction/Fantasy:
    Eftiam Legacy
      Trilogy in progress

Mystery:
    Liquid Gold (LG)

Children's Books:
    Derrick and Sierra Take Baths
    Tatiana's Shampoo
    Janel's Shampoo
    Giovanni's Pedicure
    Bella's Birthday Manicure
    Tyler Brushes His Teeth
    Chad's First Shave
    Another Sign of Chad Maturing
    A Teen's Gift
    *Scruffi Flies the Trees
      *=Soon to be published

Chapter 1

"Commander, you asked me to let you know when we spotted a possible planet," The box squealed.

"Well?" He grumbled with irritably...

"Sir, it is ... no ... sort of has Earth similarities," the box coughed again.

"Are you speaking old or new? The Commander asked, turning from his desk chair while reaching to his bunk for his hat to cover his curly sandy head. As he walked, he smiled to himself; *people have such misconceptions about space travel. Definitely not the comfort one would expect as seen of the Old Star Trek epics, or from short flight sightseeing tours around Earth; more like an old naval submarine or battleship in comparison but getting much better.*

"Sir?"

"Be right there First, you know the procedure."

"Yes Sir."

Rising from the chair, the gravity loss made him move as if on the ocean floor but without the weight of dive gear. Gravity shoes kept him from free floating, lifting one foot slowly after the other. He maneuvered the walkway awkwardly, with his broad six two good muscular frame; this added a more visual awkwardness of movement. Glad no one was offering salutes; Neil's thoughts were vexed on the six planets in this present galaxy and wondering which might be habitable. It seemed even stranger that alien had not attempted contact. Alien ships were seen on screen but were apparently not curious enough to even signal. This bothered him more than he let on. Entering the navigation center, 'Attention,' was broadcast across the bridge, and the crew jumped to their feet as gravity allowed.

"Ensign, I told you that isn't necessary here," the commander scowled head-on into his face.

"Sorry Sir, hard to break habits."

"We've been out here three years now, so BREAK'EM!"

"Yes Sir!"

"At ease;" he spoke without turning from First … *Idiot* … "Now, which world seems habitable for our people?" The Commander asked.

"This one Sir." Leaning out around the Commander Ensign pointed to the very last planet of the six on screen, which took up one full wall.

Slowly turning away from the Ensign, now sweating visibly, he nevertheless, enjoyed the spatial roominess of the nav center, where all central functions took place. Wireless comdat (computer) systems seemed to be everywhere. Truly, this was a new age, with the smallest of microfibers allowing such intricate yet invisible linkage of systems. Yes, he was fortunate to command a new age ship and he held his chest out letting all know he was proud which assured his crew, they too could do the same.

"Close in projectile," As it came up to a full view singling out the planet, "Ah… seems to be a color distortion." The Commander voiced.

"No sir, no distortion." Number one expressed.

"Purple? It's fuck'n purple?"

"Yes Sir, three different shades." Sendra offered giggling.

Logistics?" As he listened carefully, he could not help displaying a huge smile. Now chuckling, "Better set a course for this new world. HQ will not believe its color. Take pictures, although we'll wait awhile before we relate the full skinny on her."

◇

The small monitor flashed, showing a mature grey-haired man with the same blue uniform as Neil, but with extra bars on his red collar, "Neil, how're you?"

"Fine Wayne, I think we finally found one." He hated these conversations taking three fourths of his day due to relay lapse. Most of the time the TV-aped it and sent it without the long delay intervals of speech. At least he could do other things in his cubby as the relay transmission flashed on and off.

"Wonderful; beginning to think we wouldn't reap another find. "It's been almost three years. Haven't gone stir crazy yet?" Admiral Berry asked with concern.

"This new encounter will keep us occupied," hoping his voice didn't reveal his desperation to jump ship. Gathering more data and setting a course as we speak. You should be getting the data soon. We are a light year away from the planet. Say hello to everyone for us, over and out."

"I'll be in quarters, please notify me of any changes." *We could not relay in a day's time five years ago. Technology changes so fast. We should have enough food and fuel to sustain us before we must double back to Sigmet* (planet-Earth inhabited) *supply ships for foods and fuel. Not sure just how far back we will have to go to meet up.*

He set to work on the newest information the crew gathered on this planet and checked with Bré' for any overlooked areas.

<>

Feelings were electric within the ship as they entered this atmosphere of the new planet, enough for warriors to feed off for months. "Commander, a closer visual," Sendra's voice squawked from the box. *They sure can't seem to fix the squawkers!*

"Bré, any animal habitation?"

"Many species of birds, animals and other wild life, Neil," Bré responded.

"Human or Alien present, Bre'?"

"There are remains of an old decayed structure on the surface. Breathable oxygen, plants are edible and may have further value. Would you like that analysis?"

Ignoring Bré, Neil pondered aloud, "More likely they live underground or if above, it's unreadable due to protective shielding materials. The habitation is closely relative to ours." Staring at the monitor, "Whoa..., the discrepancy is strange... she sure is purple; this'll take some getting used to." *Took care of my worries about food, but fuel may be another story.*

Sendra, butted in, "A definite lavender, lilac and royal purple seem its planetary colors, Sir." He could picture a smirk from her. *I forgot to turn off the box.* As he turned off the box, "You say its breathable air, Bré?"

"Yes Neil."

"But if the air is quality, wouldn't they be above ground, Sir?" First queried, stepping into Neil's quarters...

3

"That depends on species adaptability. Make ready to deploy a search party of five, Number one. Take scoutbot (smaller spacecraft) two-away."

"Yes Sir." First turned and left.

"Bré, thanks for not going into a long description."

"You are welcome. I placed it into my memory banks; you do not like long drawn-out description, just facts, Neil."

"What would I do without you, Bré?"

"You could not, Neil."

She's getting smarter it seems. "Also keep the crew notified of the temps."

Chapter 2

Tears flowed without warning, as sudden passion overcame Efiar (daughter of Eftiar, Guide to be of Eftiam; thoughts of young years seemed long past; her brow furrowed as she pictured this sioutous (spaceship) from Earth soon entering Eftiam (planet) atmosphere. *Eftiar will set his ites* (people) *for battle. A perfect race? The Imo Macos* (passed advising images) *have not led us to believe otherwise.* Unconsciously she increased her pace. *Most Junis'* (working class) *would not land fuai* (float) *run on the ground, as they hate it, preferring to fuai despite the slower pace of floating. But Linti never complains. Only period of the dai* (day) *except for apt* (sleep), *is peace of niet* (mind). Efiar's long limbs, rare in her culture moved her ahead of Linti; a catlike expression appearing only seconds before the furrow replaced itself. *Could they adjust to life with us?* The pu (jungle) beauty of the foliage overtook her once again as she sped faster taking in the depth of color lu (lavender) to lae (lilac), then to li (pale lavender). The rushing sound of the waves told her upu (ocean) was around the next bend. Anticipation rose, with the suddenness of the view halting her as a rider who nearly dives headfirst over the saddle with the abrupt stopping of the horse. Taking in the breathless view of the lu coloring of the upu, became lae (lilac) as it cascaded over the rocks, then toward the heavens, she briefly felt the inner peace that she constantly sought. *Ah yes! Truly, Eftiam is more beautiful than any other.*

Linti slowed his pace, breathlessly arriving at her side. "Thank you for stopping so I could catch up."

Laughing, *"Linti, you usually stride with me, what happened this dai?"*

Wiping perspiration from his eyes, his upu jump suit showing salt spots, "Efiar, I am your Juni and love my job, but not this part of it."

"Really? I ... this is the only tia (time) *I have any peace and so love the pu* (jungle) *and to smell the salt of the upu* (ocean). *You really need to take some time to enjoy the beauty."* Pouting dramatically, *"I thought you enjoyed our jaunts."*

Linti did not respond instead he glanced at his tia (time) wrist bracelet grateful it was near tia (time) for them to return. Slowly they started to land fuai (run) along the lu (lavender) shore this time keeping a slower pace, taking in the expanse of the upu (ocean). Suddenly a niet avi (telepathic speech), inside her head came from Eftiar (Guide of Eftiam-Father), *"I need you Efiar! New information about these Earth ites! Why do you insist on this improper action from centuries ago?"*

"Please Eftiar, not now, not yet..."

"It must be now. We will discuss this further on your arrival at our table. Linti get her back here now!" he avid (telepathed) to both.

Rounding the bend to the hovering siout (small land craft), where they left it, "It is most likely about the Earth ites. If they realize our air is as theirs once was, we will probably do battle." Linti said.

"Do you think it will come to that?" Feeling her inner peace dissipate into the foliage of the pu (jungle).

"Only Eftiar can give those answers. I pray the Imo Macos (passed guides) give him guidance to get us through this horrible unsettling. They say there is weaponry aboard this sioutous (spaceship)."

"Weaponry? You are mistaken. They are peaceful ites."

Linti, bending grasping his knees as he gasps for air, cocks his head to the side taking in Efiar, "My Efiar, you should know of this more than I. I do not have access to the havis sig (meditation center)."

Barely showing the heavier breathing from their land fuai run, moving to board the siout, Efiar's hands flippantly waved air bound, making her arms abstract ribbons of distortion, *"This is such a joke against our weapons, I pass this into nothingness. Surely, they would not be senseless. Let us go."*

<>

She chose to land fuai (walk), not giving thought to anything or anyone around her. *They may destroy upu (ocean) and air, as they destroyed their own Earth and are now destroying Sigmet. For money and power these ites call it. Eftiar will not allow this to pass.* "Yes, yes, Eftiar, I am returning. I feel you niet avi (telepathically) probing my niet (mind). I will arrive within minis (minutes). " Effectively, she smiled knowing Eftiar was the only one to get through her havis (head gear). *Soon it will be tia (time) to ef* (mate). *Only my true ef can penetrate my havis, besides Eftiar. If not ... he must choose for me.* "*I do not understand why you choose to land fuai* (walk) *when fuai* (float) *is much faster and simpler.*"

"*Sometimes I choose not to forget how we began. It enhances my niet* (mind) *strength, Eftiar. Now may I have some peace until I present myself before you?*" She noticed a new Juni (worker). *He is different, his lu* (lavender) *is somewhat deeper, is taller, and more handsome. Eyes are the same as Eftiar's, hmmm, most odd.* "*Eftiar is that you?*" Silence: looking around, it was only she and the Juni. *Did he just smirk? No, he cannot get through my havis* (head gear). *Can he?* Shrugging her shoulders, she dismissed the interruption entering her privacy sig, her personal dome.

<>

Attired in her new upudo (dress), which enhanced her slim slight figure with just the right tones of la (royal purple) and lae (lilac) in just the right areas, she entered the breakfast area. The table was long, clear, and narrow, complimented by twelve tall clear chairs whose backs curved away. Leafy hanging plants from the pu dripped thickly from the dome, in clear artistically flared holders of multiple shapes with varied lighting for accent "*Where is Efiari* (brother-Guide to be)?" Standing before her Eftiar (father), reaching out she gave him her affectionate morn simi (morning kiss).

A huge smile replaced his tired expression as he admired his Efiar (daughter), "*Efiar that is a fine upudo* (dress), *so like your Eftiara* (mother) *wore, when we first met. Efiari will not be joining us this morn* (morning).*"

"*Thank you, for the gift, Eftiar, I love it.*" Eftiar, Efiari and their Juni Linti were her family. In her maturing years, she overheard avis (talk) of her Eftiara, being lae (lilac) not lu (lavender). This she wondered about for Eftiar would only allow efing (mating) with the same coloring; never discussed just accepted. The only avis overheard now from Eftiar were how beautiful she was with those li (pale Lavender) eyes like her Eftiara and every upudo as beautiful as she had worn.

Eftiar was worrying about Efiar, asking many questions of late. *So beautiful ... Yes, I must prepare for the change to come.* "*The Earth ites will* soon enter our atmosphere. After breakfast let us go into the main havis sig (room to speak with Imo Macos)," Alarm showed on Efiar's face, *"But first let us enjoy our meal."*

◇

Shaken, having been unable to get food down, she fuaid close behind Eftiar into the corridor. She noticed the new Juni again, *His coloring is definitely lae* (lilac); *odd most Junis' are la* (royal purple). Arriving at his main havis sig, Eftiar pressed domed buttons, necessary checking for avi (telepathy) neutrality. When satisfied, entering the doorway he asked, *"Really, why must you land fuai* (walk) *beyond your home?"*

Calmer a *lilt funa* (giggle), *"I enjoy the countryside; it brings peace of niet* (mind), *as you do here. I do as you and the Junis request. I really do not understand why you are worried. Our ites* (people) *are peaceful and would not harm one another."* Entering ... *oh my, this place is more than just for peace of niet.*

Eftiar must speak with the Imo Macos from here. The walls are covered with so many different sensors. Look at those massive compus (computers), *and oh ... this is the main havis I have heard so much about ...* turning in circle, suddenly embarrassed, realizing that she had avid all to Eftiar.

Eftiar liked what he saw within his Efiar. *Astute comprehension in only a few sentences; this child realized more than she has been told. Yes, the Imo Macos are right; she will make a great Eftiara* (Guide). *I must help her control aving* (telepathy). *"Yes this is a primary methos-sig* (meditation center) *with the Imo Macos* (Image Makers). *This will be the place of your learning."*

"Eftiar, why are you not making Efiari the one to take your place? After all he is first born."

"It is written my first-born will not be strong in niet avi (mind messaging) *apable for guiding."* Regret showed as he fuaid to the machines, working the different computations making lights dance rapidly along the many compus (computer) walls. *"I had so much hope, but you know Efiari cares nothing of such matters only of his wants and needs."*

"You have not given him a chance."

"Efiari has been to this sig many tias (times) *so I could make sure who should guide. Aspid tia* (Death time)*, is approaching and now you must start your lessons, the Imo Macos have requested this.*

"Oh? Eftiar, are you ill?" rushing to him, her avi (teleport wave) communicating her worry. It was not often the Imo Macos called upon them to do their bidding, usually they chose liaison, and his speaking of the death sleep heightened her concern.

He took her into his arms, *"No Efiar,"* He gave her a comfort hug, *"Now we will begin the process."* somberly releasing his embrace, *"Please remove your havis* (head gear) *and lie on this lounge."*

The lounge was clear and curved somewhat replicating the chairs of the dining sig. Efiar did as she was avid. *"You are now going to niet apt* (mind sleep)*."* Lovingly he reached down with an Imo Maco spirit crystal touching it to her forehead. The crystal did not seem to feel hot or cold, but a simmering glow seemed to come from the crystal as her body felt increasingly haloed in light.

<>

"Efiar, it is time for you to wake," Efiari avid, *"Come arise."*

"Where is Eftiar?" Slowly coming to terms, aware she was in her sig (room), lying in her sig- bed. Rising with difficulty to a sitting position, she felt terribly ill to her stomach. *"I feel horrible."*

"Should I send for a Juni? You have had a long apt (sleep) *since yesterday afternoon. I was beginning to think you would never wake."*

"Passé dai (passed day)*? Efiari, I was with Eft ...* Dart fuaing to the projectile sig, Efiar rid her stomach…

Hearing her regurgitate, fearing he may do the same, he hurriedly began to fuai (float) back and forth, showing more than casual interest to her problem. *"Really? Did you happen to go into the havis sig* (main center)*?"*

Wiping her mouth as she fuaid (floated) into the doorway … *Should this be known to my Efiari?* Something in the way he avid her, *"Nooo, should I have been?"* Eyes to the floor, Efiar fibbed for the first time in her life.

No, no it's just Eftiar apts (sleeps) *for long periods after he has been in the main havis sig,"* without revealing he had been in there himself?"

Still hovering in the archway, she stared, his query made her fuai (float) dart left, *"Eftiar, told me you had, why have you lied to me? I cannot believe you just lied to me! Efiari, have you been in that sig?"*

Efiari's face revealed noticeable shock, *"Ah, I was told not to tell anyone, not even you."*

"Oh? Well ... I'm sorry for doubting you, but why would Eftiar tell you to keep this from me?"

"Eftiar has his reasons for a lot of things I do not understand. When he is aspid (dead), *then I shall no doubt rule. Maybe he wants me to learn to keep secrets to be a better ruler,"* fuaing (floating) back and forth with his arms akimbo and nose in the air.

"Ah...h... have you discussed this with Eftiar?" fuai moving close to Efiari,

*"And I think it is to **guide** the ites* (people) *not rule."*

Fidgeting in flight, his bulk overpowering this extra small sig (room) with so much pu (jungle) foliage hanging everywhere, like the basin floor of the upu (ocean), *"Yes, yes, but you know Eftiar gives no answer, but it is my right, you know. I am first born!"*

"You make sure to remind me every tré minis (three minutes),*"* aving (teleporting) with her milk meow grin. *It is his birthright. So proudly he prances around my sig* (room) *in his swaggering fuai and **yikes** ...* watching in horror unable to fuai ... *he almost knocked down my new Simona lamp that took eons to find in the upu* (ocean). *Why are you doing this to us Eftiar? Why did I not tell Efiari I was in the main havis sig? The last thing I remember... oh yes, he placed the Imo crystal to my forehead. Is this what makes me doubt? I feel sick again and now my head hurts ...* Grabbing her head, feeling as if it were in a vice, slowly she fuaid (floated) to her bed, as if upu fuaing (swim ocean) in the upu. Sinking down drawing herself into a fetal position, she felt herself again in pain.

"Efiar, are you OK?" Efiari avid into her thoughts.

"I don't feel well; you best call a Juni," Focusing, briefly, she again allowed her bed to enwrap her.

Without hesitation Efiari fuaid quickly to the door and summoned a Juni, who checked Efiar quickly and left. Efiari backed away, *"Do you think you have something catching?"*

Sometimes he is such a child, "*You know there are no communicable diseases in our city. I guess I just did too much land fuaing yesterday."*

"When are you going to learn you should only fuai? I believe that is what is ailing you. Land fuai as our ancestors did, no longer exists in our genes.

"Doesn't exist? I have been doing it for trias (years) *and Junis do not fuai do they? Sometimes you do not give thought to anything Efiari."* Now desperately wishing he would remove himself.

With a smug knowing look, *"Well now that you know about the main-Havis sig* (main head gear center) *that is precisely where I acquired this tidbit of information.*

"Really?" Succumbing to her curiosity; but they were interrupted by a Juni entering with a drink of herbs prepared for her symptoms.

"I will depart and let you rest, please avi (teleport) *me and I will come upon your awakening. After all you are my favorite Efiar."* The Juni made way for Efiari, as he fuaid (floated) to her, leaning in his upudo (dress) cascaded over her body, as he simid (kissed) her forehead ever so lightly.

"I'm the only one you have. No, do not go. Did we do this in the outer city as I do now? The Junis have to do it; they can't fuai (float)*, can they?"*

Oooooooooh-oh my head... What tia (time) *is it? I feel wonderful, that herb really worked.* Going into the upu sig (bathroom), she realized it was bright of early morn (morning).

<>

Fuaing (floating) to the din-sig (dining room), she checked for the handsome Juni, to no avail. She acknowledged the kaleidoscopic glow of the dai (day) in various colors of lu (lavender) horizon. Entering this large room, with the long table of clear glass, with candles lit for atmosphere with a special scent of morn dew and pu (jungle) of li (pale lavender) throughout the sig (room) was all that was needed to make it

11

the most special of their sigs. *"Good morn Eftiar, Efiari; is it not a gorgeous morn?"*

"Good morn Efiar, did you sleep well these tré dais (three days)*?"* Eftiar inquired, as she approached to give his ritual simi (kiss)…

Efiar jolted in mid space equalizing what her Eftiar had just avid, *"What? I-I apt tré dais* (slept three days)*?"*

"You sure did!" Efiari broke in, biting an apple. *"I thought you would never wake, but Eftiar said all was well, you needed rest."* Efiari eyed both suspiciously.

"I do not believe it. I was not feeling miserable enough for the Juni to give me a heavy dose for tré dais (three days). *Must find out which Juni did that."*

"Well apparently, the Juni felt you needed it," Eftiar avid.

"Did the Juni say what was wrong with you Efiar?" Efiari avid.

"You were there, neither of us avi queried. Besides Efiari dear, why would I need to find out which Juni it was?" daring him with a smiling glare.

Efiari wisely returned to his food, *"Eftiar, what of this sioutous?"*

"It is light-trias (years) *away and heading for us…*

"What do you plan to do, Eftiar?"

Setting down his utensil, for full affirmation, *"We will be going into the main havis sig to meet with the Imo Macos after breakfast."* Both teenagers showed surprise …

"But surely Efiar has not the capacity."

"It is the wishes of the Imo Macos. I wish your Eftiara (mother) *was physically present."* Eftiar avid.

"But she is always aspid (dead)*,"* Efiari unaware of the effect that his avi made on Eftiar. *"Are we to meet with these Earth ites?"*

Eftiar smiling at Efiar's reflection, *"Thank you for the reminder. Since you both seem to have lost appetite, shall we go?"*

Fuaing to the havis sig … *Oh, there is that Juni again. Funny he is here in this area not where I saw him yesterday.*

"What is this about a new Juni?"

"There across the hall, I saw him –ah before—returning from my land fuai and I could have sworn he tried to avi me. I keep forgetting you are the only one who gets through my havis (head gear)*, Eftiar."*

12

"He is quite lae (lilac) *with lu* (lavender) *for a Juni. However, I am worried someone may have tampered with your havis. I will have Linti check into this matter, immediately."* he turned resuming fuai, but Efiar suddenly hovered, showing surprised shock, eyeing every area including the rooftop of the domed hall sig (tunnel).

"What is it Efiar?"

"I-I-ah just heard your avi message to Linti? I-I- have never been able to niet (mind) *that before."* Eftiar understanding, softened, and smiling without replying, proceeded onward.

"Efiar what is wrong with you? Are you coming?" Efiari butted in. Again, he radiated concern, *"Efiar, are you sure you are all right?*

"Ah-oh yes, forgive me I must be having problems from too much land fuaing yesterday... I- mean ... oh I am so perplexed."

"No dear, tré dais (three days) *ago not a passé dai* (past dai)," Efiari-affirmed waiting for her to come alongside.

"Eftiar you must give some explanation for all this."

"Yes Efiar, just be a little more patient."

"Efiari does not realize we are aving (telepathing) *and he cannot connect? Does this have to do with my niet apt* (mind sleep)?"

"Correct." Entering the main havis sig, aving to both, *"Here we are at last, this most special dai, meeting the Imo Macos. They are wonderful ites; you will enjoy this meeting of the niets* (minds)."

"You have changed the sig (room); *it now has tré havis' with lounges.*

"Excuse me Eftiar, but the Imo Macos are spirits not ites (people), *right?"* Efiari conveyed with question.

"Yes, since I have been the only avi (speaker), *no other lounges were required until now. You have spoken with the Imo's many tias; do you not feel a literal world sense like yourself?"*

"No, cannot avi that I have. Then why is Efiar here?"

Eftiar ignored this in an absent non- reflective manner. Removing his havis, he lay on his lounge allowing it to enwrap his body, placed the wired havis extending from the ceiling upon his head, *"Be patient; you will get all the information you require. Please lay here Efiari and you Efiar to my right, remove your havis'."* Both pre-adults looked upon the other before taking their positions beside their Eftiar, anticipating their new experience ...*"Hold my hands, close your eyes, the rest will come through my Imo crystal."*

No sooner had he avid than his crystal glowed with the color of lae (lilac) then to a soft li (pale lavender).

Efiar could see the beautiful colors through her closed lids. Beautiful Colors of her Eftiam enfolded filling her until she was one with the crystal. *This is so peaceful, so beautiful; the Imo Macos must be just as beautiful.* The crystal formed an imo (image) within the lae coloring for her to see.

"Hello Efiar," The imo (image) avid, closing in, becoming clear,

"Who are ... Eftiara (mother)?"

"Yes Efiar, it is I your Eftiara. I am here to help guide with the Imo Macos. There is much for you to learn. This may make you ill again. We are condensing lessons to you."

"Eftiar is not sharing to make clear avis (answers), *such as why not Efiari?"*

"You are the stronger for niet avi. Efiari will help with reservation at first. Already he realizes you are the te (one) *to pass the word on from the Imo Macos.* Efiar could see the colors through her closed lids first, *"I want you to relax; we will avi many tias more."*

"Eftiara?"

"Yes?"

"I am glad to finally pleasure meeting you. You are beautiful!" Efiar felt tears that could not flow.

"I have watched you for many trias (years). *You have grown into a beautiful woman. We will touch in spiritual sense, but now my imo must leave you for a while. I love you,"* Slowly fading into the lae (lilac). Efiar felt a child's need to reach out to be held in Eftiaras arms. It did not come.

The tré (three) of them spent fiftn hors (fifteen hors) with the Imo Macos (Image Makers) filling them individually and as a unit until the apt tia (sleep time) of Eftiam ites.

◇

In her apt (sleep) slide show of many imos (images) seemed to rush up, and then break as if sliding down a wall of rocks. Fiftn dais (fifteen days) later Efiar was finally able to arise without the help of Junis submerging her into the deep upu life- pool to keep her alive and to help her purge.

Moving slowly into the upu sig to relieve herself and dive into the life pool, she glanced into an imo reflector (mirror), *"OH MY IMO! MY HAIR! WHY? A BLAND* (white) *STREAK!"*

Almost immediately, Eftiar and Efiari were by her side. Looking at them, *"YOU TOO, EFIARI? I AM TOO YOUNG!"* With their stares, she realized she was not in a upudo; grabbing a sheet from the ring she desperately covered herself as a fif-tria (five year) old may do when first aware of body changes, and most clumsy with the effort of hiding oneself. *"GET OUT... AH; ah ... wait in my bed sig...oh please?"*

"Efiar sure keeps the look of the pu (jungle) *in this sig just as the roaming place out there, don't you agree?"* Eftiar avid, easing the uncomfortable situation as they glided into her bed sig.

"She has grown into a beautiful woman Eftiar." Recalling, smiling boldly and then giggling, as he played with the pu foliage, *"I had not realized, I guess I can only look at her as my little Efiar."*

Eftiar had his back to his son, but his smile was huge as he was niet aving (minding) on his Efiar. *"Nor I until now; she is most like Eftiara you know,"* allowing his private niet of her to dazzle him again. Of course, Efiari couldn't help but mimic his Eftiar at the mention of Eftiara.

"Is...is it time for her to ef, Eftiar?" Inquiring with a serious note, again playing with one of her lae (lilac) pu plants.

"I do believe it is close. I must start aving for a suitor."

Abruptly turning and fuaing up and down in the air as jumping, his upudo trying to catch up, allowing the first child syndrome to show, *"She's younger than I! Should I not be the te* (one) *to ef* (mate) *first?"*

"Efiari, you know our female ites mature before the males of Eftiam. This has not changed for many trilis (centuries). *It will be tré trias* (three years) *yet for you and from what we envisioned; she is readying within these next tix mons* (six months)."

"Maybe this explains why she's been so frustrating to get along with and why she insists on doing so much land fuaing (land walking). *It is her hormones playing a game, don't you agree?"*

15

Almost a chuckle, *"I am not sure, Efiari; I will be sure to imo (image) Eftiara; she will know how to advise us our dilemma."*

"Do not worry Eftiar; I will help to find an ef for her," his chest bulging with pride in anticipation of this task.

Now laughing heartily, very out of character, *"Help, I can use. Do you have a suitor in grasp?"*

"No, I will start this project immediately," beaming with accomplishment the tio (two) men crossed the room, meeting and shook on it eagerly.

Entering from the upu sig, Efiar hovering, eyes to the floor, aving shyly, *"Th ... thans for waiting."*

"You look wonderful in your upudo, is it new?" Eftiar cheerily asked trying to ease her discomfort.

"No, I have not worn this upudo in a very long while but seemed most appropriate with this!" pointing to her hair arrangement as if it was the most freakish ever adorned, as droplets ran down her cheeks.

"It is most becoming on you. And Efiari looks most handsome, as I once did," Eftiar avid honestly.

"Yes, I do, do not I?" Efiari's nose placed higher than usual. Boisterous funa (laughter) rang throughout the city sigs.

"You are distinguished with a streak of bland now that I look at you longer, Efiari, but do not you think I am too young for this. No one will want to ef with me now!" The tio (two) men exchanged a knowing look; they were on sketchy upu (water) here. Fuaing from side to side, then circling around Efiar, Eftiar and Efiari, rubbed their chins in a great jesting game. They went for the gusto, as she too got caught up in this playful mood.

"Well? What? What do you think? I need to know!" she now relaxed in their play, turning a circle fuai in place trying to catch sight of their imos' (images).

Playing a min more, Efiari avid first, *"Honestly I never realized until today how you have blossomed into a woman. I best watch with Eftiar and make sure you have a most suitable ef (mate). When we find him, he will see your beauty, how could he not?"*

Her hands swept to her hips, and her head craned ostrich style, her voice now in an unusual tone, *"You find him? Find me he will!"*

quickly fuaing, pushing Efiari almost into a chair, she jolted to the other side of the sig, jostling a lamp which Efiari caught and righted.

Throwing her head back, the blank streak faltered down the side of her face. She pouted, with the lower lip protruding, *"At least the Imo Macos could give us streaks of complete Eftiam coloring.* **Just look!"** Pulling hard enough to make it hurt, a sound of pain emanated, *"My streak is larger than either of yours. How could they do this to me?"*

Eftiar threw his hands into the air, spinning, into a glide, to where she vacillated and trembled, *"My dear, this is their way of making sure our ites know we are to guide, so it must be dramatic."* Cupping her face in his hands he looked directly into her brimming pools, *"You are as beautiful as my Eftiara was with hers,"* emphatically *aving,* he drew close and simid (kissed) her forehead.

"Eftiara had a streak? I did not think she could be a guide for ites,"

Looking up to Eftiar, puzzled.

"You saw your Eftiara; did you not see her streak?"

"I have been too ill to consider any of what we saw. I remember not aving with the Imo Macos yet. Eftiara was most beautiful, she was the first imo I saw, but I did not have tia with he ... r.*"* pondering ... sudden clarity as she looked into Eftiar's face, *"Eftiara did have a streak and it was larger than the one you had when we were young."*

"Eftiara had a streak larger than Eftiar; 'hardly'," Efiari countered. *"That would mean she was head guide and that is impossible."*

"You are wrong Efiari. Your Eftiara was head guide, when she went to join the Imo Macos, then I became head guide for our ites."

To get a clearer picture Efiari glided closer to capture Eftiar's facial expression, *"How? Eftiara was shading of tio* (two) *colors?"* Efiari boldly confronted, *"You never allow but te* (one) *shade for an ef, so we have been led to believe and tio is not appropriate for a guide."*

Eftiar did not noticeably flinch at the sting he felt from Efiari. *Why does this child think I would try and purposely keep things from him? "I guess you did not get a full understanding from the Imo Macos this last visit. Let me refresh your niets* (minds). *Your Eftiara was the first to guide our ites. Most all were from tio* (two) *shadings, which the Imo*

17

Macos allowed. We are chosen by the Macos; it is not us that do the
choosing."

"Did the Imo Macos choose Eftiara for you?" Efiar gave cautious
avi query.

Suddenly feeling very tired and realizing proximity of Efiar's sig-
bed he fuaid himself onto it. *"I now believe they did without our
knowledge and more. The first time I saw Eftiara we niet avid* (minded)
immediately; the only te (one) *to ever penetrate my havis. Our love still
goes on living through you both. I blamed the Imo Macos for taking her
away physically. Feeling cheated for an exceptionally long tia, I
refused to do their bidding. Therefore, I suffered the consequences for it
all by..."* refusing to precede, his head hung perhaps in regret,
apparently unwilling to divulge more. Still in a sitting position he fuaid
from the sig without acknowledging his children.

Staring after their Eftiar, the tio (two) felt even more puzzled.

*The Imo Macos choose efs or do we choose? Always the same shade of
guides. Their Eftiara, the first, Guide of tio shades? How much do we rely on
the Imo Macos'?* Efiar did not notice Efiari's departure, nor did she care.

<>

Efiar hibernated for (four) more dais (days), taking nibbles of food now
and then, digesting all that was projected to her in the main- havis -sig.
The stress was hard on her body and she found upuing (ocean
swimming) and apting (sleeping) her best medicine; dreams gave way
to her lesson's tix dais (six days) ago, with the Imo Macos. She wore
the new bland (white) and lae upudo (lilac dress) Eftiar had left for her
and giving her tia (time) alone to niet avi (meditate); *with this new
upudo, he is trying to make me comfortable when first seen with my streak.*
Niet avi meditating with Eftiara became a morn ritual that helped her
better understand her upcoming role as leader, aided by Eftiar, Efiari
and the Imo Macos. *I love being able to niet avi with Eftiara when I like.
Why not when I was young?* She knew the answer, but liked hearing
herself sort it through, wondering if the Imo Macos could consider her
thoughts for future guides. Taking extra patience with her coif; *why did
they take Eftiara away so young? Eftiara says it is written. Who writes our
lives? Imo Macos?* She fuaid into the sig corridor, keeping her eyes on

her destination with her head held high. Peripherally she saw Junis stop and gasp in acknowledgment of her bland streak. *I feel nervous, oh, Eftiara help me. I need you more than ever.* Entering the din- sig, she shakily grabbed a plate from the buffet, *"Good morn Efiari, is Eftiar coming for breakfast?"*

"He is apting still."

"Have you noticed how Eftiara and I are more la (royal purple) *and you and Eftiar are more lu* (lavender)*? Like the lu of some Junis. Do you think there is some correlation? Why do I apt so after being in the main- havis- sig? Should I feel different, I do not."* Turning in fuai, she glided to sit with Efiari.

"Speaking of apting so long after being in the main- havis- sig, I think dear Efiar that you chose to lie to me about it, like pretending to be ill."

Boldly he stared across to her in a confrontation. Understandably she had pricked him hard.

Breaking off, she sheathed her claws, *"I am sorry, Efiari. You know I never did before, but you chose to tell me a lie first. Therefore, I felt compelled to keep something from you, but I promise to never lie to you again and I hope you will never lie to me again either."*

"I too am sorry, but I did not know how to approach the subject properly. It would not be wise for us to lie to the other. After all we are to rule together."

Caution made Efiar carefully skirt this issue, *"We are to **guide** our ites not rule them, are we not?"* Efiar felt the dart of Efiari's belligerent feelings; being protectively gentle she changed the subject, *"Eftiara was so beautiful and I so enjoyed aving with her before getting lesson from the Imo Macos.*

"I have never seen her, but maybe I am schooled more on political matters," aving as he resumed his fruit.

"You will see her. You know we are not to question the Imo Macos. Did they tell you we are to guide together?"

"Sort of, ah ... you are to sit above me, but you will be fair in asking for my opinion on decisions," He looked sorrowful, slumping into the back of his chair allowing it to protectively enfold, completely.

"You are the elder. You already know my impressions. I feel we are here to guide them together, as we have always avid doing." You so want to be the head guide ... maybe in tia.

"Doubtful! It was made clear you and your off springs will do head guiding not me and mine. Fact of the matter is we do not have the same Eftiara, so..."

Shock overtook her, as she screeched her chair slamming it into the sig wall, but the wall absorbed the blow without denting, bouncing her and the chair back to the table... suddenly she fuai rose up now pacing back and forth, at the same tia keeping eye contact with him, *"What are you aving about? Of course, we have the same Eftiara!"*

As he watched her, he was the first to remove his eyes from hers while turning back to his plate, *"No, apparently that was a separate lesson. I found out this last meeting, but I will be able to help as we share the same blood of Eftiar; our Eftiaras' aspid the same tia."*

"But Eftiar has led us to believe we had the same Eftiara. Why? Is that what caused him to stop telling us of tia long past?"

"I guess, to hide the truth." examining closely a new piece of fruit, *"I think I am what the Earthlings refer to as a bastard child."*

"Efiari, you certainly are not! You are no such thing and you know Eftiar feels nothing of the sort. Ah...But...how did I know what the word bastard meant?" Efiar hovered, hesitated, hands to her hips; now sitting again; *"Eftiar has a lot of explaining to do. He's apting much too long. How long did you apt after our tia in the main- havis -sig?"*

He did not face her, *"Te dai* (one day). *Eftiar is not apting you know. He is avoiding giving answers. You are getting condensed lessons, that is why you apt longer. Just how many tias have you been in the main-havis- sig?"*

"Only the tia you tried un-apting me and I got ill, no thanks to you," spouting her avi in Efiar fashion. *"How many tias have you been?"*

"Oh, maybe fifth (fifty).*"*

"REALLY?"

"Naw, just tré (three)*,"* Efiari Funaing (laughing), *"I am glad we have this tia together.*

"Likewise," Giggling, she leaned over and simid (kissed) her Efiari's forehead. *"Tell me, what do you think of these Earth ites?"*

20

"They call themselves ites (people) *of Earth or Earthlings. They believe in waging battle war, therefore coming close to Eftiam is too close."*

"Do you not wonder about their niets (minds)*?"*

"No, it's quite primitive. For instance, they use their eating cavity to avi."

"True, but they refer to it as speaking. Also, they get to choose their own ef and some of them seem to have many efs even when properly ef'd."

"Efiar, how do you know this?"

Realizing she had spill avid this without thinking, *"Well, I- I guess in my lessons. I find them fascinating. If they are primitive, then how did they get so close to our Eftiam? Oh, and some Earthlings started as we in upu* (ocean)*, but do not continue in it as we do."*

"Efiar, do you think we are both the same specie?"

"I cannot give you an answer to that, but I want to find out, do you?"

"Together we can help Eftiar with this heavy burden. I care not to wait tré (three) *more lessons, we must tell each other everything we remember!*

Food was forgotten.

Chapter 3

Twenty-four hours later, listening to the back thrusters give their last burp, "One thing can be said for the advancement of com-tech (computer-science), we don't have to get nervous about landing and taking off anymore," Commander Gavens commented to no one in particular. "Bré, you achieved one beautiful landing per usual."

"Thank you, Commander Gavens. Shall I open the hatch for you?"

"Thanks, Bré, not at present. Crew: please run another diagnostic of the surrounding area before we choose to venture outdoors."

<>

"Commander, the away team, found something interesting."

"Bring it up on screen," As Neil still paced the com deck; the screen came alive. Looking but still pacing, "What is it?"

"Sir, there seems to have been a small craft here recently. Isn't as big as ours and left no landing marks."

"Then how do you know it was a craft?" Stopping he seated himself, with full attention to the screen.

Sir, judging from the ripples in the sand it hovered the entire time, pushing back sand and loose debris but not extensively, and there are also shoe prints appearing to be human. We have extracted every kind of sample from this area, and molds of craft emission and shoe prints. We're returning over and out." The screen went gray. *I knew there was life here, that inner feeling along with my weird dreams, hopefully friendly. The warriors are too intent on battle. Wonder what these folks look like?*

Chapter 4

"**S**hall we prepare for battle Eftiar?" Linti quizzing and closely watching the body language of his guides reply.

"Not at the min (minute). *Please be within mini* (minutes) *of readiness. The Imo Macos have allowed them to land. We must abide by their wishes. Presently, the Earth-Ites do not realize we exist."* Eftiar removed his havis (head gear), *"Efiar and Efiari are on their way now. We will spend tia niet aving* (time telepathing) *with the Imo Macos."* Making no verbal reply Linti bowed his head in honor as he backed away; the children arrived.

"I do not understand why the Imo Macos would allow this to happen?"

Efiar avi announced.

"Nor I, but they are here and we must deal with it; we best ripen ourselves on the approach we want to take," Efiari suggested as he took his chaise.

"Agreed; they automatically expect us to use mouth aving (communicating), *this will be through Linti. He is on mini* (minutes) *alert. We know why they are here, but we must go through formalities.*

"Eftiar, how long do you think it will take them to realize we live in the upu?" Efiar avid, fuaing back and forth while surveying the upu above the sig.

"No more than a dai and they will be shown into the main-community-sig, for query. Our objective is to keep them from staying on Eftiam. These ites sent out a landing party, checking plants, the atmosphere, etc., etc., and now are setting temporary habitat before trying to find other ites. Therefore, we should keep our sigs covered, especially the main- havis-sig." While aving to his children, he sent the order to keep the city covered.

"Watching them come under the upu (ocean) *will be most interesting."* Efiari avid, *"I get the feeling we are under a test from the Imo Macos. For too long we have not had anything to interfere with*

our world, not since our Eftiaras' were taken from us." He watched to see if Eftiar reacted; he did not.

"Do not underestimate them. You seem to forget the progress they have made. Never think you are more powerful than your opponent," Eftiar pronounced.

"Some of their ites are also niets (telepathy). *To what degree is more a wonder, after all they speak with their eating cavity. I'm sure they brought some with them. This may be a problem for us. I am unable to niet with Eftiara since they entered our atmosphere. Have you Eftiar?"* Efiar quarried.

"No, only the Imo Macos can give and there has been absolutely no discussion process. I am very disturbed. A plan we; will actually need to lie."

Chapter 5

The entire crew exhausted after the changes in atmosphere from Earth/Sigmet similarities and now working to acclimate after the landing, made ready a survey station on 'Purple,' now planet designation for obvious reason. After taking samples, now awaiting analysis they now had time to enjoy this strange land of purple water, trees, and plants. Birds and other animal life were abundant looking very similar to Earth except for the different hues and combinations and of purple. All wondered if they too would become purple color after ingesting the food and water. Yes, some were exhausted so sleep came quickly.

In quarters, "Well Bré do you still believe there is life on this planet besides vegetation?"

"Yes, Neil."

"Affirmation?"

"They have been trying to probe my brain, Neil."

Neil jumped to his feet, pacing while deep in thought, "For how long?"

"Exactly one light year from this planet, Neil." *As in my dreams...*

"I take it the probe has not been able to get through or you would have advised myself or First. Is there something I need to do to help your brain after –ah-this probing?"

"No Neil, thank you for asking."

"Any indication as to where the people of this planet are located?"

"The probe comes from a large body of water, 8,000 yards from our ship, so naturally this is their habitat." *Yes, the water.*

"Thank you Bré. Make sure this information goes out promptly. Ah-Bré can you give me some idea as to the looks of these people we're about to encounter?"

"No Neil."

<>

"It felt wonderful to be on land, Sir. The animal life we encountered is different shades of purple too," First, reported. "Don't you find it odd how everything is different shades of purple?"

"Yes, the entire crew seems to like the fact they can move about without running into each other. What…"

"Neil, we have a signal from the water."

"Patch through to them Bré."

"They want to speak with you, it is coming by hologram."

No sooner stated than a soft purple haze blinked in front of all on deck. The form was also the color of purple, but a much deeper shade, uniform slightly lighter, more like a dress. A better description is a flower turned upside down. *They look like us except for coloring. Didn't think about it before, but damn, again, as in my dreams.* Neil looked around peripherally to see how his crew reacted. They're fascinated. "Greetings Earthlings, I am Linti, head speaker for the ites of Eftiam. I would like to know your intentions. We offer assistance of service to get you back on your travels."

"He's getting straight to the point. They don't want us to stay." First, remarked. "And how did they know we're from Earth?"

"That is correct." Linti spoke.

"I thought this was a hologram?"

"A upu-gram, technology is advanced; hologram to your video phoning."

Linti stated without further explanation.

"Thank you, Linti," The Commander jumped in face flushed with embarrassment at First's outburst. "I'm Commander Neil Gavens, Earth Ship 'Bramble' and would enjoy council with your leader or leaders, could this be arranged?"

"Commander Gavens, Guide has asked me to acknowledge presence and give assistance for departure. Guide spoke of no meeting; again, I ask how can we expedite your travel?"

"Please tell your Guide, we'd enjoy meeting, say right here this evening tor dinner, say 1900 hours. And we look forward to discussing the vegetation of your beautiful planet."

"Advise I will. Commander Gavens." The upu-gram (water-gram) dissipated. Complete silence falls throughout the deck.

"They definitely don't want us to stay, so this may be somewhat a problem. All here on the com deck; you're not to speak to another of this matter, understood?"

"Yes Sir." The full crew reported back.

"First, join me in my quarters, the rest of you carry on and notify me of the slightest change." Not waiting for a reply, Gavens leading the way.

<>

Neil went straight away to send a message to the Admiral, turning away from the comdat, "It will take some time for us to get a wave from the Admiral; we can have a cup of tea and muddle this over."

"Sir, do you think they'll meet with us?" First queried, sitting in the only chair.

"Not sure, but it's worth a try. Would you want someone to land on Earth or Sigmet, knowing how it would affect them or our planets? Shoot look what we went through to live on Sigmet. Is it right to take a planet away from another when they're born on it? We are supposed to be peaceful, but ... are we? Like, walking in and taking over Sigmet because it didn't suit our ideas? We must put ourselves in the Purples', shoes looking at it perceptively, or at least try; there is much to consider." Handing First his tea, he seated himself on his bunk. Quietly they sipped, contemplating their thoughts.

"If this is the way you evaluate, then most likely we won't find a planet to inhabit, Sir." First, struck, eyeing his Commander. Staring back ... *God, he is just as bad as the rest. He would go in with the troops and take over without thought.* Considering, he could not remember ever taking on another brutally, only when backed into a corner ... when *bringing my defenses forward. Today's young take pleasure in battle. Surmise it is from brain wave pattern change in the twentieth century; the more war like for the taking of planet, they kill each other off at the slightest thing, just because it's wanted.*

Smiling catlike, "Well now, the last I looked I still carry more bars on the collar, so it won't be done the way you desire, but feel free to speak with the higher up, when the call comes through."

Running his fingers through his brown waves First, began to grind his teeth, wishing for words he lacked; looking to the awaiting screen; it was still fuzzy. Neil awaited a reply and did not give a damn about the silence between them. First's teeth grinding grew louder; *They always took the planets this was heartily boasted during buzz sessions at the academy. Were they fabricating stories? All do brag, but was impressed for us to conquer!*

"Ah … this is my first real planet find and not the first for you...so maybe I'm being too hasty, Sir."

A picture burped on screen, calling their attention. A figure appeared,

"Yes, Commander Gavens, how can I help you?"

"Admiral Berry, please," Neil turned away, "More tea, First?"

"But ... Sir?"

"Oh, don't worry those words will take a while to reach Sigmet, then to Earth." Walking to refresh his cup, he did not wait for a reply.

<>

Hours passed relaying messages back and forth with Admiral Berry; in between both catnapped as conversation lagged. "Neil, a upu-gram (water-gram) coming from the water," Bré announced.

"I'll take it here."

Linti did not appear again, but could be heard within the Com-room, "Commander Gavens, Guide will meet with you in our main-community-sig for query in sixt minis (sixty minutes). You and tré ites (three ites), and a Juni will come. Linti's voice dissipated quickly.

"Bré, what does he mean by tré, sixt, ites and minis and Juni?" First asked.

"First, tré means three, sixt means sixty, minis are minutes, and ites … estimation … are people. Old English version with new planet variation is spoken," Bré announced. "I do not have a definition for Juni."

"First, you, I, a telepath and scientist will make the meeting."

"Sir, wouldn't it be wise to take warriors instead of a scientist and telepath."

"Thank you First, you have your orders." *Idiot … And I was given to believe he was the best?*

"Sir," First clicked his heels, and turning he strode out, showing dissatisfaction.

<>

Opening the hatch, they saw nothing. Even striding down the plank, it seemed there was nothing, but soon they saw a misty fog circling then surrounding them to form a clear four individual transparent bubbles.

"Well, I'll be damned, they look like soap bubbles; impressive transport." *Will this really be our ride?* Neil cleared his throat, keeping the crew from realizing he was ready to crap his pants, "Seems each one of us has one." Reaching out to feel the bubble, "Feels like a wall. Are you getting this Sendra?

"Yes Commander. This is fascinating. Looks like those bubbles we used to blow out of soap pipes as kids. Not sure you're ready for this; Bré says; it's organic."

"Do you have a name?" querying the purple person, in the fifth bubble.

"Juni is enough."

"Well ok Juni, envelope us or whatever you do with your bubbles, ah—transport." The Commander said.

The siouts glided sideways through the air surrounding, not adhering, or breaking when enwrapping its guests, clearly allowing them to see one another in their bubbles of palest lilac. The Juni was pressing buttons seemingly on a keyboard, but one could only imagine where the rest of the PC was. They had lifted from the ground, guided away from their ship toward the water with the Juni bubble taking up the rear.

"Sir, do you think we'll be going under water?" First showing great apprehension.

"Yes, I do," Neil professed with glee. "Are you picking up any signs Spencer?"

"Nothing yet Sir, other than First isn't enjoying his ride." Spencer smiled, as she spoke.

As they floated above the ocean, a fog ascended each bubble, instantly dropping them to the floor... instant slumber.

"My God, they're gone!" Sendra exclaimed.

<>

The party of four awoke to find themselves before hundreds of purple males and females. Linti, a mature royal purple and royal purple male with the palest lavender almost white hair, a young teen more the coloring of the adult male, and a female of delicate lavender were seated before them on impossibly clear glass throne like chairs. It was hard to make out their features, with a protective waterfall separating and surrounding them in a special area. The room also was clear walled or so it seemed with surrounding water. Planters of elaborate artistic design hung from the ceilings. A soft water flow surrounded by varied foliage familiar to what they had seen above on land, with dramatic lighting added serenity in appearance and feel. Linti broke the silence, "Commander Gavens, this is my Guide Eftiar, son Efiari and daughter Efiar."

I ... believe I have seen them in my dreams. "Very glad to meet you; I would shake your hand, but I can't seem to get out of this bubble or whatever you call this ride. Why did you put us to sleep in transport?"

"What is the nature of your visit to Eftiam?" Linti inquired.

Here we go again ... "We're checking out different planets for life compatibility, perhaps to trade with each other for resources; basically, this is what we would call a public relations crew." As the Commander threw out the bullshit, Spencer gave Neil a glare letting him know they were not buying his speech.

"If there is no mechanical difficulty, then Guide suggests you and your crew leave Eftiam within a dai (day). There are closer planets to Sigmet and Earth for trading."

"Why doesn't your Guide speak for himself?" First butted in; instantly he was put back to sleep, hitting the bubble floor hard.

"Ah ... Forgive my young officer he speaks before thinking at times."

"Commander we are aware of weaponry and warriors aboard your ship; you have te dai (one day) no more; this meeting is concluded."

Linti pronounced. Almost immediately the party was asleep again; waking the minute the bubble removed itself from them and dissipated; finding themselves before the hatch door of their ship.

"We'll meet privately in my quarters," The Commander said getting up from the ground moving at a dead heat they entered the ship.

<>

The fundamental part of Earth public relations as they call it, is out of the way. They are lying about their presence. They want to seem friendly and exchange information. I feel I made it clear we want no relationship." Eftiar avid.

"Then why do the Imo Macos want them here? They give no answer?" Efiar avid.

"Efiar, I know not, why ...with all this... public relations." Eftiar avid, closing his eyes as if to block out everything.

"We thought you knew until the other dai (day)*,"* Efiari floating closer to His Eftiar. *"Then…"*

Eftiar raised his hand, *"I understand doubts. I spent much tia* (time) *in the main- havis-sig, but alas no answer is given other than we were to let them land."*

"Eftiara did say changes are now; no longer will it be the same. I understood the aving of when Efiari and I were to guide Eftiam. Perhaps she meant we will no longer be alone on Eftiam starting with these Earth/Sigmet ites. Niet avi from her is that we will need their help," Efiar avid.

"I agree with you Efiar. Too long we did not ask, only accepted," Efiari avid. *"But as for their help I doubt it. Earth ites are not peaceful."*

Looking one to the other; all three flew down the corridor into the main-havis-sig, this time for questions to be queried and answered.

Chapter 6

The three names on the thrones Eftiar, Efiari and Efiar sound the same; maybe it's their way of identifying family as we do with last names," First commented, standing in the corner while Spencer and the Commander took the bunk and the Scientist held the chair.

"Linti received telepath messages, but from where I couldn't tell." Spencer commented.

"Most of the foliage was the same as on land. The beauty sleep was to keep us unaware of how to get in or out. The tables and chairs looked like glass, but I can't be sure and they were so clear, without flaws, just like spun hand- blown glass from where I was standing. And the chairs formed to their bodies as if alive.

Believe me I checked all and there was no wiring showing; the head gear of the three leaders was also crystal clear, perhaps their dress marked them as leaders, but I believe they're telepaths and this head gear doesn't allow anyone or anything to enter, only what they choose to allow." Scientist Chambers voiced. Spencer nodded her head in compliance.

"Also, the three-prominent had white streaks in their hair and that's the First color differential we've seen on Purple. The female … ah … Efiar had the largest one, yet Linti introduced her last. Possibly to throw us off to the real leader or maybe females have larger streaks?" the Commander wondered aloud. Many of the people had mixes of purple skin, guess from inter breeding.

"The old guy didn't have a white streak, it was all white," First commented.

"No, it's pale lavender with a white streak." Spencer looked witheringly at First for his ignorance. "They must have probed us with a mechanical device. I'm sure they're aware I'm a telepath."

"Sir, Bré was right, about how differently they spoke. Like proper English, with word variations," First noted. "Are we leaving in the time period they demanded?"

"Before I make that decision, download all into Bré any little detail you can think of; see what comes of that and who knows, maybe in that period they'll reconsider. I'm sending out two scoutbots (small ships) to the other areas of Eftiam. For now, we are finished, be on call; First, I would like you to stay." The others left quickly; the two officers alone, "Now we are going to have a very long and very deep discussion."

<>

"Sir it's been four days and no word from the scouting party," the box squelched.

"Have you been able to pick them up on scan?"

"Not since First met up with the scoutbots, Sir," the voice resonated.

"Keep trying. I'll be on deck in a matter of minutes. Bré, have you reached Number One or any others?"

"No Neil."

"They're out there Bré, keep looking."

"Yes, Neil."

Entering the com- deck, he sensed the disapproval of his crew, for not sending warriors to immediately take over Purple; the discord was spreading throughout the ship. He couldn't tell them of his dreams of this planet. *How can I explain a gut feeling and odd dreams?*

"Sir, in- coming by upu-gram (water-gram)," Bré announced.

Linti appeared before them, "Commander Gavens, we found your Number Te (One) along the upu (ocean) banks minis (minutes) ago. Junis are mending his injuries. A siout (small land craft) is waiting. Bring the same members as before." he dissipated.

Jumping to his feet, "Bré order Spencer and Chambers immediately to transport. Franklin you're in charge while I'm gone." The door closed behind him. *First injured? Hmmm ... how would they find him and why care for him after they are so adamant about us leaving? He called the transport a siout; guess it is their word for a scoutbot. Remember when we called them air buses on Earth. Their technology is better than ours in every respect.* "Bré, did you not get readings of First's whereabouts? Have you assimilated the information on the Purples' mode of transportation yet?"

"Yes Neil, at the same time the upu-gram contacted me. The siout is organic matter; in layman term; plants and water."

"Organic matter? Did you give this information to anyone else?"

"Yes, Neil, Dr. Chambers has this analysis."

"Why is everything purple?"

"An asteroid hit this planet causing many different gases to mix, leaving the plants, water, animals and humans the color purple."

"Humans? Did you say humans such as homo-sapiens-sapiens?"

"Yes, Neil."

"Then you're telling me they're of Earth?"

"Correct." The door opened.

Before departing the elevator, "Bré, has this information been given to any other?"

"No, Neil."

"Good, don't give this info to anyone without my permission and I want a complete analysis of everything you've sent and to whom since we've landed. I just can't figure why you didn't tell me until now."

"Yes, Neil, to your order, secondly, you never asked."

"Bré, why couldn't you read the scout party and the scoutbots?"

Bré did not reply.

◇

Neil awoke in his pale lavender bubble in a hospital room; First was also encased in a bubble but with bed and machinery. Warily he tried taking a few steps. Walking did not seem problematic, as he neared First. *Oh my God, he has been tortured almost beyond recognition. Wow, they have really taken care to handle his wounds nicely. I'm sure he looked worse when they brought him here?* "First?"

Talking stiffly with a broken jaw, that definitely was wired shut or so Neil surmised; like through gritted teeth, "Commander ... you were wrong ... these ... aren't friendly. Warriors ... couldn't ... begin to ... ah ...

"Don't try to talk, just nod your head at my questions, ok?" First tried nodding his head but could not. "Whoa, ok...ah...just blink your eyes, once for yes and two for no. Are you telling me these Purples did this to you?"

"A yes, blink."

"A different tribe?"

"Two blinks."

"The very same ones we met?"

"Yes again."

"Well, I'll be damned. But these folks are taking superb care of you, from what I see. It doesn't make sense ... looking to First again; he was sound asleep.

Linti entered the room, "This way Commander Gavens." *Was he listening at the door?*

Turning away from First, Neil followed within his bubble contraption, "Where are we going? I'd like to speak with someone about First and my crew members and where are the other members I came with?" Linti not heeding proceeded forward. Gavens realizing he was getting nowhere turned his attention toward the corridor they entered. *Not going to get any answers from you.* Looking up as they moved; *under water, they do live under the ocean. Top of their domes are rounded and covered. Wonder if they keep them covered all the time? A .... puffer-fish...well sort of. Plants and lighting everywhere ... this tunnel also has the look of real glass. Lighting goes on and off as we pass by. Bet we'll enter that door at the end of this tube.*

"Enter Commander Gavens." Linti stated, stepping aside. *Sure enough...* Gavens stepped toward the door; it slid sideways into the wall. Looking up again; *every room is domed, probably for water flow. Fish viewing me as if I need to be swimming with them; looks to be about the same specie as those of Earth. A gorgeous body of water; purple but so clear, I can see for miles.* "What the...it can't be...stepping forward to spy, his hand touched the wall....

"Commander Gavens, why have you proceeded with a further search of our planet? Linti asked. Turning Neil jumped at the dramatic outburst. The wall held him, allowing him to quickly recover. He spied Linti and his Guide Eftiar; now he really stared, he went pale... *He's raised a good foot off the floor! His robe must be hiding machinery. Oh my God, I've definitely seen him in my dreams...what...*

"Commander, are you, all right? Suddenly the bubble surrounding him dissolved. "Here sit," Linti took his arm, guided him into a chair. Upon sitting he immediately had an adrenalin rush and jumped from it; it seemed to be pulling him into it, as if it would dissolve him. "Please Sir, the chair adjusts itself to fit your person, it will not harm you." Neil sat, reluctantly, allowing the chair to accommodate him, taking the drink that was offered.

Shaken, he drank half not bothering to taste, or give thought to the drink possibly being drugged. Looking, he realized indeed the chair formed to him. As thinking to himself, he spoke aloud, "This is the most comfortable chair I've ever had the pleasure to sit in. How do you get the chair to mold like that? Ah Eftiar is it; how are you able to float and not walk? I saw someone out there in the ocean…."

Taking a seat on a chair that seemed to appear out of nowhere Eftiar mind-spoke to him, *"Another time possibly; why did you send ites to other parts of Eftiam?"*

Neil was shocked at this man who glides finally speaking to him, *He's a telepath, not moving his mouth,* "Well ah … by ites I guess you mean my crew; we always do this to see if there are others willing to trade or purchase possible items," proffering words from memory. "Why did your people hurt my team and try to cover by mending one of them?"

Eftiar and Linti looked to one another and then at him with seemingly innocent shock. "I assure you we would never harm your Officer or any other of your ites," Linti spoke with sincerity.

"That's not what my Officer tells me."

"He is wrong there are no other ites on Eftiam

"According to First, it was the very same people we met in your so-called welcome arena. I sent my crew in scoutbots to the dark side of your planet, where your people confronted them."

"Sir, we did not harm your ites and we do not go beyond our farms," Linti stated.

"Never go beyond your farms? Hell, how can you be sure there aren't others living on this world? Aren't you at all curious about your planet?"

No sooner had the words flown from his lips when he grabbed his head from the excruciating pain. After a few seconds it stopped, but he knew Eftiar produced it. After the pain subsided, "When will my mate be ready to travel?"

"He is ready now." Linti answered, as a Juni escorted First into the room, walking of his own accord.

He could not hide his utter shock. Wanting to stand, he reconsidered for fear he couldn't after taking so much in such a short period, "First? Ah … how are you feeling? *My God, he was in no condition twenty minutes ago. It was twenty minutes, wasn't it?*

"Great Sir!" Turning to Eftiar and Linti, "Thank you for caring for me; I will never forget your kindness."

"You are welcome," Eftiar avid while inclining his head, then gestured to Gavens, *"Your dais* (days) *are ended; departure from Eftiam is imminent. This Juni will escort you to your sioutous* (spaceship)." Suddenly Spencer and Chambers appeared through another wall, also without clear bubbles surrounding them, escorted by a Juni. *"You must leave Eftiam immediately!"*

"We need to talk…my dreams; you've been in them for over a year."

"Please follow Juni, he will escort you to your sioutous (spaceship)," Linti pronounced. Neil tried to hang back to get Eftiar to communicate with him, but a Juni pushed him forward leaving no alternative; they all proceeded.

Chapter 7

Neil, Spencer, and Chambers collaborated over coffee awaiting Firsts medical evaluation. "You know he's more than medically fit. Their technology is far superior to ours," Chambers marveled.

Still shaken with all that went down, Neil managed to keep his voice even, "Yes, but they did alter something in his brain matter, that's evident. When I visited him in the hospital room hooked to machinery, he was sure the Purples' we saw in the greeting hall beat him. I don't yet know about the other crew members, nor has Franklin given me any news. Now I don't know if First will ever tell us, but we'll interrogate him and Bré will record. Those Purples told me they never go beyond their farms. Why wouldn't they? They evidently have no idea what their planet is about. Or are they too afraid of something? Also, I think, no, I know I saw…"

"Neil?"

"Yes, Bré?'

"Doctor Simms wants to see you."

"Thanks, Bré." As they moved toward medical, "By the way where were you guys?"

"We awoke in a domed room without our bubbles and were kept there until we met up with the rest of you," Spencer stated.

"While there, I got to check out their chairs, walls and planters; just as the scoutbots, all organic," Chambers offered excitedly.

<>

"First is in perfect health, like he never had an injury in his life," Dr. Simms conveyed, "From the injuries you spoke of, I couldn't have saved his life. Can you believe it; they've removed every scar from his body. Could I get into their medical labs? This is too good to pass up."

"Right now, I'm more interested in his brain. Did they alter him in anyway?"

"There's no way to tell, matter of fact like I said, you'd never know he had any injuries or even diseases; maybe interrogation will give us answers; he's waiting," Simms stated leading the way to his cubicle.

They entered the small room, which resembled an old 1950's boob tube detective show set. "First, Doc here tells me you're in fine shape."

"I feel fantastic, Commander. Those Purples really know their stuff."

"Do you remember me coming to your hospital bed?"

"Yeh, we each had our own bubbles, Sir. Only mine had lots of machines. As beaten as I was, I sure didn't think I would live, now…tears coming into his eyes…just look at me."

"Do you remember who you stated beat you?"

"Yes, the Purples, but…"

"Why then, aren't you angered?"

"Because Sir, now that I've had time to consider everything, or so I thought, I really don't believe they're the same Purples as I first thought. They weren't the exact color as these Purples, so I think it was another group dressed to look like them and well … the other Purples were more tribal like and the meanest S. O. Bs'; even our warriors couldn't deal well with them. They made mincemeat of us, Sir… and … shifting his sitting position… "Their eyes were white and red. Also, there was one with a white streak like the Efiar woman we first met, but it was reversed."

"White and red eyes?"

"Yes Sir."

"Do you know what happened to the other crew members with you?"

"No Sir, when captured, we were put separately into electrified cages. We were unable to communicate with some sort of metal devices over our mouths. I couldn't even remove the device with my hands and I really worked at trying to get it out of my mouth; everyone tried around me too. Also, we were taken away separately, and, in the time, I was there I never saw anyone brought back to the cages. God, we could hear them being beaten. It was horrible, they never laughed or even spoke, just tortured."

First gave a shiver in remembrance.

"So, you're saying they never even tried to interrogate you?

"No, Sir."

"Was the other crew there also?"

"Yes Sir."

"Did they offer food or drink?" Chambers questioned.

"No Sir."

"Who was the leader of this tribe? And did they speak telepathically or verbally?" Spencer asked.

"Ma'am, it was the female Efiar. But like I said even though I knew she was in charge; she never spoke to them at all."

"I believe you've had enough for now. Just keep debriefing your dialogue to Bré as you remember incidents of any kind that might be helpful. A lot more may come to you later. We will get back to you and go over all again. You can go back to normal duty." They all rose to leave.

"Sir... Sir, the head Guide Eftiar ... well as ... he ah ... spoke with his mind ... he helped me understand that warring of planets isn't always the right answer. Therefore, I apologize for my statement to you, Sir."

Silence ... "Ah...Thanks...apology accepted. That's enough for now, please get some rest, First."

<>

Back in Neil's quarters, Spencer had the chair, Chambers and Neil took the bunk.

"You don't believe it was the Purples our crews met, do you, Commander?"

"No, I don't I do believe First."

"So that means other Purples are present on this planet, for some reason to take on the look of the Purples we know and blaming them for their deeds," Chambers stated. "But when he spoke of their eyes being white and red, I pictured a robot."

"I agree and I'm sure the rest of you do. After First, dwells more on what occurred then we'll possibly have something more to work with; you're dismissed."

"Oh, Spencer could you stay a moment,"

"Yes Commander?"

"What do you think of these Purples?"

"Sir, they're not a warring people. From what I feel and waves I've received they're givers and could easily become friendly. Plus, they seem guided by someone or something else, I really can't explain it. Like the head gear the three wear. I believe it's for keeping other telepaths from entering. Have you given any thought to them being robotic?"

Neil felt amazingly comfortable with Spencer, more than he'd felt in years. So much so he leaned back against the wall slouched on his bunk. "No, Bré has made that clear to me, they're not robotic. What would you say if I told you they were human?" Speaking, he felt a slight stirring in his loins as he took in Spencer's profile.

Spencer re-took the chair without asking. Digesting this information briefly, eyeing him, moving uncomfortably while wringing her hands; "Then we need to talk Sir, as I've had waves from you, I've not divulged, and I know these people have a connection with you. You made that clear when we met up with you in front of Eftiar and Linti, about seeing them in your dreams?"

Neil froze, *a sharp statement*, "You did telepath me without my permission?"

"No Sir, you gave waves to me freely without your knowledge," Spencer now blushing, wanted to look away wishing her hair was long enough to cover her eyes, and to keep her feelings from showing. Clasping her hands in her lap to keep from wringing them, she braved a look into Neil's eyes, "Really Sir, I would never use telepathy unless given permission. I think we're more connected than most others on this ship."

His loins swelled fully, as he stared back into those clear blue pools, her short auburn curls delicately framed her flawless mural, and those bow full lips inviting him to kiss. Without thought, they seemed to meet in the middle, she jumping from the chair, he from the wall landing half on and half off the bunk, *"I've wanted you from the first day I saw you,"* Speaking with her mind.

Staring in disbelief, *"But how ... I just... try...* "And I, you; how is *all this possible... speaking this way? We aren't struggling to converse."*

*"Let's not think of whys just now...*unbuttoning his shirt, her hands pleasurably roamed his chest, while he removed her shirt, and unsnapped her bra enjoying her gorgeous full breasts....

<>

A few hours later, they lay fully nude on Neil's bunk, caressing each other heedless of time. Giggling, *"Neil, have you been taking your pills? I have, but they don't seem to have worked."*

"Now that you mention it, yes, I never forget them. I now *wonder if others of our crew are having this problem. We aren't even supposed to think about sex taking those damn things let alone, get turned on by a nude picture. It would be interesting to probe this area for information?"*

"Sure, why not have Bré do a survey. It's all in the line of study for the future." Neil offered with a wry smile.

"Ah...Spencer, your file, says your first name is Jean. Is this what you go by? I don't know many of the ship's crew by first names."

Laughing heartily, *"It's Jean. And it's understandable with a crew of two thousand."*

"Jean, eh ... do you think we can do this telepathy because of this planet?"

Adjusting her pillow, spooning herself closer to Neil, *"I've been receiving your dreams for about a year now. You've kept me awake many a night."* Neil became very still but kept hold of Jean's breast. *"How could I come to you and say, Commander I need to tell you I'm reading your dreams, when I wasn't sure you were recalling them. I know it now, from coupling with you and what you stated today in front of Eftiar and Linti. Call it woman's intuition if you like or telepathic intuition, but I'm right, aren't I?"*

Unsure how to react, Neil took his time answering, *"I...I...I've never had anyone tell me they'd read my dreams."* A wry smile...his hands still holding her breast, *"Since you and I are speaking telepathically, then we too have more than just a slight connection here with this planet. I'm not so sure, this would've happened on Earth or Sigmet for us, or maybe we could and weren't aware, because it's not* common. *But shouldn't a telepath be able to tell if another is telepathic?"*

"Yes, but you and I never came into contact until we were scheduled for this jump. So, no, we wouldn't have known. I received your dreams maybe because I am the only telepath on board. We never even saw each other until you requested, I be present to meet the Purples."

Still toying with her breasts, he turned her toward him, *"Oh, but I've seen you many times on Earth, and Sigmet and aboard this ship. I knew I wanted to meet you and be with you exactly like this."* No other words were needed......

Chapter 8

*"**M**y Eftiar, why did you let the Commander know you avid?"* Efiari avid.

"I really cannot say, but for him to actually think we would brutally hurt their crew angered me to the point I let him also have pain. I have never let myself show anger in such manner before; it appalls me. His frustration showed physically as well as telepathically. He already seems to know more than he should; he saw one of us in the upu (ocean). *I did not acknowledge this. Somehow this Commander Gavens is connected to us. How do you feel about the Earthlings?"*

"My Eftiar, I want them to also leave; they bring disease of every kind wherever they land. I still do not think we should have removed their transports."

"Yes, but we can learn from them," Efiar avid. *This Commander Gavens and Ms. Spencer are blood related to us through our Eftiaras'. This was given in lesson recently. I believe therefore the Imo Macos chose them to be on Eftiam. The Imo Macos feel they will do us no harm if this is the true understanding, I have acquired."* Father and son looked at Efiar with great perplexity. *"I want to see the inside of this sioutous* (spaceship) *that is so different from our siouts* (small land craft). *We really have nothing like it. Our siouts cannot go into outer space as theirs, why is that?"*

Now choosing to rise and fuai float in place, *"I always wanted to stay just on Eftiam, but now, the excitement of gaining new knowledge to help guide our ites, gives me goosey bumps. Would you not like to see other worlds?"* The silence was deafening in the sig for many minis, as Efiar finished.

Finally, Eftiar avid, *"Considered venturing off Eftiam? No, I have wondered about other planets, yes. And the information I acquired through the Imo Macos does seems repetitive."*

"You are right Eftiar. In all the lessons of other planets I get from the Imo Macos, it seems to sound the same," Efiari avi offered. Suddenly an alarm went off in all the niets (minds) informing the

cognoscenti the Imo Macos' were compusizing (computerizing). But how could their Eftiara be a part of the compus when the compus were developed many trili (centuries) before her time, or were they? This was the most vexing of all. *"This makes me wonder if the Earthlings are right about other ites on the dark side of our Eftiam. It could also be why we are not to go beyond our fields. Let us allow the Earthlings to investigate the dark side and enable them to find the rest of their crew. My, my this is quite an adventure, and on our own Eftiam,"* Efiari now fuaid around the sig with excitement.

"We should upu-gram (water-gram) *Commander Gavens for dinner aboard their sioutous,"* Eftiar avid. *"So finally, I know where your leadership qualities lie. I must make sure to have you spend tia* (time) *with Linti, my Efiari."*

Chapter 9

Sunsets were not ordinary in Earth/Sigmet sense. The absence of pollution caused variations within the sky as the sun set in the opposite direction of Earth's norm. It went down fast as if one was on the ocean watching a sunset; it just seemed to plop. And there were one and one-half- moons and absolutely no stars.

Neil, First, Chambers, and Spencer greeted the Purples under a canopy of the temporary station on Purple. Neil felt this would frost Eftiar. They wouldn't be able to get inside the Bramble; after all, Eftiar did give him great head pain and now seeming to have had a change of heart, Neil, pondered what they had in mind. *Yes, I've seen all of you in my dreams, but one seems to be missing... Eftiar's mate?*

As they arrived in a scoutbot (small craft), which was quite different from theirs, Chambers couldn't help wanting to reach out and touch it wishing he wasn't standing at formal attention. The craft hovered in place as they stepped from the craft; no one shut the craft down. It seemed to look alive, as though it could see and feel the Purples. In addition, the three Purples with head gear floated before them in their so-called tulip dress, while Linti walked. Earth/Sigmet warriors were placed silently in the background perimeter at the ready, weapons hidden; mouths gaped at this sight before them

Linti performed the semi-silent introductions. In turn Commander Gavens re-introduced his three comrades: again, thanking their guests for healing First. Linti stated, "Commander Gavens, for you all to know; my Guide Eftiar avi speaks, of which you are aware and also his children."

"Avi speaks?" Commander Gavens questioned as if not understanding. Hopefully, this would clarify the message; he didn't want the rest of his crew aware he could now telepathically speak himself.

Before Linti could respond, Eftiar's hand came up, letting Linti know he could step back. *"Good eve to all of you."* The warriors and dinner crew rocked on their feet with surprise, hearing these words in their minds. *"Since your arrival on Eftiam, we have encountered changes, some frightening, some enjoyable. We are ites* (people) *of non-warring and choose to remain so. Some of you may be able to communicate with your niets* (minds) *and some will mouth avi* (speak). *Efiar, Efiari and I only communicate with our niets. Ms. Spencer, it is grand to meet a fellow niet avi* (telepath). *Do you carry a title?"* Bowing his head to her and smiling.

"Sir, it's most endearing for me to have the pleasure," Spencer offered, *"On Earth and Sigmet my title is Doctor Spencer."* Eftiar made sure this communicated to everyone all around. Each kept looking to see if the others were also hearing with their minds. Warriors placed their hands to their guns automatically, and then thought better of it, not having been given orders. It took a good five minutes for warriors and other crew members to calm. This was definitely a first for the entire crew.

Commander Gavens stepped forward offering a proper salute and his hand to Eftiar. Hesitating, Neil lifted Eftiar's hand, but Linti immediately jumped between them. Both of Neil's hands flew into the air in a 'hands up' gesture. "Hold it Linti; I was just going to show him how to shake hands, which is a welcoming custom where we come from. Slowly he took hold of Linti's right hand, "Here let me show you," He saw some sort of weapon was in his palm, so quickly dropping his hand, he turned to First and signaled him to demonstrate the hand shake. All the others joined in the demonstration ... Then he proceeded again to Eftiar, "Welcome to our temporary land station. I thought with the beautiful evening having dinner outside would be more pleasant than in our confined quarters. As for our meal, we can only offer pre-packaged items from our commissary." *I wonder where their guards are hiding. I know they're near; feel them. Neat weapon the palm device; never saw anything like it before. Shook me up; broke a sweat.*

"We also brought foods with us, for you to try," Eftiar said to all. *"We will keep your secret, Commander."*

"How do you do that? Ah ... you know ... separate who you talk to? There is so much ... I don't know where to begin."

"In all good time, Commander, in all good time; now, I do believe everyone is awaiting seating."

47

Embarrassed, Neil quickly stepped aside for his guests to sit down. While taking their seats, Efiar brushed Neil ever so gently. He felt her pressing his mind.

<>

The first encounter was going exceptionally well. The foods of the Purples tasted similar to those of Earth, after getting past the fact all the foods were different shades of purple, but of course chemically unaltered, and oh, so fresh. The taste buds of the Earth/Sigmets came alive, enjoying them immensely. However, the Earth/Sigmets' foods were only politely tasted by the Purples. When dinner was finished and the preliminaries out of the way it was time for politics. Neil felt this would be difficult, for Linti was the only interpreter and he sure couldn't let his crew know he Was now able to communicate telepathically.

Efiari was the first of the teenagers to mind speak since being introduced, "Commander Gavens, please tell of these ites you encountered on the dark side of our Eftiam."

Silence now was prominent. *Therefore, they're here. This one goes straight for the jugular.* "My crew encountered a very unusual situation. From what your father has told me, you never go beyond your farms. Has this always been so?"

"Yes," Linti answered for Efiari.

"This we don't understand for we investigate every area of a planet we live on or visit. So, you're telling us you've never seen these other people or ites as you call them?"

"No Commander Gavens, we have never been beyond our farms as we explained, and we are not aware of another te (one) on Eftiam." Eftiar avid.

"Truthfully, these people looked very much the same as your people.

"How do you mean?" Efiari questioned.

"The people looked exactly like all of you sitting before us and many of your other people we saw the first day in your home." Neil offered looking around, then proceeding, "Right down to the white streaks in your hair." Unease settled around the table. Their physical sitting patterns immediately changed. Neil and Jean knew the three telepaths were talking to each other mentally and they knew not to mind talk for fear Eftiar, or the siblings would overhear.

"This is of great concern to us. We have never seen nor realized other ites besides those of our city are living on Eftiam. My insides also tell me this is an untrue measure." Eftiar avid.

"Didn't you interrogate First, about the encounter? And what do you mean by untrue measure?"

"Commander, we are not at battle with you, so, no. Our concern was to heal his wounds, not how he got them." Linti retorted.

Eftiar explained, *"Untrue measure is a falsehood in your way of niet aving and mouth cavity aving* (speaking).*"*

"That isn't normal," Neil retorted, realizing the Eftiam drink was making his lips loose. "We definitely could teach you a few things about war.

Raising his hand, before the rest could speak, "I can only presume no one else has landed on this planet. Then who's to say someone else wouldn't land here with war in mind and you would need to protect yourselves. I'm surprised you've lasted this long without others landing here. As for untrue measure do you think these others are robotic? Once verbalized, Neil knew he had made a grave mistake; the evening was ended.

Linti struggled for a few moments with Efiari and Eftiar's commands in his mind. "We cannot avi what this is, other than what is avid at present."

"Commander, I suggest we meet again, with your party privately, so we can share ideas and see if we can help you find the rest of your crew."

Rising and floating above his chair as he spoke, signaling the evening's end, Eftiar offered, *"Linti will upu-gram* (water-gram) *you."* The rest of Neil's party also rose; Neil and Linti shook hands first. Eftiar following suit, hovering in midair, *"Commander, I feel we have much to discuss and learn from one another. If I may ask, did you have a relative who also flew space sioutous* (spaceship) *as you?"*

"Yes Sir, my Great Grandfather. I carry his name. What makes you ask?"

Looking out over the assembled crew, Eftiar spoke to the entire present crew, *"Thank you for your hospitality, it was a most enjoyable evening, however, your foods do have many chemicals, we could not taste the true flavors."* Laughter broke out.

"Sir, we've eaten chemical preserved foods for so many years, it startled us to enjoy the true taste of your foods, making our taste buds come alive as you could tell from the way we devoured everything you brought. We do wish to experience more in the days to come." First once again did his usual blurting out. Again, laughter broke out, this time having a considerable calming effect to finalize the evening.

<>

Without a word, the four headed straight for Neil's quarters. Chambers spoke, "I wanted to touch that scoutbot/siout or whatever it is; badly. It's organic; I just know it!

The Purples are perplexed by this chain of events that happened with me and the rest of our scout party," First commented. "Oddly, I seem to be able to feel that." Jean and Neil eyed each other.

"It's also amazing Eftiar is able to broadcast his mind to all or individually. This is not a normal phenomenon," Spencer volunteered, with certainty.

"Do you think we will turn purple from the foods?" First queried.

Well, that is finally out. A complete quiet reigned in the quarters with the three expecting an answer from their Commander. Instead, he questions, "Bré?"

"Yes Commander?"

"Could you give your analysis of this evenings undertaking?"

"Linti and Efiari are of warrior minds. Eftiar and Efiar are Guides of the people of Eftiam. They do want our help to learn of their planet. There is another presence."

"Do Eftiar, Efiari and Efiar receive messages telepathically from this other presence?"

"Yes Commander. This is the only way they communicate."

"Wait ... Are you saying these folks are human as in Homo Sapiens Sapiens?" The Doctor of science butted in.

"Yes Doctor, Bré, has concluded they're human."

"Then that…

"Ah Bré, are these three using machinery to float rather than walk?" Neil quickly asked.

"No Commander."

To no avail, First, butted in, "Bré, we have eaten of their foods; will we turn purple as they?" The quiet filled the room, all seemed to shift position awaiting an answer that never came. "Sir, is there something wrong with Bré?"

"Maybe she hasn't an answer," Neil replied, keeping his eyes to the floor.

"Presently no; but I do believe in time this would be the case," Chambers offered, clearing his throat, "Scientifically speaking."

Well, I … I'm not eating another bite of their foods," First declared.

"I guess you won't be going into negotiations with the Purples," Neil proffered. "Is there anyone else who feels this way?"

"Sir, I…it's just…

"Bré, do you feel this presence is a machine or a person of Eftiam," Neil carefully asked, staring down First.

"Both," Commander," Bré reported, claiming their attention.

"So, then you're saying this is both man and machine, Bré?" Chambers asked again, to make sure what he heard.

"Yes, Doctor Chambers."

"I'll be damned, it's a comdat (computer), they're relying on," Chambers almost sang.

"Jean, do I tell these two of our findings or do I wait? I so need your opinion."

"Neil, I think we should wait a while longer to see what we are up against with the other unknown Purples. Chambers is already putting things together anyway, but I think First is too quick with words."

"My feelings exactly, thank you. It's wonderful having someone to share with."

<>

Thirty minutes after the upu-gram (water-gram) arrived, they were in bubbles floating out over the waters, and they did not induce the sleep mode. Whatever the Purples did to First so far seemed for the better. He

51

was not fearful of entering the waters. Plus, Dr. Simms could not find anything in brain scanning in conflict with his brain; at least nothing known to Earth/Sigmet technology.

Entering the ocean, the bubble surrounding them let out its own bubbles as a submarine submerging and glided sideways. Chambers and Neil both watched as the Juni worked his controls while First and Spencer focused on the plant and sea life, which seemed to have almost the same look of Earth with only slight variations. Gliding over the city, they now could see within the uncovered domed houses, except for those areas that required privacy. It was a huge populated city whose inhabitants moved about in tubes, going to and from with daily life as on Earth and Sigmet.

"Sir, they look so human from up here; like they do the very same things we do daily," First stated to Neil. The party could not help but laugh. "You know what I mean," First reiterated embarrassed.

"Wasn't this so with any planet you encountered in your academy studies?"

"Yes, but one never looks at it quite this way until experienced."

"It's a whole new world for you son; probably why I put up with your outbursts, but then I myself sure made plenty of mistakes."

As they arrived this time in the transport area, they could see the entire goings on. A large circular landing port noted two devices with five arms reaching out to capture each bubble individually. This made Gavens wonder if they placed them into other types of bubbles to accommodate travel within the city itself. The Commander's and Chamber's heads were revolving trying to take in every inch of this landing hub. Purples were walking about this area, taking little notice of their arrival except for those securing the bubbles. All seemed to dress in the same manner as Linti.

Linti arrived as their bubbles dissipated. He offered a shake of hands as he had been shown the night before, "Commander Gavens, we are most happy you and your personnel could attend, please follow." Not waiting a reply, Linti strode off.

"Neil, they trust us completely."

"Yes Jean, I pray I don't get orders to do harm to these Purples. This welcome has not happened with any others we've encountered."

Linti led them down an exceedingly long tube, the ocean floor was not visible as in the other tubes and rooms they had been in. Turning a right, they entered a bright and cheery room with masses of plant life hanging from the ceiling. The table and chairs were clear as seen in the throne room on their first day meeting the Purples. A long buffet was set to one side of the room, also clear as the table and chairs, and set with variations of foods and drink. "Please sit anywhere you like, except for the largest chair at the end of the table," Linti stated. Sitting, Neil's three comrades suddenly jumped up as they experienced the strange enfolding of the chair's phenomena. Linti and Neil looked to each other smiling with remembrance of his first encounter. "It's ok guys, the chair doesn't bite it molds to you and it's very comfortable." Slowly they eased into the chairs, finding them remarkably comfortable. One could be ensured with the smiles crossing their faces, but also with puzzlement of the chair workings.

Another door slid into the wall revealing Eftiar, Efiari and Efiar. All rose standing at attention to greet their hosts. Commander Neil had taken one of the chairs closest to the larger chair to be close to Eftiar, whom he presumed intended, him to have this chair. Before seating, each offered their greetings, shaking each hand. Neil's presumptive seating was correct.

"We are pleased and welcome you to our home world. My Efiar felt it more comfortable for us to meet here in our dining sig." Waving his hand at the buffet, *"We took the liberty of placing foods for you to enjoy while we meet,"* Eftiar avid.

Thank you, we're glad to be here and your thoughtful accommodations are enjoyable," Commander Gavens said, looking to Efiar, who seemed to blush through the purple.

As they were seating, Efiari, jumped right in, *"Commander, just what did happen on the dark side of Eftiam?"*

"First should be the one to relate his findings on the dark side," Neil spoke looking at First to commence.

"Sir, the minute we went from light to dark, we knew someone was watching. We couldn't see the Purples … ah … people, but we could see their white with red eyes. They let us go about five kilometers before capturing us. This is where we met with the rest of our crew, each given a separate cage. These people are brutal. They didn't give us food or water, nor did they speak to us. They just tortured us. We had mouth devices preventing us from speaking and we could not remove them. We desperately tried, but they did remove them when a person was to be beaten. I think it was to make us feel more apprehensive, like they really got off on it. I never saw any crew members returned to the cages. From that point, I only remember Linti saying Commander Gavens was notified that you were caring for my wounds. I still question why I was the only of our crew found."

Efiari asked, *"What is this getting off?"*

"Sir, it means enjoying the situation."

"You say their eyes were white and red. Do you mean like a machine?" Efiari avid.

"Yes Sir, I do believe they are machines or robots as we would refer to them, but they look like you and their skin feels real. Sir, would you allow us to return to find the rest of our crew?"

"Yes, we would very much like you to try to find the rest of your crew members, and we too will send battle ites with you." Eftiar stated. *"I also suggest we use our siouts* (small land craft).*"* Before Gavens could protest, Eftiar raised his hand, *"Our siouts are quiet and yours seem to make…noise."*

Gavens smiled, "Perhaps you can give us insight into how to make our scoutbots less noisy."

Hearing this, Chambers leaped to his feet anticipating being inside a siout, barely able to contain himself. "Shall we set out immediately? The more time wasted the less likely we're to find our crew members." He strode to the door anticipating the others to follow.

"Agreed," Eftiar avid and Gavens spoke simultaneously. The troops rushed off.

Unruffled Eftiar avid, *"Commander, while our warriors are looking for ites perhaps you and Miss Spencer can share time aving of other matters. I believe this will be a fruitful gathering, and at the same time we can keep tabs on our scouting party."*

<>

Doctor Spencer and Commander Gavens spent almost two hours on a comprehensive tour of the city, marveling at what they saw. Tunnels and sigs were alike with multiple plants hanging from the walls and ceilings, with lighting better than they had ever seen; truly enhancing the plants.

Play areas made for the children were much like that of Earth/Sigmet, but again the plants were designed to entice rather than to distract from play.

Although the framework was of dark purple it had a see-through appearance. All Junis wore clothing of the same color of purple. The only ones different were the three wearing the head gear. Their clothing resembled an upright umbrella with legs instead of a handle, or possibly a mushroom, because the two were not sure petticoats were part of the dress.

One tunnel access was denied to them, which stimulated Neil's curiosity about the unseen.

<>

Back in the din- sig during lunch, Gavens took a closer look at the utensils. They too were of this special see-through organic material. *It seems that everything is downright organic. Boy, would I love this technology to take home to Earth.*

"Commander Gavens, you stated your great-grandfather was also an aviator. Did he encounter new adventures such as you?"

"From what I've been told and read, he was a very adventurous person to say the least. However, his whereabouts are still unknown." Putting down his fork, gesturing with his hand, *"My great-grandfather's last ship called the 'Preamble' is yet to be found. His crew of six hundred-some fellow travelers and Scientists who all disapproved of Earth's insidiousness, including my great-grandfather."* Eftiar, Efiari and Efiar, looked at one another. *"Before he left Earth, he was considered the best of all fliers. Today his name is considered unmentionable because of this act of treason, but somehow I find myself still believing he did well wherever he may be."*

"Dr. Spencer, your family is also telepathic?" Eftiar avid.

"Yes, I come from a long line of telepaths, and many of my ancestry were also, on the 'Preamble." Surprise showed on Neil's face, Efiar catching the exchange."

"What made these ites leave Earth?" Efiar avid.

Neil and Jean looked at one another; *be up front.* *"Earth was in turmoil with the ozone layer growing so large. Global warming caused great havoc everywhere. The United States was once the power of Earth, and then it became the weakest. The US spread too much greed around the world and at our weaker point other countries took advantage. No one would listen to what the Scientists predicted would happen to Earth if man did not listen. The Environmental agencies could not get through to our people, so NASA sent out ships to try and find new planets to inhabit. Making a long story short this is how we came to settle on Sigmet,"* Neil explained.

"And now that Sigmet is having these same problems you are navigating to find a new planet for your ites," Efiari declared. Neil just nodded a given. *"Thank you for being candid."*

"I have seen all three of you in my dreams for over a year now, but I feel one of you is missing. I feel compelled to be here but telling my crew would make them think I was loony."

"What is loony?" Efiar avid.

"Crazy...insane." Jean avid.

"Jean ... ah ... Spencer here says I telepathically sent her my dreams. Also, we're speaking in this manner seems normal now, but I've only been able to communicate with my mind recently. Spencer here has done this since birth. I however feel it has something to do with your planet." Neil got up from his chair and started to pace, *"I want to know so much about your people, and your planet, but I know we do have a problem with Earth/Sigmet wanting to inhabit your planet. Since we are both Homo-Sapiens-Sapiens we should be able to live well together; teach each other so much. But looking you as a people and a planet Earth/Sigmet can inhabit, I fear that no regard will be taken."*

"What is this homo-sapien-sapien you avi?" Eftiar avid.

"Same race, human, humanoid, specie, alike...the only difference is our color."

"You are different shades of purple and we are white, black, brown, yellow, oh, and they always refer to an Indian as the red man, but few if any are truly of red skin, at least I've never seen one. I believe this saying has to do with the fact they can't handle alcohol and they get

very mean when drinking, but that is my theory, I've no proof from any history I've read." Jean looked questioningly at Neil. *"I don't know why I'm telling them all this Jean ...I guess...I ...really need some answers to all this ... this... weirdness."*

Efiar rose and walked to Neil, and, raising her hand, she placed it on his shoulder, *"We do not have all the answers, but I want you to know that I too have seen you in my dreams. I believe we are distantly related, and therefore, we are able to avi."* A twinge of alarm went through both, and they quickly separated.

"Yes, we in this room are related," Eftiar avid calmly, but those in this room knew he was not, as they all turned in query for more information.

"Doctor Spencer you are related to my Efiari's Eftiara, and Commander Gavens, you are related to my wife Eftiara."

"How do you know this?" Neil avid.

"Aving with Eftiara a few hors (hours) ago, she let this be known." His children showed surprise to his revealing this information.

"Where is she? I would so enjoy meeting my distant cousin or Aunt," His excitement overcame his inability to consider the ramifications.

An uneasy silence filled the room, *"At the min* (moment) *this is impossible; another tia* (time) *perhaps,"* Eftiar avid. *"Our ites are at the line of darkness, shall we go to one of our imo-mirrors?"* Without waiting for answer, Eftiar arose and fuaid rapidly from the room. The others scurried to catch up.

<>

Neil and his mates were surprised encountering other Purples entering this sig; all were watching the imo-mirror (movie screen), which took up the entire wall. It was definitely the largest com-mov screen, the Earth ites had ever seen, and their awed surprise was not hidden. The screen seemed to be part of the wall, unlike most com-mov screens of Earth or Sigmet, which would be separate from the wall and or wired behind another wall.

"Don't you keep this sort of knowledge from your people until it is necessary to give them information sparingly?" Gavens avid.

"Certainly not! There is nothing to hide. This includes them." Efiari avid in dismay turning; eyeing Gavens with a forward stare.

"Excuse me, but I've never looked at it from your viewpoint; it's customarily done that way on Earth/Sigmet," Neil avid, feeling most apologetic.

"Well maybe that is a piece wrong with your governing as you refer," Efiari did not hesitate to offer.

Eftiar went to the front of the huge imo-mirror screen to speak, *"Ites of Eftiam, the Earth/Sigmets have found on the dark side of our planet an unknown source of ite which may be harmful to them and us. We are not sure, what you will see; some possible battle war graphics, so we ask all young babe-ites go to the nurseries and other areas."*

Without word, the smaller children carried by larger children met up at the doors; adults then removed them to other areas of the city.

Jean remarked, *"It's amazing the culture here is so advanced from ours; all is peaceful, no dissension of any kind. I find it soooo...hard to believe."*

"It took many centuries, but our ites had to be close to survive. Our ancestors fought hard to bring this to fruition. Excuse us," Efiar avid.

Linti was on the imo-mirror screen with First at his side. Warriors behind them were armed and ready, along with siouts (small land craft) in front, beside and behind them. As they paraded slowly into the line of light to dark, it seemed uncanny how these siouts could maneuver slightly above ground and so quietly. Breaking formation a siout came forward and went into the dark side as the others remained in waiting. The siout had cameras, presumably infra-red, brushing aside foliage in its path without damaging it. At exactly five kilometers, a laser of fire came from the side of a tree and red and white eyes were seen. The laser seemed to bounce off the siout. *"Neil if these crafts can ward off laser fire, then why didn't our warriors stay in the siouts?"*

Eftiar answered to all present, *"In order to make a complete assessment of these dark ites, we must have our battle ites go in on foot."* Eftiar seemed to pause, returning his concentration to the wall imo-mirror.

After an interval Eftiar again turned to his ites, *"We will now proceed into the darker side of Eftiam."* Almost exactly where the siout first encountered fire, more fire broke out from both sides of the pu (jungle) foliage; all eyes were glued to the imo- mirror screen. The siouts fired toward the targets without turning; dark side Purples flew out from the pu foliage and fell quickly, but no cry of any kind came from the Dark Purples.

Linti ordered, *"All Eftiam and Earth warriors to the ground!"* The ites watching the screen also went to the floor except for Gavens and Spencer.

Shots coming from the siouts again downed Dark Purples.

Spencer and Gavens looked around in disbelief. *"My God, these people aren't used to war; they're engrossed as if watching a com-mov* (movie), *or do they feel no emotion?"* Neil wondered. *"I've never seen such huge beams of infrared light. I didn't even realize the siouts were so lethally armed. I'm convinced the Darks are robotic by the way they move, and their eyes are a dead giveaway. And look at the white streaks in the hair, they're opposite as First, described and the insignia is reversed on their uniforms; probably for identification purposes by the ones who made them, making it easier to tell Darks from Lights."*

"Yes, they do move rather strange, but look so damn real," Jean avid. *"I can only imagine what these people are going through right now, seeing themselves, yet not themselves. We do have to help these people, Neil. Ah ... Neil ... ah, look more closely at the floor, these people are all connected."*

"Connected?" Quizzically ... Neil took a closer look, with trepidation at her comment. *"It's like looking at a hive of bees but holding hands, no... not hands ... what ... God, they're hands are webbed!"* Minutes passed between them, not believing what their eyes perceived, *"Their feet too!"*

Staring still in disbelief automatically Gavens pushed a button on his wrist, "Bré, are you getting anything like maybe a fix on this?"

"Yes, Neil. The Dark people are machine and human as I described before. I am receiving electronic signals from one systematic area of the dark side, underground. I can give you a trajectory on your return."

"Great, I also will try to bring one of those machines with us for analysis. But Bré I'm taking pictures right now to send you ... ah ... from the assembly floor of the Light Purples. Then give me an analysis."

"Yes Neil."

"Neil we, shared meals with these light purples and I do not recall them not having hands like ours. Do you think they are able to block various information from our minds?"

"Jean, I've never seen their webbing before except ... when I saw a Purple in the ocean. It wasn't wearing clothes or scuba gear." Before Jean could reply ... *"Eftiar, can you make sure to bring a couple of those robots back with our crew?"*

"Of course, Commander Gavens, they will be returning soon. We should not proceed further until we know more about these machines, but your First wants to proceed on...

"My God, it's Brill, he ... he ... he's got red eyes ... they've made him into a machine!" First yelled from the imo-mirror screen and he fired once, then again and again, until finally Brill fell. "Pull back, pull back immediately." The siouts stopped flipped into reverse and all backed away from the dark forest along with the warriors and battle ites making sure to stay within the encirclement of the siouts.

All eyes again were on the imo-mirror screen. The Light Purples got up from the floor, but still held hands. Not one spoke, they seemed to be in a trance.

"Yes, we are returning Eftiar," Linti said.

In supreme silence the entire assembly of Purples, Guides Eftiar, Efiari and Efiar included, leaving the room in webbed hold, some walking and some fuaing. Jean and Neil watched silently, mouths agape.

<>

"That was quick thinking on your part First," Gavens stated for all to hear.

"Thank you, Sir. I was taken back by the way Brill looked. I knew it wasn't the Brill I knew. He was a good warrior. Sir, do you believe the rest of the crew is dead or made into one of those things?"

"Well First, what better way to get to know your enemy, than to take their minds and adapt design them to your liking," Gavens commented. "This may be a problem for us in getting those out, who hopefully haven't been transformed into robots. We should get back to our ship with one of the alien robots and have Bré and Chambers run a full analysis, then return to speak with Eftiar and his people. We probably will need Dr. Simms involved, since they also seem to be half human. At this point I can make no assumption that all are dead. We could try to get into their habitat and destroy this type of bad seed that has manifested. Do you agree Efiari and Linti?"

"*I agree with you,*" Efiari avid. "*In the meantime, we will run our own diagnostics then compare. Of course, you are better trained in battle than we, so we will rely heavily on your expertise. Go back to your sioutous* (spaceship); *we shall make sure there is nothing left of this bastardization of our ites* (people)."

"Yes, I also agree." Linti stated, "Eftiar shall we place battle ites at the edge of the dark side?" No answer came from Eftiar.

"I must say we've all had a very severe eye-opening ordeal today," Dr. Spencer stated.

Gavens looked around the room but did not see Eftiar. "*Ah...where are you?*"

"*Our ites need rest after such a long ordeal, but I want to assure all that we will purge these Dark ites' from our Eftiam; this I promise you. We will not let this disease harm our ites.*" in the voice of a hurt and baffled man.

Chapter 10

"**Y**es Neil, they are human and machine. The inner body is machine and the outer is human skin."

"Your projection shows this. Would they be able to function physically as a human Bré?"

"From my analysis, yes, the eyes have immediate recognition, followed by functional movement of the body. This also could be mechanically altered. A machine model like this was designed in early 2020 by Dr. Henry Salinger and Dr. Justine Harper."

"They're Earth design?"

"Yes, Neil."

"Get this information to Dr. Chambers now."

"Yes, Neil."

"What about the Light Purples' webbing of hands and feet?"

"Early settlement took them mainly to water, for Eftiam had more water when they arrived. Some were drawn to land and some to sea, but calculations it was the presence of this other entity. Therefore, adaptation occurred as needed for all."

"So, I was truly seeing someone swimming in the ocean without scuba gear?"

"Yes Neil."

"They must need the ocean for survival."

"Yes Neil."

"Bré, do you have the names of the crew that was on the "Preamble?"

"Yes Neil?"

"Were these two scientists' part of the crew?"

"Yes Neil." Everything I already knew; must start listening to my gut and dreams.

Please see to it that Chambers, Spencer, First and I receive projections of the crew members of the 'Preamble'."

"Yes Neil."

<>

"The robots are machine inside and human skin outside. Also, these machines are of Earth human development by Dr. Harry Salinger and Dr. Justine Harper in the 2020's. They were on the passenger list of the 'Preamble', so I feel it's our responsibility, to make sure this planet is rid of the DPs'." Commander Gavens stated.

"Do you feel the LP's will be in agreement with ridding Eftiam of the DP's?" Dr. Chambers asked.

"Well, Efiari and Linti definitely are. However, Eftiar and Efiar may have some problems, after all this is part of the early genesis of Eftiam. But we're responsible for this problem."

"Why are we responsible? Even though they were part of the 'Preamble', this doesn't mean it's ours to take care of the problems of the past." Chambers added.

Gavens looked to Jean; he knew this question could not be avoided. With a sigh, "My great-grandfather was Commander of the 'Preamble'. Yet, I can't tell you fully why this has occurred now, other than we did go to the dark side, which in turn caused the robots to go into action. When I have more to share, I will do so. Now we must meet with the LPs' and compare analyses, and go from there, but I wanted you to be abreast of the situation. Don't give out this info until we know exactly where this is going. Understood?"

"Yes Sir." All replied, uneasily.

"Sir, what makes you say they are genetically related to the LPs'?" First asked.

"Bré shared upon first arrival that some of the people went into water and some stayed to land. Why or how is unanswered yet. Also, why, some of the land ones are half man and half machine is a question to be dealt with. I asked Bré to withhold this information until I deemed the time for explanation was right."

Dr. Chambers rose to get himself a cup of coffee, knocking into chair backs as he went. Setting his cup under the spout, it started to fill, "Theory tells us we too started in both land and water at the beginning."

He turned to face the group again, "I'll go into this further with Bré, to see if this can be helpful." lifting his cup to drink he tried to contain his excitement as a scientist.

Chapter 11

*"**T**hen we are in full agreement. Send the robots back into the dark side; monitor them, cameras included to evaluate their habitat?"* Eftiar avid.

"Aye," Came from the Purples and Earth/Sigmets.

"We should get underway immediately." Efiari affirmed.

"All battle ites' are at the ready. We should also be at the edge of the dark side." Linti proffered.

"Most certainly," Commander Gavens stated. "Let's get underway." All started to rise, but Eftiar and Efiar held back.

"Do you not think it wise Commander Gavens, to stay here with the imo-mirror to be ready for any other situation arising?" Efiar avi queried.

"No, I don't, besides it's my men out there and I plan to make sure they get back here safe, that is if any are left," stating this as he headed for the door.

"You know best about battle warring, we do not." Eftiar avi commented, now fuaing toward the door with Commander Gavens and the rest of their party.

Efiar and Dr. Spencer did not rise with the others. Efiar looked to Dr. Spencer, *"So you agree with me?"*

"Someone has to be here to pick up the pieces for the Boy Scouts."

"What is Boy Scouts?"

Sorry, I keep forgetting you don't fully understand our language at times. In other words, all men love war and must go into battle. It never seems to change. They get a great adrenaline rush from it. Boy Scouts is a national club on Earth/Sigmet for children to learn about nature. It's just men never seem to grow out of it. Most Women would never start war, only men."

"Yes, I do niet avi (think). *We can get to know each other better even while we observe the imo mirror."*

Both women seemed to accept each other as they left to watch on the screen and Jean also gave considerable thought as Eftiar's more frequent use of Earth/Sigmet phrases.

<>

Finally, able to be in a siout Gavens could not contain himself, *I want to know every nook and cranny of this craft. So much so, it's hard to keep my mind on the matter at hand. Chambers was right this craft is alive.*

"I can hear you," Jean breaking into his thoughts.

"Eee-gads, from where you are?"

"I'm with Efiar and the rest of the LP's watching from the imo-mirror. We've had quite a visit so far. Felt I could do more from here."

Immediately the scene changed, the two robots encountered other robots; unnoticeably they joined. Those in the siouts and the imo-mirror sig (image screen room) seemed so quiet, as if all held their breaths at the same time. Without realizing; the Earth/Sigmets in both areas, grasped their hands to the webs of Light Purples; their minds meshed to form a larger mind mass muscle to encounter the machine Purples.

Despite the dark surrounding them they could plainly see the infrared cameras planted in the robots' eyes as they proceeded to the robotic habitat. An exit and an exit door showed in a small clearing. Down they descended into an earthen tunnel. The robots made absolutely no sounds other than their footsteps. The tunnel seemed to go on forever; there was no structure that appeared to hold it up to prevent cave-ins. Finally, the tunnel opened into a large cavity, which had minimal soft blue lighting on some sort of metal walls. Machinery and wiring hung from the ceiling over tables, with robots lying in wait to be worked on. As Eftiar watched the imo-mirror from his siout, he opened communication to all; this was felt and readily accepted. *"Commander, how do you want to proceed?"*

"We should wait and try to find the main artery of implementation. Can we get these robots to move into other rooms if there are any? From here I can't tell if there are."

"Yes, I believe we can." Slowly the robots turned in a circle revealing more of this cavity, causing other robots to bump into them as

they broke normal formation. They recovered without being knocked aside. *"Yes, there are other arteries."* Eftiar gave the order to move the robots along into an artery. They entered into a room which had a bed, desk, chair, and old-style laptop on a table, about the size of Gavens' cubicle aboard ship.

The robots exited into a new artery, an alarm blared, lights flashed in red, and the room seemed to seal itself with a door sliding across. The robots were held half in and half out, making it impossible for them to proceed despite numerous attempts. The cameras went dark; all knew that the robots were still struggling to free themselves from the sliding door. All had a sensation of pain, although not hurtful in the physical sense; their hands webbed together more tightly so as not to lose sense of the other.

As suddenly as it started it stopped; all let go; exhaustion took over. *"We will return to our Sig City."*

<>

"Why return? We could have gone on," Neil asked, even though he too felt exhausted along with the rest. However, he had been in battle long enough to know that one went on despite exhaustion, when necessary, but no reply came from Eftiar.

The return trip gave the three Earth/Sigmets and warriors time to examine their escort siouts in greater depth. The crafts themselves were not noticeably large; when touching the wall of a craft it felt as though their hands entrenched through, but was held fast, just as the chairs held them.

Definitively they had organic seat materials, but the seats were not clear, but a dark yet transparent purple. They heard sounds of flipping comdat switches or keypads, one could not see whereas a hand slid into a tube up to the elbow while entering code. They were similar to an I-stick or con-wheel but almost silent due to hand-downloading controls. Gavens noticed the Juni piloting them also piloted their bubble transports. This Juni slightly nodded his head in recognition of Gavens. A smile crossed Gavens' face as he returned the recognition. He marveled that no wiring was visible, and the ship could maneuver up, down, vertically, horizontally, turn over, and he did not know what else, other than boggling his mind. No one dared ask what source powered the ship's operation, although this thought occurred to all Earth/Sigmets. Powered by fuel? Water? Water and Hydrogen? Nuclear cell? Upon entry, a metal grate removed all debris on their footwear, and a slightly felt suction took care of their clothing. Gavens mused that these crafts, unlike scoutbots were not designed for off planet or even overnight trips.

Eftiar made sure to take them by their farms on the return trip, discussing the different varieties of food and other types of crops. He told them of their growing seasons, which seemed to be year-round. This ensured a very mild climate pattern, meaning that tropical storms were non-existent.

Water came from the early morning moisture and two months of mild to heavy daily rains, much like in the tropics of Earth; these soils were rich.

Eftiar explained the upu-gram and how other integration of water and plants produced various products such as furniture and walls, which Earth/Sigmet had been imagined and semi-tried but never successfully.

While this was being explained ... *My superiors will want to take this planet right here and now. I must keep this from happening; this is such a new and young thriving planet. How can I keep this from coming about? These Ps' are advanced in many respects, yet so naive in others; fascinating, like those who grow up in the streets and never see a classroom but in reverse. Eftiar doesn't seem upset or urging for battle with these others from the dark side, why? The inside of that habitat seemed familiar...we didn't lose any present warriors...we have got to get back in there ... maybe...* "Commander Gavens, may we consult?" First asked, looking distressed.

"First?" Gavens looking about realized the siout had landed; doors were opened on all siouts and now First entered his siout.

"Sir," Fist spoke almost in a whisper, "I think I know what those robots are living in?

"Really?"

Shaking his head in a puzzled way, "It ... this is going to sound crazy ... but well ... Sir ... I think it's the 'Preamble'. Not waiting for Gavens to speak, he went on, "It has been re-designed into the main artery of a mine. The interior arteries I got to see resemble the ship.

What I don't understand is why would our people make robots? And mean ones at that? They sure didn't have to protect themselves against Eftiar and his people...Sir; it just doesn't make any sense."

Neil knew First was looking to him for answer, but he had none to give other than he too felt down deep in his bones a cold affirmation. "I believe you may be on to something First. I don't have answers to give, so until we know more, we should keep this to ourselves."

"Commander Gavens and First, shall we?" Eftiar avid. Without word, the two left the siout. *Their English is starting to sound like ours. I guess from hearing us so much.*

<>

All Earth/Sigmets seemed famished and proceeded to eat as if they had never eaten before, while the Purples left to rest. After eating the Earth/Sigmets then snoozed wherever they sat.

Efiar and Efiari were the first to enter the din- sig along with Jean. All those sleeping in the sig awoke and jumped-up demonstrating confusion.

Efiar frightened, jumped fuaing straight above their heads, hovering not sure what to do. "At ease," Doctor Spencer announced. "It's ok Efiar, come back down." Slowly she returned.

Gavens fumbling for composure, "F...First, would you please make sure our crews get back to our ship?"

"Yes Sir." striding out as he threw orders to his warriors.

"Efiar and Efiari, I want to thank you for feeding our warriors before they went back to our ship, but I sure didn't plan on any of us falling asleep."

"No need to apologize, you will always fall asleep after joining in an avi *transmittal centrifuge Commander,*" Efiari avid, fuaing to his chair.

"Why is that?" Gavens asked.

"You can niet avi now, Commander; no one is present that would know." Efiari avid.

Neil completely relaxed, *"Oh good, it's getting so this is the only way I want to converse. Why's that?"*

69

"Maybe it is more conserving of energy, or more like rejuvenating after an exhausting process using total avi strength or I believe you call niet strength," Efiar avid.

"Well, if that's conserving then we shouldn't sleep after transmittal centrifuge, I believe you called it."

"It's a different way of aving and extremely taxing to the body. Efiari, Jean and I have been aving about the habitat of the mechanical-ites; we find this is much like the inside of your sioutous (spaceship). *What is your estimation?"*

"That's a different way of referring to robots." Eftiar looked perplexed.

"Ah, mechanical- ites? Yes, First, brought it to my attention the minute we landed. We both believe it's the 'Preamble,'" Neil couldn't help himself; he looked straight at Jean when he spoke those words. *"I ... I don't know why or how this'd happened, but I feel we have landed here for special reasons. It feels very right that it's my great-grandfather's ship."*

Efiar, skillfully fuaid, immediately catching hold of the buffet ... she could not understand the sudden feeling in the pit of her stomach. *"Are you ok, Efiar?"* Jean and Efiari avi yelled.

No answer came from Efiar ... she looked straight into Neil's dark eyes with desire ... *but why? This is an Earthling not of Eftiam ... I really must have not rested enough,* but looking his way again, she realized she wanted him as her ef (mate). *He already has Jean as an ef, but Earthlings have many efs, I remember the imo's* (images) *I have seen. Why would I want one who efs with many...this is not custom?* All she could know, and feel was the need to ef (mate) with this Earthling. Again, she tried to think rationally but could not, the animal part of her came alive! She was completely overtaken; with a hunger she had never felt before. *Is this what it is like? I must speak with Eftiara immediately; she will know how to handle this.* *"Excuse me, I feel faint."* Fuaing rapidly, she left the sig as she avid.

Looking after his Efiar, Efiari tried to explain her unorthodox behavior, *"I am sorry, Efiar must have imo-niet avid more than she realized. We should wait until morn for further discussion. Linti will upu-gram you."*

"*Yes, perhaps you're right.*" Jean stated. Looking to Neil, they strode from the sig, as a Juni entered to escort them.

Chapter 12

"*Jean what did you make of Efiar's episode?*" Neil asked to make conversation.

"*It has to do with you; like, maybe being here for a reason.*"

"*Well, I do believe it. This is absolutely no coincidence we're on Eftiam. We were led to this planet, but our ship wasn't overtaken as Grandfathers. We're already observing this galaxy.*" Neil paced his cubicle. Jean could not help but giggle quietly to herself ... he missed the chair with every turn. "*Did you notice how Eftiar didn't seem the least bit bothered about the robot situation or take precaution against them? Instead, they all go rest and leave us alone and we eat food and fall asleep, as if nothing had taken place. This is just too weird. You would think they'd keep us under some sort of surveillance. No, no something isn't right here, and I can't put a finger on it.*"

"*Does the habitat really resemble the 'Preamble'?*"

"*Yes Jean, you saw what I saw. Think it over or do you just need to hear me say it's the 'Preamble'?*"

"*Point taken,*" Silence again fell upon them, but Neil still paced. "*Eftiar trusts you implicitly; therefore, he has no reason to place you under guard. All right, now how do we go about rectifying and helping the folks here on Eftiam?*"

"*Eftiar didn't give an answer to your suggestion of a guard on the DP's line either. I think I need to sleep on it.*" Jean got up to leave, but Neil gripped her by the arm pulling her close to him. "*No, please don't leave.*" She folded herself into him without question.

<>

"Neil, incoming, Linti upu-gram," Bré announced.

"I'll take it on main deck, Bré, thank you." Grabbing for his pants throwing his legs in before leaving his bunk, Jean too scattered for clothes realizing they slept late. Placing his finger to his lips to warn Jean, he looked through his folding door to see if anyone was in the walkway. Instead of looking back, he gave a thumb up behind his back. Finishing with buttons on his shirt and running his hands through his curls for a semblance of neatness, he moved toward the bridge. Jean scurried in the opposite direction. Arriving on deck, "You may patch the upu-gram (water-gram) through, Bré."

"Yes, Commander."

"Good morning," Commander," echoed throughout the deck.

"Morning all."

Linti's figure came into view, "Commander Gavens, Eftiar, wishes your usual party to attend a meeting in fiftn minis (fifteen minutes)."

"That's perfect, we'll be there." *I hope he has something like food, I'm starved.*

"Bré, have Chambers, First and Spencer in five minutes, meet me at the landing site for siout escort."

"Yes Commander."

In the elevator, "Bré, do you have an analysis of the robots?"

"Their skin is human, and they are completely mechanical, as in the 2020's. However, the two new robots differ. The newest one has skin like our present warriors, but the other skin is about or near one hundred years old. Would you like me to do a further analysis, Neil?"

A hundred years old! Wow! Ah ... no ... not right away. I want to do some other investigating first." *Eftiar's sciences may be able to, outdo her.*

"Oh, have you sent out any finished analysis to Earth or Sigmet."

"No Neil."

"Please wait to send out the material analysis. I may want to add something more to what you already have ready to go."

"Yes Neil."

Efiar fuai floated back and forth avi speaking with Eftiara, *"I cannot understand why this ite* (person) *affects me so... Eftiara ... I ...; suddenly I wanted to ef* (mate*) with him. Most embarrassing: I have never felt like this before. I must ef with an ite from Eftiam, not from Earth. What do you think, Eftiara?"*

"My Efiar, you are just coming into womanhood; this Earthling is just showing you, that your chemical hormones could easily lead you to ef with another, but yes, you must learn to control your emotions. It is only your emotions that you are letting control you. Taking an ef is more than chemical emotion. Their physical attributes are helpful, but not necessary, for to truly have a great ef relationship, one needs a best friend. Does this ite have the same principals in life as you and how about brain ability? The ef and you must like most of the same things in life, for if not, there is not a thing to keep an ef linked with you. Do not let this worry you, for it is not an Earthling you will ef with, it truly is an ite of Eftiam."

"How do you know? Are the Imo-Macos deciding whom we all ef with?"

"To those of us in the guiding of Eftiam, yes, the Imo-Macos definitely decide on our efs'."

"But Eftiara, I should be able to choose my own ef. They do not know to whom is better for Efiari or me," Dramatically her hands flew into the air as she fuaid. *"I will not allow this for myself."*

"Eftiara laughed heartily, *"Eftiar and I love you both very much and want the best for you and so do the Imo-Macos; it is your destiny. Ergo, the silver cord never to be loosed."*

"What cord never broken and why silver, what is the meaning?" So many words of late, my head hurts from all the new words and lessons. I know, I know, you are going to tell me, in tia (time) it will all come to a sense niet avi (mind thought) sense."*

"Efiar, my capacity is to guide you, but I cannot do the work for you. This you must do."

Finally sitting on her bed, *"I cannot show my face to our guests this morn."*

For an interval, no avi came from Eftiara. Firmly yet gently, *"You will not shirk your duties, you are to be head guide; this I command as your Eftiara!"*

Efiar did not make a sound, her legs spread, feet coming together in pigeon fashion; arms were crossed, but mouth hanging agape. Anger started to arise, so much so she began to rise from her bed in this unusual sitting position. However, she knew she best quell this anger, from the way her Eftiara avid. Also, in her niet avi, she now saw clearly that the Imo-Macos were right beside and behind her Eftiara, *"Why so important a matter with these Earth/Sigmets'? You Imo-Macos wanted them to land here, but you have yet to explain more about that. Now we find they were part of our past."* Her niet avi was precise and extremely forthright.

"They truly have not learned to stop battle warring and or how to care for their Earth or Sigmet and now we know they are here to take over Eftiam? We are not good at battle warring and this would make it so easy for us to succumb. Did you bother to avi on that?" Efiar was now avi pacing again, *"I also want to know if you Imo-Macos knew of the mechanical ites on the other side of Eftiam?"* No reply came from the Imo's; this irritated Efiar more. *"Well?"* Still no reply, *"Until you can give me some kind of avi, I will be in my life upu,"* Off she fuaid without an answer. *Just who do they think they are? They cannot tell us what to do; they are only advisors. Why has Eftiar succumbed to this? I believe now he has totally used their advice to guide our ites. This he should not have allowed, but who am I to say, I have not the experience of my Eftiara and Eftiar* (parents). *This leads me to wonder if I am truly capable of doing guiding.* Instead of staying within her life upu, she opened her door to the other realms of upu and quickly took off for depths unknown. With webbing enhancing her speed, feeling free for the first time in weeks, her mermaid fashion quickened.

Chapter 13

"Juni, we are not going to the ocean floor, why?" Gavens requested.

"Eftiar requires your presence at the farms." All four looked questioningly at each other. Neil shrugged his shoulders knowing the Juni was following orders, so he decided to enjoy the views. *Now I am aware why they sent a siout, not bubbles.* Looking out over the pu (jungle) *Even though this planet is different shades of purple, it grows on one. The shades of color are soft to the eye; it's almost the same feel as when on Earth. I've not felt comfortable on Sigmet in all these years. It would be easy to live here. The trees are abundant with fruits, the soils produce almost every crop known to us by nature and then some that are not...Oh! A Jaguar... It's gorgeous...wow a fawn the spots appear almost white, but the light refraction gives a hint of lilac... animals are also in great abundance. I know I must give Berry a report, but I'm not able to take all of this away from these LP's. Is it because we are distantly related? No, there's more to it than that. Look at First, he no longer wants to take over their planet, brainwashing? Or did they just show him another side of life, or because they saved his life? Myself I think it's the latter.*

"Oh God!" Doctor Spencer shouted.

Shocked out of his reverie Neil looked in Jean's direction. She was looking to the ground, along with the others, even the Juni.

Taking in the moment ... "Juni, what has happened down there? There are bodies all over the place ... without awaiting an explanation he jumped up next to the Juni, let me speak with Eftiar now, please. Something is seriously wrong." *He's the first one I've seen show any emotion, it's in his eyes.*

"Just avi to him Commander, Eftiar will answer, he knows we are here."

"Oh? Ah...Neil didn't know why, but he closed his eyes, *"Eftiar, this is Neil, what's happened?"*

"The mechanical battle ites have taken to killing our farm ites. At present, we have found sixt ites (sixty people) *aspid* (dead). *They are beyond recovery. Please avi your sioutous* (spaceship) *for more battle ites* (warriors). *Linti has arranged siouts (small land craft) for them."*

Without hesitation, Neil used his arm transmitter speaking to his acting deck command, ordering all warriors, since he did not know the full extent of casualties. Then he directed Bré to give him a full translation of the Purple interchange. Doctor Chambers and Doctor Spencer looked pale from the happenings on the ground. *This is truly their first encounter with violent death, in such numbers, and it's their first mission of this kind.*

"Sir, I thought the Dark Purples never went beyond the dark side," First stated.

"Well frankly First, I assumed nothing of the kind, but our hosts apparently felt the same as you. It wasn't my place to step in front of Eftiar, but this changes everything. If you were in charge, how do you think you would handle this matter?"

"I would have placed warriors at the borderline to be sure, Sir."

"Good, I expect you to do just that when our warriors arrive. I will leave you to choose those placed in charge."

"Yes Sir, thank you Sir. I'll await further orders."

"Doctor Chambers, I expect you to give help wherever needed and you Doctor Spencer will help in counseling; these folks will need help. This is their first encounter with death of this kind. Doctor Spencer you may also want to take Efiar with you, so she can learn from this experience. I will counsel with Eftiar, Efiari and Linti. We will need to take every precaution from here on out. Juni, when will we arrive?"

"We are in approach now, Commander Gavens."

Linti and Efiari were waiting for them at ground level. The siout hovered; quickly they assembled around one of the fallen, while the others left for their duties. *"Robots used laser. It was quick. No suffering."*

Linti, "Te (one) alive not conscious; a niet probe is being used."

Efiari saw the question on Gavens' face, *"A niet (mind) probe, feeds our compus (computer) information about the event. We do not have to wait."*

This probe was placed at the temple.

"They have everything provided for but battle. Is Eftiar with you?" Gavens asked.

Linti blurted, "Absolutely not! His safety is of vital importance, but he is within avi range and making use of imo-mirror (image- screen).

"Efiari, have you placed warriors at the edge of the Dark Purple section?"

"No, Commander Gavens we did not?" Efiari showed puzzlement.

"I've just placed this order into effect through First, so we have secured the area for now. Do you have any idea what made them leave the dark side?"

"We found the skin of te mechanical ite (one robot), *to be from te of your fallen battle ites and its brain changed, they also wore your battle clothes. Since you chose to send your battle ites to go to the dark side, they are learning and moving into the rest of Eftiam. They no longer need to stay in Eftiam dark."* Efiari avid with malice.

Looking at Efiari eye level, *"Oh Efiari, I was afraid of this. Don't let on I 'm speaking to you in this way. I need to speak with you and Eftiar privately."*

"Yes, I agree."

"I don't know for sure how all this came about, but I believe explanation is unfolding. We should counsel to decide our next approach." Gavens suggested, *"We can counsel on the Bramble. Is this fine with you Eftiar?"*

"I will meet you at your sioutous (spaceship), *Commander Gavens."*

<>

"This sioutous (spaceship) *is so large, how do they find their way around? We will surely need a guide to show us back to our siout* (small land craft); *we have been fuaing for so long. Everything is of an ancient metal; it makes such a horrible sound. It is so cold, it must be why the Commander places his hand to his head as he moves through his sioutous,"* Efiari avid to Eftiar and Linti, *"And why is Efiar not present?"*

"I believe it is what they refer to as saluting their Commander, and he must return salutes. His arm must be tired by now." Linti whispered.

"Yes, this metal is of passé (passed) *generations. It must be needed to go off planet. Surely, they are not still using these methods, although Commander Gavens avid he had the newest of planetary travel craft*

78

and he was very taken with our sigs, siouts and furnishings. I know he wants our knowledge of how we go about using natural science. Maybe this great-grandfather could have saved their Earth. Efiar was not in her sig or in any others; apparently in need of life-upu. After the display you avid she made; it was desperation. So much placed upon her these mons (months), *is wearing on her. Eftiara is also concerned."*

"Well, she cares nothing for battle. It is best she is not here," Efiari pushing his chest out further, *"You notice how their lighting glares; it hurt my eyes."*

"I feel it is from so much metal, but then too, I must agree, so much of their science seems passé. What say you Linti?"

Speaking normally, "Yes ... he found his voice echoing ... he now whispered, "Yes, I agree with you both. Even our battle ites noted how passé their science, but it does make one wonder how they have proceeded so far into space. Could it be their will power?"

"I do believe you have a point there." Efiari commented. *"Oh, I wish we could avi together Linti, rather than your mouth avi."* Linti made no comment, but his jaw seemed to stiffen. *"Oh look, we are coming into an open area."*

The room was round with other tunnels leading elsewhere. Commander Gavens took the time to introduce their guests individually to the crew on deck. They all stood at attention, in unison, saluting, before offering their hand of welcome to Eftiar, Efiari and Linti. A small, long table had chairs appearing most uncomfortable to the Eftiamrs, like the night they ate outside this sioutous (spaceship). "This is the largest area of our ship, so, this will have to do for our meeting," Gavens stated, "Please take a seat."

Eftiar, fuaid in place looking around, then, *"Commander Gavens, since your crew would have to stand the entire tia* (time) *we are seated, would it not be advisable to take our meeting outside under canopy?"*

Efiari queried, *"But before we do take this meeting outside, could we possibly see more of your sioutous, ah...ship, I...we are quite anxious to see the rest of it?"* The entire deck broke out with raucous laughter.

"Efiari very good thinking on your part at a politically delicate tia (time), *"* Eftiar avid only to his son. Giving a coy smile and nod of his

head Efiari, did not avi for fear it would be overheard, since he did not possess his father's gift.

<>

Out under the canopy, there was a light breeze, a lot of humidity but bearable, and the birds had quieted some. The usual entourage was seated for discussion without any warriors on guard, or at least not one visible.

"As I explained to Commander Gavens, the skin of the mechanical ite (robot) *is changed, and they now have the brain of human ites, resulting in the killings on our farms. Probably they will be coming further beyond the farms very soon. Oh yes, and these dark mechanical ites are wearing the battle shields of your present battle ites* (warriors), *"* Efiari stated. The silence hung letting the information digest before anyone moved or spoke.

Gavens studied the group before him, "Yes, we Earth/Sigmets faced the fact that we are the cause of the robots leaving the dark side." Not waiting for anyone to rebut him he went on, "Now getting to business, we must get back into the habitat. The robots should by rights not be able to reproduce themselves, so that leaves humans are accomplishing the changes. Eftiar, is there anything we need to know about your beginnings here on Eftiam, such as splitting of groups, or people being banished from the group?"

"Not that we are aware of, but I will discuss this with Eftiara you can be sure." Gavens noticed the grimace Efiari made at the mention of Eftiara.

"I agree we need to go back, but we must leave these matters to our battle guides and of course your expertise. You have the use of our siouts. I do not think the Dark ites will attack in the dai (day). *"*

"Couldn't Eftiara have joined us for counsel; this would make it easier to understand what we are up against? But as far as the DP's go, I believe they'll charge at any time since they've met with success on their first venture."

"What is DP's," Linti questioned.

"Sorry, that means the Dark Purples, we just shortened it to save words; we've mangled the English language." Gavens stated.

Laughter broke out in the gathering all except for Eftiar. Emotion showed on him as never before acknowledging an error partially spoken. *I am so used to being able to avi freely. Will they understand? Imo-Macos please help me now.* He braced himself for Commander Gavens' query.

"Well, Eftiar can we have Eftiara here and I apologize for not asking about Efiar's non-presence, please forgive me."

"Efiar has other matters to care for and she, like me, trusts in Linti and Efiari and the guidance of yourself and your counselors for battle decision making. I assure you if Eftiara could be physically present, she would. I will imo her the min (minute) *I return and upu -gram the result of conversation immediately."*

Neil considered this. *What is he hiding? Physically present? Imo her?*

Stunned with his revelation Neil, pushed his chair away from the table and started to pace, now running his hands through his hair … *Do I embarrass him here … he's a lunatic … she can't be …?* "I think we should take a small break. Ah, Eftiar, may I speak with you alone before we proceed further.

"Of course, Commander."

All rose to give the men time to separate themselves, leaving the others to take more foods and drink. Slowly Gavens walking and Eftiar fuaing, *"Eftiar, are you trying to tell me that Eftiara is dead and if she is, how long?"*

Looking frustrated in his fuai, *"Neil, what is dead? Our words are not the same."*

Neil stamped his foot, *"Come with me. We'll settle this problem right now."* Not waiting for an answer, Neil strode abruptly up the plank into the ship with Eftiar in fuai catching up, leaving the group quite perplexed.

In his chambers, he invited Eftiar to sit in the chair while he took the bunk.

"Bré?"

"Yes Neil?" Eftiar could not identify where this sound came from, as he scanned the room quickly.

"I have Eftiar, head guide of Eftiam with me. Seems we have a communication problem. You are the best I can think for clarifying language."

"Of course, Neil."

"This comdat (computer) *is the head brain of our ship, so she should be able to help. She believes she knows everything, but she doesn't,"* smiling slyly. "Could you explain the word dead to Eftiar?"

"The word dead, means a human having passed away, or in Eftiam language aspid." Eftiar's eyes lit like a light bulb. *So, this is a compus* (computer), *they speak to with their eating cavity. I need to study this English language more.* Neil also realized the meaning of Eftiar's use of word aspid previously.

"How in the hell can you talk to a dead person ... ah I mean aspid person?"

"Through her Imo."

"Bré?"

"Neil, an imo in Earth/Sigmet language is image."

"A picture?" No response came from Bré. Eftiar sat watching Gavens face for a reaction, but only saw him get up and pace in his small cubicle. Eftiar was amazed at how he maneuvered this small area without running into an object.

"Does Eftiara speak to you in this imo?"

"Of course, she avis with me and advises me. She was head guide before her asping."

Curiosity taking over, *"When did she die...aspid?"*

"At *the birth of Efiar; I would not be alive, could I not speak with her every dai."*

"So, you rely on her to tell you how to guide?"

"In most cases yes; she is with the Imo-Macos, who truly are our Guides."

"Bré, define Imo-Macos."

"Yes Neil. Imo-Macos means Image-Makers, perhaps similarity to God."

Neil sat up abruptly on his bunk, baffled ... *So, they take orders from others here on Eftiam. Is it the dark side group? This is getting complicated. "Eftiar, I'm trying to reason this. Do you also talk to these Imo-Macos, and do they also have faces?*

"Of course, they are the tes (ones) *who wanted you here on Eftiam."*

That's it! There's someone else here on Eftiam. Handle this carefully; we don't want to upset him. These people don't realize they're being used. "Bré, define tes.

"Commander … the closest definition is the number one plural."

"Ah … can I talk with them Eftiar?"

Now it was Eftiar's turn to fuai the small quarters; his upudo (dress) would not cooperate, so he placed himself back on the horrible chair.

"I have not given thought to this matter. I will ask their advice on aving with them. I have no qualms with you aving them. Now I believe we have others awaiting us and need to get present problems cared for." Eftiar did not await an answer, but fuaid up and through the door.

Neil followed but did not hurry. *"Are you Ok Eftiar?"*

Chapter 14

Gliding like a lightening streak, through the upu (ocean), gave Efiar elation she so badly missed; close to the same elation she felt land walk fuaing through the pu (jungle). Her pores were so open allowing the salt to penetrate deep into her cells with every breath, washing her clean and allowing for better niet aving (thinking). Suddenly reality stepped in…*how far have I come? My upu tia* (ocean time) *is near.* Making a slithering diving turn down to the upu floor bottom she joined a school of Kamich (grouper-like fish). They surrounded her waving support racing along to their hearts content. *"I have missed you also. Thank you for helping to bring me back to my upu roots for niet avi tia* (mind time). Sensing the emotional excitement, was now tiring her, all the Kamich now hung under her to help return her more speedily to the land resurgence tia (time) her body required, but it was far. *"Thank you; I do need your help. I avid Eftiar, he will send a Juni."* Even though she slowed her maneuvering the Kamich maintained their speed, many staying under her, taking the load to carry her. She could feel and hear the Kamich calling on the Dolfia (like dolphin); they sounded distal. Her webbing now slowed, floundering and her intake mix for breathing was shallow … *cannot seem to niet* (think) … *Eftiara, I am sorry…*

"Efiar you must help more please try." Eftiara enticed, "I too imo'd Eftiar."

"You and Imos … look concerned … fine … Juni … Dolfia coming… breaking into her avi … someone there … Juni… You? Understanding, Efiar did not struggle, she relaxed completely as the Juni *wrapped* her in a hy-oxy-sig ((bag of oxygen and water) He set the dials to give her the breathing mix needed to return her to her upu-life-sig (ocean pool). Dolfia took over for the Kamich carrying them both back to the sig. Once she was back in her life -upu-sig Efviari knew she would be fine, but he could not bring himself to leave her. He waited for her to regain consciousness.

Instinctively he knew he was not to stay, after all he was only a Juni. Efiar was royalty, he was not to go near her, yet he could not stay away from her. *I could ef with plenty of female, you are beautiful, and I yearn for you, why?*

"Your Eftiar is of tio shadings, as I, why could we not be ef'd? I do believe we should be te (one). *We will be te. I know you heard me that te day I took a chance to be closer to you; I did get through your havis* (head gear). *By Eftiam policy, that does make me your ef. It is my right to be here with you. You are soon to be head guide. I too can mind avi as good if not better than any of your family. We would be good together." She is coming around. I best leave her pool.* Now positioned to the side of her pool, the only webbing left showing was his feet, still connected into the life upu. He watched Efiar carefully.

"The handsome Juni? ... Yes, I do believe it is he ... looking from shaded lids ... yes, tio (two) *shades ... my ef?*

Gently he started un-wrapping her hy-oxy-sig, letting her slide into the life -upu -pool ready if survival help was necessary. Her webs kept her afloat, but she realized her strength was nil. "You were under great duress, my lady."

As she worked desperately to flip to the side of the life -upu-pool, he helped by removing the hy-oxy-sig completely. He laid her up on the side of the life- upu -pool as though she were a dead fish. *He is strong not requiring the help of another Juni. Your eyes are gorgeous like an oplatic diamond. What is he smiling about?* Efviari could not contain himself; boisterous laughter now escaped him carrying throughout the sig and tunnels for several minis, until he had to hold his stomach. Angrily Efiar, now tried desperately to rise; *"What ... is so funny ... to you Juni!* Her breathing finally acclimated and becoming stronger ... *Thank you for saving my life ... with the help of the Kamich and Dolifia, but I can do just fine now.... Please leave."* Controlling her frustration, now embarrassed by her unclothed state, she turned away from him, still unable to rise. His laughter stopped. Without a word, he picked her up in his arms. She still too weak to fight back. The Juni carried her to her bed, dropped her on it and strode from her sig, smiling hugely. Mouth still agape Efiar, could hear Eftiar in the back of her niet (mind). Finally answering his fear call, *"Eftiar, I am fine, just weak. I challenged the upu today thoughtlessly. With help from Kamich, Dolifia and Juni, I'm in my bed- sig resting; do not worry."*

She called upon her sig Juni. Upon his entry, he inquired as to her health, giving her drink and food. *"Juni, can you tell me the name of the Juni who rescued me?"*

"His name is Efviari," The Juni spoke with surprising venom. "I am sorry, it was my place to come for you, but he is much stronger than I and he was the better candidate.

"I take it you are not fond of this Juni. Why was he here in this part of the city? Where does he usually give comfort?" His name is not usual of a Juni.

"Efviari does not comfort anyone but himself. He seems to feel he can go wherever he pleases. We have tried many times to keep him out of the royal sigs, but he seems to find his way again and again. Although this dai I am truly pleased he was here in this tunnel sig when Eftiar avid the plea for your life. Is there anything else you require?"

"Ah, no, thank you for your kindness." Giving a slight nod of his head, he withdrew.

Goes where he wants when he wants? Does Linti know of him? Sleep came easily.

Chapter 15

Channels were open to all siouts for speaking. This was recently added since the Earth/Sigmets, arrival. Linti and First each were in their own siouts and two others assigned by First. Neil realized he had the same pilot for his siout. Neil took advantage of this opportunity, "Pilot, do you have a name, and I don't want to hear 'Juni.'"

The Juni looked curiously at Commander Gavens, showing teeth, "Efviari, Sir."

Gavens smiled, bending his head in acknowledgment. *Odd his name is similar to Eftiar's family; relative?*

"Commander Gavens, we're ready," First announced. Gavens was pacing within his siout; he turned to see Linti and First standing in the doorway entry.

"Very well First. Linti, why'd Eftiar leave so suddenly?"

"Commander Gavens with all do respect, it was an emergency, and there is no more to be said."

"Well, was there an attack on our ship, your farms or city? If so; shouldn't I be informed?"

"I assure you we are not hiding anything from you. This is a personal matter. Efiari is with Eftiar also."

"So, who the hell will give the orders through telepathy when we go in, did anyone consider that?" Gavens shouted now pacing more rapidly than ever, running his hands through his damp dark curls. The humidity was dripping from the leaves of trees and plants and all in uniform were showing marks of perspiration. Even the siouts seemed to be dripping water. *It must be a problem with Efiar.*

Linti smiled, "You will Commander Gavens. Eftiar assured me you could give those orders."

"I'm not a frig'n telepath!" Gavens shouted at the top of his lungs.

Linti did not move a muscle and did not wipe the smile, "Sir, just give it a try."

Neil stopped in his tracks, taking in what Linti asked of him. First and many others that were in hearing distance stood stupefied.

"I ... I ... Neil plopped into a seat letting it grab him thoroughly. *This is too much ... way too much ... Jean needs to be here to do this service. I just barely do good min-aving* (small telepath) *with Jean, Eftiar, Efiari and Efiar. Linti does not seem the least bit concerned. He believes I can really pull this off. God, help me, this sucks, sucks, sucks! I think I'm going to vomit!* Wiping his brow with his sleeve, taking a huge deep breath, he closed his eyes, *"Ah ... Hello out there ... ah ... this is Commander Gavens."* Every warrior and battle ite stopped what he was doing; some mouths dropped, some hit another on the arm and gave a thumb up while those of Eftiam accepted and waited.

Gavens opened one eye to see what or if he got through. Linti, First and all the Junis in the siout smiled and nodded their heads in affirmation. *"I, did it? I, really did it? Well, I'll be damn."* Again, he rose and started pacing back and forth. *"Damn I, really, did it? Really Linti, I, did it?"*

"Yes Sir!" Heard by all in every siout; laughter soon broke the heat discomfort. Embarrassed shuffling his feet and clearing his throat, he tried again, *"Eftiar has been called away, and ... ah ...Earth/Sigmet warriors together; perhaps we should have each battle ite pair with one of our warriors in case we have a language problem. I may get a little excited and you definitely wouldn't understand my heated orders."*

Laughter broke out again, but only with Earth/Sigmet warriors. This brought the Eftiam battle ites to hurry to work together to understand the Commander's aving, easing the tensions of their forth coming battle.

If the robots were watching from the dark line, it was not detectable.

"Those in charge, please remember the black box or the main comdat we are looking for. Try not to make battle, but if it comes your way, do not hesitate. Break a leg. Oh, for you Eftiamrs this means good luck in Earth/Sigmet language." Raising his right hand and looking at his wrist of the other, *"Gents, set your watches. At the top of twelve we will follow our siouts* (small land crafts) *in."* After a seeming eternity, down came Neil's arm. Slowly forming up the party moved into the forest of the dark side.

Entry was different this time; the siouts carried all the warriors and battle ites into the interior, making a pathway with laser beams.

Looking into the imo-mirror, *we still don't know the type of ray these LP's use. I must find out. These siouts take down anything in their paths.* Orders were given for the pairings.

There was no response from their prey. Did they sense the ray could hurt them or was it their sleeping hour? Only a human could guess.

Exchange of fire suddenly began. The leading siout seemed to drop slightly as if grounding, but regained lifting once again, as it returned fire.

"Commander, we have taken a hit, but are able to keep it air bound. Damn sir, it's already repairing itself and still firing!"

"Ack ... uh ... Acknowledged. Is it DP laser fire also?"

"Yes Sir, we are on equal laser ground so far with the DP's," The Officer answered. Gavens was so surprised at himself for being able to avi transmit his complete conversation to all that he broke out in a cold sweat and realized his hands were shaking. Efviari gave an affirmative smile with head nod, acknowledging his success, building a comradely feeling.

Gunfire seemed to come from all sides now, their progression slowed but remained precise. *The LPs seem to have no doubts, they feel these ships will take care of everything, but I know that can't always be the case.* No sooner had Neil's thought passed when the lead siout exploded along with everyone inside.

The eight siouts stopped in midair almost colliding with one another. As Neil righted himself, he could see that this shook his pilot Efviari along with Eftiam battle ites. *They are not used to this sort of exchange or even the slightest of battle.* "Keep moving, men; don't let this stand in our way. We have a goal here, remember your goal."

Linti's voice heard fully in all the siouts, "Listen to your Commander, Eftiam battle ites, we must destroy these of the dark side!" Efviari and Linti's pilot reacted immediately with their siouts out skirting the other siouts, hoping the others would follow in course. They did.

"Thanks, Linti."

"Do not think it is you, they do not listen to, Commander. Sir, well ... this is our first battle ever."

Holy shit! *"You are giving me this information rather late, but I believe from here on Linti, we will start with morning battle exercises for everyone."*

"Agreed; we lost twenty-five battle ites Sir. Along with the farming ites, we need to make sure we win this battle for Eftiam and our ites. The Imo Macos have spoken." *Again, I hear of these Imo Macos, but I thought they only spoke to Eftiar's family?* "Commander, we're almost through. How would you like to proceed? Looking out Gavens could see more DPs' coming from the exit door hand fighting, but to no avail against the siout. Neither ships, scoutbots nor any other sort of heavy weaponry other than guns were evident, although some sort of makeshift knives were being used by the DP's. Suddenly from the top of the housing came laser fire and this did make contact once again with another siout. It did not disable it entirely but stopped it from progressing further on. The leader of the siout opened the doors and had his men move to the outside for further battle.

Now DPs came from the habitat with guns. These guns emitted laser beams, aimed at the LPs' that left their siouts. *"Focus your lasers on the DPs' with guns. We must get inside to get to the comdat box."*

Focusing, their lasers struck down the robots as if they were toys, falling within a domino effect. The battle ites started cheering. The Earth/Sigmets smiled, understanding the full implication for these people.

"Efviari, could you navigate this siout, sideways to their door entrance?"

"Yes, Commander!" Within seconds he had the siout in front of the door.

"All right warriors remember we only counter attack if necessary. You know our goal. Carry on." *This seems strange not going with my warriors.*

"Ok, Efviari, we will now move away and let another siout come in." Neil was giving the orders before his pilot reacted.

"Yes Commander."

It has been more than an hour. Neil paced the entire siout while running his hands through his wet curls and rubbing his eyes. Now he watched the imo-mirror comdat that illuminated the fighting within. It was hard to identify battle details; lasers and swords were seen, soldiers or robots fell, but in the chaos, it was almost impossible to see if progress was being made or not made. *Now I know how it was for my superiors to sit, watch and wait. Waiting sucks...*

Chapter 16

Eftiar and Efiari fuaid faster than ever before! They entered Efiar's sig with a large gust of air which engulfed Efiar so that she awoke frightened.

This had never happened to her upon awakening in all her years. Realizing the mistake before Efiar could avi; Eftiar clasped her into his arms, squeezing her to the point of pain. *"Eftiar you are hurting me, please I can barely breathe."*

"Efiar I...we were so frightened when you avid," Eftiar explained, letting go while his hand examined every inch of her to make sure she was all right.

"I am fine the Kamich, Dolfia and that new Juni saved my life, but I already explained this to you. However, this new Juni stayed with me until I fully acclimated once again to land life from the upu (ocean). *I went too far. I was terribly upset with myself and also with Eftiara and the Imo Macos, and the Earth/Sigmets', I needed the upu for free aving. Seems I did more than I should have, tia* (time) *got away from me."*

"We must find which Juni saved your life," Efiari avid, *"And send an avi of thanks to the Kamich and Dolfia."*

"I was able to thank the Kamich and Dolfia, I was still semi-conscious, but yes, it would be good for you and Eftiar to send avi thanks to all. Oh, I know the name of the Juni who saved my life."

"You do?" startled both avid simultaneously.

*"Remember the Juni, I told you about, Eftiar, the one I saw on my way to my sig, and again in other areas of sigs, and thinking that he had niet avid (*telepathed) *me? Well, his name is Efviari." Not sure why, Efiar did not continue, but waited for Eftiar and Efiari to react.*

Eftiar's eyes became large marbles, *"Efviari? Family? But this cannot be all our family history is aspid except for our immediate family, so we were told by the Imo Macos."* Letting go of Efiar, Eftiar uplifted and proceeded to fuai back and forth in front of Efiar's bed. Both teens watched their father in motion, unsure how to react to his perplexity.

Breaking the silence, *"How did you come to know this Junis given?"*

"It was the strangest of avi; I asked my Juni his given, and he became slightly upset. He explained that Efviari is not to be anywhere near our sigs, but no one could keep him out no matter how many tias (times) *they tried. Plus, he does not do Juni service, and no one knows how this man survives. He seems a mystery to all Junis. I even got the feeling of respect or even worship when my Juni spoke of Efviari, even though he tried desperately not to allow this niet avi* (thought)*. Then I wondered if Linti has spoken of this man to you Eftiar... however, I am glad he was in the sig area after what my Juni presented to me. I would not have survived otherwise. Admittedly I went too far out and apparently, Efviari is the only Juni capable of the distance let alone bringing someone back unconscious. I do owe him my life."* Efiari and Eftiar looked to the other for support of this heavy avi even clearing their throats although their mouth cavities are not used for aving as are Junis' and Earth/Sigmets.

Again, clearing his throat while fuaing, *"Linti, has never mentioned this Juni to me."*

"Eftiar, have the Imo Macos never niet avid the given of this Efviari? It does resemble our given, does it not?" Efiari avi requested.

"His given is a family name, but no, no mention. We believed all aspid except for our immediates." Efiar could not express how this odd statement affected her body chemistry, a pang of loss? Yet, his given is a sign of a relation. I do feel we must meet this Efviari, to investigate this relationship and to give thanks for saving our Efiar. What type of reward should be given this Efviari?"

"Truthfully Eftiar, I am more interested in fact if he is a relation." Efiar, avid with sorrow ... This focused both men's eyes ever so closely on Efiar.

<>

"Commander, we have found the black box!" First exclaimed, showing up on the imo-mirror screen. "Also, leaving there are no heavy casualties on either side. Odd, once we retrieved the box, the robots

93

quit attacking, see …" they stopped in their tracks as he panned the room."

Sure, enough the robots were paralyzed. *"Was the box connected to a comdat?"*

"Yes Sir."

"This is how the robots were navigating. I placed two siouts at the line of forest entry for precaution's sake. Also, I placed two siouts in the farming region with warriors. Even though they are stopped doesn't mean a backup system override of the main comdat could bring them running again. The siouts will be at the exit door for you to board. We will confer on our return to LP base."

"Sir… something's happening … the … LP warriors have dropped…"

No sooner said, then Neil saw the siouts stopped in their tracks, and all the Junis hit the floor of his siout. *"Hello what's happening with your siouts? Pilots? First?"*

"Here also; there's got to be a connection with the DP robots."

"Linti?" Neil waited, but no answer came. *"Eftiar are you there?"* No reply came. He tried the two youngsters, to no avail. *"Ah … First, gather all LPs', both injured, deceased, and unconscious and get them back to the LP base. I will take two of the siouts and check the farms for any other LPs' and return them to base."*

"Yes Sir."

"Jean? Jean, are you there?"

"Yes, Neil, what's wrong?"

"Get to the LP base with as many of our medics as you can and anyone else available. We have a severe problem. You will find LPs' unconscious or in coma, not sure yet, but it has to do with the robots somehow. I'm going by the farms … checking there … First and warriors are bringing in injured, deceased, and comatose. No time to explain more, just do it."

"What are you saying coma or comatose? The rest I relate to, but….

"Look Jean no time to go into explanations other than it refers to the black box. I need the medics to verify their condition, that's if they can. They need help fast and it's the entire population of Eftiam. The longer in this state the worse it'll be for them and us. Also, it's the best

place for scuba divers to try and get into the Sig City, as the bubbles aren't available to us. Get all to the water edge for us to transport them into Sig City. I'll have First come with his siouts and get most of you. We will pick up any left after we check the farms"

"Yes Neil."

Neil had some of his warriors try to get a handle on the siout controls, but to no avail within his craft so he put out an avi, *"Do we have any Earth/Sigmet warriors who have piloted space craft?"*

"Aye Sir", came from about five different locales.

"We'll head for the siouts and try to get them flying so we can get everyone back to base. It may take some doing, but if you've piloted before it shouldn't be that difficult." Neil could see different soldiers moving toward the siouts. One approached his.

"Sir?"

"Get in here and try the sucker, no time for talk."

Scurrying to the control center, he placed his hand in the cuff, while his eyes watched the board, "Better all buckle in Sir, don't know what might happen?" After he fiddled with the controls, the siout took flight, but immediately dropped to the ground, jostling all within. Again, he played with the controls, repeating the same process. From his seat Gavens could see through his seat view finder imo-mirror screen others, were having the same problem.

"Attention Pilots… this may sound strange, but I want all of you to stop what you are doing and close your eyes. Leave your arm within the cuff."

"What the hell?" Came from Gavens' Pilot, *"Ah…sorry Sir, but…"*

"Pilots, just do as ask." As they obeyed all seemed to calm, *"Now pretend you are in your old cockpit; you know this baby so well; you want to fly with the birds or out under the stars as always."* Waiting a few more minutes, he let this sink into their minds. *"Ease slowly back on your controls and your ship will rise to your touch."* Neil could feel the change in everyone within his siout and those in the other siouts. *I can feel every heartbeat.* Without a doubt, he knew they would be capable of flying these siouts. For the life of him he did not know where the instructions he spoke came from, but hell it was going to work; he just knew it. Yes, yes, they were lifting the siouts, *"Now gents, let's get our business completed."* A few skeptical pilots were still

having trouble, but he knew they would eventually control their craft. *"Pilots, we need to get to the farm,"*

Gavens alerted his pilot and another siout, also giving out their orders, *"See you back at base First."* *I still can't get over how I'm able to separate my thoughts and giving communications without thinking about it. It's like I think and it flows, a phenomenon. This box had better give us the information we need. I must get a hold of Berry now that I have more to go on. I will be up for two or more days. Can I hold out?*

Chapter 17

The siouts were loaded with unconscious farmers; there were not enough stretchers left let alone beds, so they were just unloaded and moved to areas of floor space, creating a makeshift hospital. Gavens' troops scouted the entire city to bring other Eftiamrs to the hospital set-ups. The entire city was down. They found many Eftiamrs floating on the water or on shore that had attempted life revitalizing in the ocean and lost their lives.

So far, the death toll came to one thousand. Those injured weren't seriously ill, and there was no worry about the supply of pain killers with them all in an apparent comatose state. Doc Chambers requested a robot brain from the DP side so he could establish brain connection with the LP's. Chambers was trying every angle to figure out the connection. Doc Simms even started coming in to help Chambers, with the physical side of things. Both worked well together in their goal to get a final analysis to help all on Eftiam.

On their arrival into the main sig with the largest imo-mirror screen, Doctor Spencer related, "Commander Gavens, most of the LP's were here in this room webbed together watching the wall screen."

Gavens, First, and Jean sat down to investigate the box. Anticipation was high in the room they now called LP base. Purple plants, furniture, dishes, and lighting now seemed part of their everyday world. Even the warriors seemed to feel at home with no thought of eliminating the LP's.

Tables and chairs for discussion were added to the room, along with its use for medical purposes. Holding most of the city people who were comatose, it was an eerie feeling to walk around the area and see many bodies lying on the floor. *"I'm not sure we will find much of anything to hear or see on this box, it being so old. Plus, they may have erased most of the data since it was used in conjunction with the comdat (PC). We can only hope."*

"Sir, why're you still mind talking?" First questioned.

"In case Eftiar and his people possibly can still hear us, even though they are unconscious." Gavens gave a nod to First, who dimmed the lights enough to see the projection. Everyone seemed to lean slightly forward in their chairs to ensure getting a closer look.

Jumping into immediate view was an image of Gavens' great-grandfather conducting the usual takeoff procedures. The sound was good; one could even hear the clicking of switches around the deck. Finally, the former Commander Gavens began to speak to the entire ship, "This is Commander Gavens speaking. If any of you have a change of heart about embarking on this great adventure, please gather your belongings now, and go straight away to docking, give your name to the Ensign in charge so we may remove it from the roster. Otherwise, for those of you going on, buckle everything down, we disembark in fifteen minutes."

"Now I see where you get your good looks." Jean mind spoke, smiling at Neil. He returned the smile, without comply.

The speech went on about how the craft maneuvered smoothly and how they were encouraged in their quest to try for a new galaxy, to gather new information and find a new home where their science could be used in a better environment to improve living conditions for all concerned, especially those left behind on Earth. *Even though they cast you out, you were till trying to help Earth.* The com-mov went drudgingly on and on to the point all were tiring and ready for naps. Even Neil was ready, but he knew he couldn't fast-forward for fear they may miss an important point.

Suddenly all was chaos ... one could see the boards lighting without any manipulation by the crew on deck. "Sir, something's ... getting ... taking control of our systems. We can't navigate on our own."

"Same here Sir." All were reporting that controls were not responding.

"Oh my God, we've been re-routed to a different galaxy!"

"Are you sure?"

"Yes Sir!"

"Well, I'll be damned ... Can you get control again?"

"Sir, it seems someone wants us badly. Not a damn thing we can do about it either; our hands are tied," as his hands flew across the keys trying to manipulate, things to take over control of their ship again.

"Are the earth ships still following?" Neil's great-grandfather questioned.

"No Sir, they dropped back a good three hours ago."

"Well, they've at least given up. We're now in the hands of the new Aliens, or maybe it's just a magnetic pull."

"Ah Sir, they've literally taken over the ship and set brand new coordinates."

"Ok … let's get a look at these coordinates and try to make sense of the galaxy we're set for. Also, see if this system has planets that can accommodate us. Check with the main computer to see if it can get a reading. I would like to find out why the computer didn't pick this up before and try to give some kind of an alert. That new tool that was added didn't work. Earth would like to know that. We are in close enough range still try to relay that to Earth."

"I'd forgotten in that time era we didn't speak to our comdat," Gavens mind-spoke to all. *No one seems to consider it out of the ordinary now for me to mind speak. Changes can happen in one's world so quickly. …* Listening … *The main comdat didn't find a new planet or where they were headed.*

Former Commander Gavens spoke directly into the imo-mirror screen. "It's been four weeks and still we are being guided by this unknown force. There are those on-board ship that are fearful. You can see it in their eyes. Others are regretful for having come along because they didn't want to disappoint their spouse. But the rest of us aren't afraid. We knew coming into this that trying for a better life had its down points. Hell, we're surprised we're still out here in good shape." He paused.

"We've been busying ourselves with picturing galaxies different from our own. It truly looks as if we're headed for a new unknown galaxy. We're taking the time to imagine and draw up new worlds as we experience them. Maybe it will be centuries before anyone gets a chance to see this record of our adventure, but for those of you that do, I hope it gives you insight."

The screen blacked momentarily. All thought the recording had finished, was empty, when Commander Gavens suddenly jumped back on the screen in full view. He was sporting a beard. The date on the screen showed a month later; as First was ready to play back thinking they missed something Commander Gavens spoke, "No don't touch your dials folks; I've taken the privilege to reprogram the box to recording once a month. Reason being, we don't know how long we'll be out here, so I don't want to take up space with nothing to report. Good thinking, eh?" A slight wry smile, "Anyway, in this month, I have married three couples. And they've agreed not to pro-create until we find a habitable planet. I just pray they're good for their word. We're still unable to pilot our ship. It's unknown where we're going."

His monthly reports droned on and on for two years before any changes came about, "Our signal is stronger now. As you know we divided our ship into small cities with a governing council in each." Former Commander Gavens took on a perplexed look. It looked as though this excursion to an unknown galaxy was beginning to break down his demeanor. "We have divided into four separate groups; each has a council. Not sure if I told you of this, so please bear with me if I already have. Then once every two months all the councils meet to discuss any major problems requiring governing command protocol. Many of our citizens have been complaining of headaches and odd dreams. Can't say they're nightmares, but in discussing the dreams, they seem to be of the same nature. Before I give you further insight on this matter, the Doctor and his Staff are still researching." Jean and Neil's eyes locked, *"We never thought to check with any others on board. Chambers never mentioned anyone coming to him with headaches ... did he?"*

"No Neil, but you couldn't nail down what was going on, so I suppose if anyone else was, they'd think it weird to talk to Doc Simms about something so minuscule as dreams; although, it would be a good idea to have Bré check into this. I really didn't realize how great we have it with comdats such as Bré to help with major research and ship navigation until now. We take them for granted."

"We sure do. Hard to believe so much has changed in such a short period."

First turned the box on again; "One wouldn't believe this if they knew our two main scientists on board the Preamble, but they fight everyday over any little thing. Just to argue a point. I guess it's to keep their minds active. Heaven knows we all need activity now. We've got required exercise for all areas every morning. Games for the young and old, but with our everyday tasks curbed to a minimum since we aren't piloting this vessel, we now just maintain it and we're definitely going a bit stir crazy. It's very dark out here ya know. Anyway, I married them today, but Justine refused to take Henry's last name. She kept her own, as she puts it, 'after all she is a scientist.' The best part is on Earth they wouldn't approve, but out here, who out here is to argue?

The date changed to a month later; "This is Dr. O'Brit, assigned to the Preamble. My Staff and I have done an extensive study and find a most unnatural prevalence of headaches and odd dreams, throughout this ship. The oddity we find is that the dreams are exactly the same for all.

The headaches occur two hours before the dreams and the personnel involved are related by genetic birth. There is nothing in our research to show any sort of significance, except we found this does occur in twins, and some theories state the supernatural, which is not considered scientific theory. Another similarity we find is when the signal that seems to be driving our ship is strongest, the headaches tend to occur, and the people take naps two hours later, no matter where they are or what they're encountering. We will keep recording this information and if there is any change, we will alert Commander Gavens."

Neil entered the date and times in his handheld, along with his other notes of reference; so, did Jean and Chambers, who by now joined them. *There is a pattern similarity to mine and Efiar's.*

"I think we need a break; you have fifteen." Everyone took off immediately, probably for the restrooms. A few headed to get refreshment; Neil himself wanted coffee hot and black.

On Jean's return, she came straight to Neil's side, *"Neil there is a pattern to your dreams, but I don't recall you having headaches."*

"I agree," Chambers mind-spoke stated from behind, *"Excuse me for eaves dropping."* Both looked at Chambers quizzically. *"What's the matter?"*

"Chambers, you're speaking telepathically." Spencer transmitted.

Chambers looked at Spencer as if she was giving a freak show.

"It happened to me the very same way," Neil offered. *"Did you have any relatives who were on the Preamble?"*

"Y...Ye ... oh shit ... I'm really speaking this way, aren't I? It's so ... damn weird. But yes, I've an Uncle; he was the Doctor you just heard speak. I must try to get to his notes. I'm sure we'll find them; he took great pride in his work."

"I think we should check and see how many from our ship had relatives on the 'Preamble'." Gavens suggested, then spoke into his wrist transmitter, "Bré, please send a question to all aboard the ship asking if they had a relative or relatives on the 'Preamble."

"Yes, Commander Gavens."

"Well then, how many of us at this table have a relative or relatives that served on the 'Preamble'?" five at the table raised their hands. Gavens smiled, *"I think we've something in common. If it hasn't started. Believe me it will. Chambers just found out he can send telepathy."* Of course, surprise showed on the five non-believers. *"I found out a year ago I could speak with my mind. This occurred with Dr. Spencer and me. I don't know if it happened with all of you at that time or not, but I do believe we should try to speak it right here and now to one another."*

Commander Gavens had each one try to accomplish telepathy, with Dr. Spencer first, then with himself and then with each other. Two were able to achieve it immediately and the rest had not caught on to mind speaking yet.

"Are we all telepathic? And will we be able to mind speak as you and Eftiar do Sir?" A warrior asked.

Smiling, *now that's a born leader.* Before Neil went on, he made sure to repeat the questions asked by the warrior to the others who were having mind speaking problems. *"You know as much as I do about this. We're all learning. Anyway, I feel it has to do with this planet and those of us who had relatives on the 'Preamble'. Matter of fact why don't you try to speak to all with your mind right now, Gates is it?"* The warrior tried to no avail and began to laugh, for the only one hearing him was Gavens. *"Keep working at it. Let's try and complete this film, we have a lot of people who need our help."*

Monotony ruled for another twenty-five minutes into the film; the Commander appeared with an exceptionally long scruffy beard, uniform wrinkled, un-manicured hands and pallor skin, "We're entering their galaxy; I'm sure. I've one hell of a headache. Yes, I'm one of those aboard getting headaches and they're constant for me since entering this galaxy. This morning I also received a message from this group through my mind. They told me they are the Imo-Macos. We will be landing on the last planet within this galaxy, of which there are six. The landing however, will not be good. We will crash, but all will survive. They give no explanation as to why we will crash and not land with our ship intact. I feel it's because they wouldn't know how to land it, even though they took control of the guidance system. I tried reasoning with them, but they will not give us back control of our ship to land it. So, knowing this as I do, I'm not going to tell my ship's crew, for they would get hysterical to say the least. Plus, we may never be able to return to space and or Earth. Fortunately, we really didn't plan to be able to return to Earth anyway. This was such a gamble coming out to find a better place for survival without pollution. Shit, we've been destroying our beloved Earth for centuries, over and out."

The entire room was silent. Even those working on patients stopped to look at the screen now blank, awaiting the next communication ... time seemed to drag, even though it was only seconds, "Hello again, sorry the lapse was longer this time, but my head is hurting so much. The Imo-Macos say once we land the headaches will stop, but we will all communicate now through telepathy. It will only be a matter of hours before we have crash landed on this planet. Get this; it's purple in color from this distance. Not sure if this is a distortion or if it will remain purple or if it just has something to do with gases seen by the naked eye at this time."

The lapsed time brought another face, "This is Dr. O'Brit. Commander Gavens is in sickbay. He is comatose. Matter of fact all those that have endured headaches and dreams for the past three years are in an unconscious state. I too have endured this off and on, but I could hear the Imo Macos telling me to wake, so I could care for them all. Hell no, we don't know what to make of it. Commander Gavens told me personally it is the Imo-Macos causing the headaches, whoever they are, and they will subside after landing on the planet. The screen seemed to start jumping up and down. "Oh? My, my … shit … we're entering their atmosphere! I … I'll try to resume this after we've landed."

The imo-mirror screen showed a planet so covered with water, there was only a small island showing. "I wanted to show you what we're up against here on this planet. The messages I'm receiving are from the waters surrounding us; exactly where I can't tell. All of us with headaches are requested to enter the water and completely immerse ourselves. Who knows what will happen after this? However, these people will come before the box in threes to let you see their faces." As each one passed, all at the table recognized some of their family members from pictures of yore. As they watched, the people joined hands as they entered the water.

"It has been ten hours; not one of the crew members has emerged. I do not know what to gather from this undertaking, but I will keep you posted. Commander Gavens and I decided that if they did not return in twenty-four hours, we would consider them lost. This is Dr. O'Brit. Oh, the Imo Macos' told me I will enter the waters after the others return."

"This is Commander Gavens, yes, I am speaking to you and I might add I will be speaking telepathically from here on. We spent twenty-some hours with the Imo-Macos. This Eftiam with the Imo-Macos teachings, te (one) cannot explain how wonderful and fulfilling our lives will be and already are. Everything on this planet is various shadings of la, lae, li and lu, (royal purple, lilac, pale lavender, lavender) of course you are not color blind. Here are my new gills … turning he showed the openings for breathing on his back and neck and showed the webbing of hands and feet. … All of us who entered the upu have experienced this body change. It will be our responsibility to help those not chosen by the Imo-Macos with their other responsibilities and show other methods to live here on this planet. Those that were not chosen can still earn the Imo-Macos trust with hard work of service. It is rather hard to explain. A major problem occurred. The Imo-Macos have chosen only te of our head scientists. There is now heavy dissension between Justine and Henry. I fear something major will come of this. I will try to give updates, but now that I am part of Eftiam, we will not give, I should say share as much as if we were still Earthlings. We must protect Eftiam; after all this is our home now!"

"Stop the com-mov (movie). *I believe we just found the main problem here on Eftiam."* Gavens pronounced.

"The scientists," First stated.

"Exactly."

"Ok, but who are the Imo-Macos?" Chambers requested, mouth speaking for the others not yet receptive to telepathy.

"Doctor Spencer..." this way I don't use her first name ... *"And I have been asking that question since we got here. Eftiar and his kid's talk of them constantly, but never give any information about them. Lately I've been hearing from the Junis of these people called Imo-Macos, but they too refuse to give out information. It seems when the Junis speak of the Imo-Macos, they look around cautiously like they are not to speak of them at all. Maybe they're not supposed to know too much information on them, but they do anyway. You know what I mean, like the help seems to listen, without authority. But they do discuss privately amongst themselves."*

Gavens slid back his chair, then rose and started pacing back and forth. So far, he was not running his hands through his hair, so he was evidently quite calm. Now Chambers also pacing, but in his strides, he managed to go to the refreshment center and grab an Eftiam drink. Picking up the drink, he looked at his skin to check for color change, as though he was running an experiment on himself. Gavens took notice of this but didn't comment.

"Your Grandfather Gavens mentioned that those not selected had to perform services to gain a chosen place with the Imo-Macos," Dr. Spencer commented. *"Maybe they've attained this level but don't want to let it be known."*

"Now why would they do that?" Chambers queried.

"Well, Eftiar and kids are the Guides here on Eftiam. Maybe the Junis are secretly planning a takeover," First stated, sliding his tablet on the table. It got very quiet, causing First to look up from his thoughts. *"What ... what's wrong?"*

"First, you are mind talking," Spencer avid.

"Oh ... WOW!"

Gavens explained for those still unable to mind talk, smiling, *"First projected that the Junis could possibly be planning a takeover. First, you have a valid point there. Like ... ya know ... it could upset the way of life here on Eftiam and the Junis aren't ready to make their move."*

"You do mean a takeover?" said Dr. Chambers, apparently unbelieving.

"Why would such a thing matter?" Dr. Spencer interjected.

Slowly First took time to think after speaking with one of the warriors he had placed in charge while still sitting at the table. Now speaking to all, "Primie here tells me that he has become good friends with some of the farmers. They speak of a new coming that the Imo-Macos promised."

This stopped Gavens and Chambers from pacing. All turned to look at First, then to Primie and the other warrior Colt at the table.

"Tell us more Primie."

"Commander, it's not so much what they say, but how they say it. From what I've gathered amongst the Junis there's a chosen one. He will lead for all the Junis, but the time is not yet right. That's about it in a hen pack."

"Raised on a farm, were you?"

Yes Sir, but how did you know"

All could but smile, *"Just a lucky guess; thanks for your information. Before we go jumping to more indefinite conclusions, maybe we better get back to the com-mov (movie)."*

The date showed a month later. *"We have erected temporary sigs* (housing) *from the wreckage of our sioutous* (spaceship). *Some from downed trees nature has discarded. These are only temporary sigs until the Imo-Macos bring us together to complete our lessons for permanent sigs. We are learning about new materials that blend with Eftiam and not hinder the planet and or its ites. Justine is doing splendidly. The Imo-Macos chose the right scientist to teach all operations. Henry, however, Has chosen to go off on his own with some of our ites* (people). *He refuses to partner with his wife or any other ite* (person) *on Eftiam. I know this is due to the fact the Imo-Macos chose Justine over him."*

"The wreckage doesn't look bad and all did survive," Gavens shared, as they kept watching. *"Also, I think we have all noticed my grandfather is speaking using Eftiam vocabulary."*

"Commander Gavens, Dr. Simms needs to see you immediately, concerning Eftiar," Bré announced.

"Thank you, Bré. As Neil rose, knowingly he was tagging along, *"We will finish this later, you're dismissed."*

Chapter 18

Entering the room Neil could see that Eftiar was moving ever so slightly, *"Has he regained consciousness?"*

"He's coming out of his coma. I felt maybe with you here the process might be quicker, but what caused the comas we still haven't determined. Man, I heard you were talking telepathy, but I really didn't believe it until now." Dr. Simms chuckled, "How does it feel?"

"Actually, it feels wonderful; like I've been mind talking all my life. I find it easier than mouth speaking. If you and Chambers want to look into my brain after all this; be my guest. It may help us understand everything better. The main reason for speaking this way is for Eftiar hopefully he might hear me in his unconscious state." Both men simultaneously looked at Eftiar.

"I don't want him to think we're trying to keep anything from him and his people. The information I've acquired so far isn't enough to give you help either. As soon as I have something, I'll let you know.

"Thanks Doc."

Neil had never been in Eftiar's private quarters, plainly furnished with bed, comdat, and a picture, which Neil figured to be of his wife, for she looked like a more mature Efiar. His thoughts wandered to how the children were doing in their comas. There were a few other pictures of Eftiar when he was younger, but nothing out of the ordinary. He moved to where Eftiar lay and sat on the chair next to him. *"Eftiar, can you avi with me?"* At first, Neil did not see a change, but soon realized the small physical movements Eftiar made was certainly a way of communicating. *"Tell you what; try to move your right hand for yes and left hand for no, oh sorry, I mean webs."* Looking at Eftiar's hands, he waited for a reaction ... the slightest of movement in both hands? *"Well don't let it worry you. I'll still keep trying to get through; you're doing just fine. Your kids and all of your ites' are in coma. Do you have any idea for the cause?"* His left hand moved. *"Have you been able to niet avi me during all this?"* There was no movement from either hand. *Oh God, I was so hoping you'd hear all thinking taking place.* *"Don't let it* worry you; we're trying to get to the bottom of the problem. Everything points to a connection with the robots and the beginning of your ites (people) here on Eftiam. You must be hearing me sometimes. So far, you're the only one we know coming out of coma. I'll check back with you soon my friend."*

<>

Setting up to watch more of the com-mov, *"It looks as if Eftiar is semi-conscious. Yet we still don't know what's causing the comas."*

"Sir, I've been think'n about what happened when we were inside the robot compound. Those robots came to a complete stop when we took out the box. Then we're hear'n about all the people going into comas, so if we replace the box, then most likely, these folks will be fine." Primie postulated.

"You're right of course, but this still doesn't explain why they're connected in this way. There's a question if we put the box back, will it have repercussions. Say, could it hinder or cure Eftiar, his family and their ites (people). *That's what we need to find out. Shall we get started?"*

Neil nods to First.

"Excuse me for waiting so long to get back to this diary, but we have been so busy; and oh, it is glorious indeed. As you can see behind me, we have beautiful new sigs. Today we finished the last connection of all our sigs. We divided ourselves into different groups based on what we could offer to the community in the best way to serve. Let's see, it is ten groups. As we completed projects involving services that would no longer be required, we divided down to five, and will probably scale down again. By unanimous vote, I am to still be head guide for this community."

"I am sorry to report Harry has been redeveloping the robots he and Justine were working on before leaving Earth. He has become more and more unreasonable. We wonder if it has anything to do with Eftiam, such as living in the 'Preamble' instead of listening to the Imo-Macos wishes."

Neil interrupted the recording, *"Let's stop there; we now have our answer as far as who is at fault. All we must do is get into the main comdat of the 'preamble' and have Bré be the carrier to go for the sig community comdat. I believe this will get us to the bottom of things faster. We will finish this com-mov later; dismissed."*

Chapter 19

Neil tried to get some sleep, but it would not come, so he rose only to pace the floor. Antsy, he transmitted to Admiral Berry, getting him out of the bed, now heedless of the enormous transmitting distance. Berry did not seem to mind, not showing that he was either expecting Neil's call or fuming about the delay. Their talk expanded into a twenty-four-hour period to bring Berry up to date on the happenings of Eftiam. He was surprised to find himself letting his feelings come out about the situation.

Coming to a final close with Berry, as he went to hit a key, he noticed one of his fingernails was a light lilac... *well I'll be damned, I'm turning purple.* ... He was not frightened. Finishing, he got up and went into his small shower cubicle to check a mirror. Was anything else changing color?

Sure, enough his eye whites were a lilac ... *it's taking effect. I wonder who else is experiencing this. Hope they don't freak out. Best let Berry know about this also. He's been extremely sympathetic to this; rather unexpected for him. It may change once he speaks with the council.* Chuckling ... *he was really surprised to see me speak with my mind. It truly bothered him. I could read his mind too. Must not do that all the time, something I need to work on, but I needed to find out if he was kosher with the way I've decided to run things here. I'm becoming more like Eftiar daily. Did the Imo-Macos or Eftiar plan this? Jean's most likely changing with me. We've been exposed the longest. I feel so guilty that my great-grandfather started all this happening. I pray I haven't let on how it's affecting me. I want to right this wrong, but maybe this wasn't his idea after all. He may have commanded the ship, however, someone else could've hired him; possible. Another question unanswered. But he did say that those who did not want to go could jump ship before take-off, and all along in the com-mov he sounded as if he was part of the true planning. The further we get into this the more perplexing it all is. Too long his shadow has hung over me; grandfather's landing here intentional, those Imos whoever they are, are responsible. Why do these people let them rule? Well shit, that is not a question, that's how they began ... hello! The best thing now is to get us into the habitat, get into the comdat and go from there. Yes, I did make the right decision.*

"Commander Gavens, sorry to wake you at this hour, but there is a problem in Efiar's quarters," Sendra, squawked through the box.

"Did you say Eftiar or Efiar?"

"Efiar, Sir; seems to be an intruder."

On my way, an LP or one of ours?" Now why would I ask that when all LPs are comatose?

"That's all I know Sir."

"Notify First to meet me at transport. We'll go straight to her sig. Man, this is wonderful not having to use the wrist transmitter, but that will change now since I'm going back to Sig City so soon."

"Yes Sir."

◇

They each took a different route to Efiar's sig entry. First was speaking with the guard. *How the heck did First beat me? "First, your assessment?"*

"Sir, the Juni slipped away."

"Juni? Did one of the Junis regain consciousness? Slipped away? How?"

"Apparently this Juni hasn't been seen by our people before by the description I received. We've checked throughout the entire clinic coma areas to make sure. Maybe there are some Junis' not affected, or we didn't know about, so they might not be accounted for. Funny thing is the guard happened to hear a voice while on guard at this door. No one passed before him to enter Efiar's sig, but when he got inside, he noticed some of her bedding moved and the floor wet, but whoever this guy was he disappeared through the pool in the bathroom. The guard jumped in to retrieve him, the guy wasn't anywhere to be found, except the water is a salt water pool and there is also an open door at one end of the pool base, leading out to the ocean." Neil looked over at the guard and realized he was wet from head to toe leaving a great puddle on the floor.

"Send him to get a dry uniform."

First turned, released the guard, waited till he was a good distance away, and turned back to Gavens, *"Sir, do you think it may be a robot?"*

112

Neil smiled to himself realizing First was copying what he did in the beginning. He did not want the guard to know of his telepathy ability. Without fully answering his query, *"Or maybe it's one here in the city."*

As if they read each other's thoughts in conversation, they turned and proceeded into Efiar's quarters. *I can't figure out why this person wouldn't be affected like the rest. Probably it's a robot posing as a Juni? What would his interest be in Efiar and especially when she's in a coma?* Quietly, both look in all areas of her quarters and at Efiar, who looked like a sleeping beauty lying in her bed. The bedding was wet.

"He definitely came in through the pool. More like someone who cared for her was sitting here." Reaching out, *"Her cheek is even damp. But why hide? You'd think he'd want to help his people. We've got another puzzle. I suppose you've already put out a bulletin looking for this person?"*

"Yes Sir."

"Commander Gavens and First you are needed in the large imo-mirror room."

Looking around in surprise, *"Bré?"* How the hell are you broadcasting from our ship, through this city?"*

"Commander Gavens, I am Bré two. Main Bré programmed me to communicate verbally throughout our sigs. This helps Earth/Sigmets to understand."

The two men were somewhat at a loss, digesting this before Neil replying, *"Ah, thank you,"* Bré Two. Do ..." clearing his throat ... *"Ah, do you know the problem we are needed for?"*

"Yes, Commander Gavens; the black box."

Jumping like a shot, both took off running down the sig tunnel corridor, First shouting orders into his wrist transmitter. They almost missed the turn into the large imo-mirror-sig. As they entered, force of old habits brought all those working within this area to stand at attention, while Gavens and First almost fell over the comatose Eftiamrs. Neil noticed that the lights were dimmed, *"Ah ... ah, oh ... at ease ... Do we still have the black box?"*

Everyone in the room looked blank, and then alarmed, except for one person. The guard stepped forward, still in semi-formal attention,

"Sir, I was just about to notify you and Sir, to First how … how did you know?"

We were notified by Bré … ah I mean Bré Two."

Now the guard looked at him doubtfully, "Sir?"

Oh shit … this is what I was afraid of … "Bré Two, how did you know the Officer was in need?"

"I did not Bré notified me, Commander."

"Are you saying original Bré notified you or Bré Two?" First asked, for full confirmation.

"Yes First."

All started conversing at once, not sure what to make of the entire situation; Gavens and First stared at each other while the buzzing went around the room, standing at attention now fully forgotten. *"Thank goodness for telepathy, Sir."*

"Maybe, you remember Eftiamrs speak to their comdat in this manner."

"Oh? … Ah yeah."

"Warrior, do we have the black box still?"

"No … it was taken by the Juni, Sir. He got away. We chased him into the corridor, and he disappeared into a wall. We couldn't get through the wall. I already sent warriors to the robot compound in case the person is planning to try to put it back into the comdat without your orders, Commander."

"Thank you, we also placed orders to have warriors added to that area. By going into a wall, you do mean a door slid open, do you not?"

"No Sir, he went into the wall."

"Ok then, I guess you better show us the area where this Juni entered the wall … please," a confused and doubtful look on his and First's ganders.

"Follow me Sirs." Arriving within the area the wall seemed solid, even though it was made of organic materials and or substance, possibly both.

Gavens ran his hands over the wall looking for a line; not finding anything, *"Thank you, you may go back to your duties."*

"Yes Sir." He saluted and left.

"First place guards everywhere, there's to be no one passing without our knowledge. Bré Two, did you see the person who went into this wall?"

He allowed First to hear his conversation.

"Yes, Commander Gavens."

This knowledge made both uneasy, although they tried not to show displeasure, *"How did he accomplish this task?"*

"With a hand device, Sir."

"Thank you, Bré Two." The two men stood staring into each other, eyes silent, each afraid to speak. Now slowly turning in a circle, they looked for cameras. None was visible to the naked eye. *This is going to take heavy scouting. Paper ... need paper to write on, shit, we haven't used paper in over twenty-five years ... need to get topside on land to speak without the comdats hearing us. What a developing challenge this is ... I knew Bré would one day be able to achieve this goal. Every sign was there. I must ...*

"Commander Gavens, First, they need you at the mechanical ite compound," Bré Two announced.

"Thank you, Bré Two. Do you know the reasoning?" *I hope she didn't catch how grateful I am.* Both men smiled and sighed knowing how they needed to talk privately.

"Yes, they have the Juni and the black box."

Chapter 20

*E*fviari?" *But I saw you in coma with my own eyes. When did you recover?"* Gavens asked, allowing all to hear his interrogation as he paced in front of the robot habitat in front of Efviari, and his warriors. *"Plus, how did you get away without anyone noticing you? It's not like we have the same color skin going on here?"*

"So, you are still able to speak telepathy. I do not have time to explain, except that I must place the box back into the compus in order to keep my ites alive or they will die. Please, Commander Gavens let me do this now. Unman me now!" Efviari struggled to free himself from his bonds.

"To keep your ites alive? Most interesting. How do you know this will keep your ites alive?"

*A*ll could tell Efviari was struggling with exactly how to answer Gavens, his eyes darting from one ite to another, now looking at the floor, "I ... I ... was asked to do this by the Imo Macos for my ites. Now please let me do it, I am begging you."

He's sincere ... embarrassed to demean himself in this manse ... a very proud man. ... *"So, there are more of you awakening from your comas? Then I guess it isn't necessary to replace the box if all are coming out of their comas. Apparently, they won't die."*

"No, no you do not understand. I am only conscious and Eftiar is now semi-conscious," now looking at Gavens directly.

Neil stopped pacing, looking right into Efviari's face, *"You seem to know quite a bit. I bet you're the one who was in Efiar's room."* Efviari blushed through his two skins of purple and looked to the ground: his hairs now disguising his eyes and face. *He's in love with her, I'll be damn I wonder if she's aware? "No one can hear me but you right now Efviari. You know I'm not going to hurt you or any of your ites. I'm trying to figure out what's happened here. All I know is when we pulled the box, the robots stopped functioning and all Eftiam ites became unconscious. I'm afraid if we put the box back it will kill your ites and I don't think you want this to happen either."*

Efviari brought his head up to meet Gavens eye to eye, *"I too can speak telepathy, and I am the chosen Juni you have heard of to save the ites of Eftiam. Yes, I was in coma and the Imo Macos brought me around. They are the tes* (ones) *who have asked for the box to be replaced."*

Gavens rocked back on his heels, showing his uncertainty.

"Commander, are you, all right?" First asked.

"Yes... First... I'm fine." Without looking at First, he gave him an order.

"Release the prisoner."

"Sir?"

"You heard right, release the prisoner." First cocked his head to the warriors; they removed the bonds. Unconsciously Efviari rubbed his wrists. *The warriors are loyal to him, that's good; it's for what is to come. .... what made me say that, premonition? Man, this planet is changing all of us ... Efviari knows more than Eftiar, I can feel it...*

"Thank you, Commander Gavens; I am bound to you loyally. Please help me bring my ites back to consciousnesses. The problem is the mechanical warriors are bound to Eftiam as we under upu ites (ocean people). Therefore, we need to keep them active, just re-program them. We could use them in many various ways here on Eftiam. We do not have much time to replace the box. Possibly your main compus could help in this matter, to reprogram the mechanical battle ites. She has already been into both compus' databases."

"You have a point my friend," responding truthfully. *How ... wait a minute did you just say databases? You did; you just said databases. That's an old Earth term. How did you know the word's meaning?"*

"I do not know." sounding perplexed himself, "I guess ... from being with our Imo Macos."

"You speak more in tongue as if they're ... Gods. How often do you speak to them and do you do exactly what they ask of you?"

"Commander, I have no reason to doubt them. They are here to help guide, not hinder, this I know for sure. Why do you doubt what I avi when you know they brought you here?"

"I've never spoken with these Imo Macos or seen them as you, and Eftiar's family. For many centuries, we have been at war. I know only to doubt and try to figure the questions to make it right."

"You have been given mind speech by the Imo Macos. It hasn't anything to do with our planet as you believe," Efviari held up his hand ... "Let me finish, I know this because the Imo Macos give me these answers. They have told me many things to come and how we are to guide in the future of our sacred planet. They apprised me of this, only since unconsciousness."

"Ok ... ah ... pacing again ... so you're saying they speak to you in your sleep?"

"Sometimes, and sometimes I'm very awake. I do not need the main havis sig as Eftiar and Efiari and now Efiar." Rather than let Gavens pace alone, Efviari, just turned and started pacing alongside him companionably. They began to wear a path in front of those listening and looking on. It seemed even the animals stopped to watch.

Stopping in his tracks, *"Havis, what's that?"*

Turning to face Neil, "A havis is the clear head ornament that is worn and the te (one) main te in the special havis sig. This was made for Eftiar, because his Eftiara was our true Leader who was requested to join with the Imo Macos."

"Oh?" They began to walk away from the warriors to be alone, totally unaware, but unconsciously they did need space for privacy.

"Commander, we must get the box into the compus now. Can you not get your main compus to do the re-programming now? I am more than willing to tell more, but first things first... please."

Neil looked into Efviari's eyes, *"Bré?"*

"Yes, Commander Gavens?"

She can even hear me from out here, wow ... "We are going to replace the black box for now, but can you work with the robot comdat to re-program the robots to be non-violent and able to communicate in a more serviceable way? Also, we must do this quickly from what I'm to understand the LPs' vitally need this part of our black box for survival."

"Yes, Commander Gavens."

"Approximately how long do you think this will take?"

"I am in process now; it should take no more than forty-five minutes, Commander Gavens."

"Let me know when you're finished. Oh, and thanks Bré."

"Yes Commander, you are welcome." Looking back to Efviari, "She is re-…

"Yes, Commander I do know what she said, I too can read the same way. As you see Compus Bré Main, can also communicate telepathically now.

"What?" disbelief written on Gavens face, thinking; *my gosh he's right. I just communicated with her in telepathy. This is becoming so weird.*

"Yes, she is an extraordinarily strong compus, but she is not out to destroy or take over as you imagine. The Imo Macos say she is the first of her kind to have emotions and feelings or I guess you could say sensitivity. Those of your making have given this to other compus before, but their configuration was too complex to allow this to develop. Whoever bred Compus Bré Main, bred her properly. She will serve many throughout her time."

This really threw Neil for a loop … staring into Efviari, he finally broke down laughing as he ran his hands thru his hair, *"Man, my head hurts the most, but my body too, I haven't slept much lately. My friend, from the information you've divulged, in just a matter of minutes, I feel very stupid about everything. May I call you friend? You may call me Neil, but of course not when my crew is present."*

"Yes, Neil, I am your friend and distant relative."

Laughing heartily, but nervously, again astounded at so much information so fast, *"Oh we must get to sit and talk over a drink, but right now I think we best get to our crew and tell them our plans and prepare to replace the box."* Not awaiting a reply, Gavens turned back toward the habitat, *"I guess we walked a good way from the others."* They hurriedly made toward the warriors, when Gavens jerked to a stop and pulled Efviari's arm, *"You said Eftiar, Efiari and Efiar need the main havis sig."*

Efviari smiled, proceeding on, *"Come we have much work to do, let the Imo Macos help along with Compus Bré Main; we will have plenty of time to catch up."*

Neil's mouth gaped, now looking at Efviari's back as he fuai sped ahead.

<>

Neil spent much of the hour briefing his people about the sig city situation and what would be expected of them. From what Neil could gather the people would wake, returning to consciousness at varying speeds. He knew the first to be expected would be Eftiar and his family, so he made sure, they were placed in one location and that Jean and Dr. Chambers would be there to explain things to them to best of their knowledge.

It had been days since Neil saw Jean and he felt it a lifetime. He didn't even have time to mind speak with her, except in short spurts. He so wanted to talk and hold her. He remembered, when he first saw her years ago, knowing the fascination then was there, but never allowing the thought of being with her to factor into his life since he was, truly off planet more than on. Now that he'd lain with her, being without her was as if a part of him was missing.

This planetary adventure is completely out of the ordinary. He did not feel that Earth or Sigmet would believe what presented itself on this planet. How could they, they too had never known anything of this sort. *Bré, now the controller of all the comdats on Eftiam and helping to reprogram robots! What is it that the robots have that the other Eftiamrs are relying on?* Something with programming he could only guess. *Efviari did say they were tied to Eftiam. Why are these Imo Macos controlling these people and why was I sent here by the Imo Macos? Yes, Great Grandfather crashed, by the Imo Macos hands, but it didn't mean that I should have to come here too. I was just looking for a new planetary habitat or so I thought. Did the Imo Macos really give us all the ability to speak telepathically? Was this the Garden of Eden for Eftiam in comparison to the Bible explanation of Earth?* Looking around Neil was beginning to feel his mind was maxed to its limit, he felt lost. *"Do not give up Neil Gavens; we are here to help you. Soon we will meet."* Startled to say the least Neil panned the room to see who mind spoke to him. *It was more than one... a unison group.* Everyone was going about their duties; there were no lookers his way. *Was that the Imo Macos? Man, this is so damn weird ... "Efviari, I think I just heard from the Imo Macos. Do they mind talk kind of in unison?"*

"Yes, Neil they do. I know you will meet them soon. Is it not about tia (time) for Bré main compus to be finished?"

Just about, she did say one hour and forty-five minutes. I really want to know what is in the comdat here; I was not able to acquire all the information from the box. Now Bré can give us this information more readily. Oh, I noticed you walked this ship like you knew it from stem to stern, do you?"

"Commander Gavens…"

"Yes Bré?" Neil projected for all to hear.

"The male and female mechanical people have been re-programmed."

"Thank you Bré. Are they able to speak?"

"Yes, in time we can program them to be productive to full extent of human capacity. At present, they're able to say hello and shake your hand.

"Each robot does have a name."

"A name?"

"Yes, their names were given to each upon mechanical birth. Many carry the name they arrived with on the 'Preamble'."

"So, they also used the brain configuration of the individuals along with mechanical capacity?" This could be why the Imo Macos need the robots.

"Precisely, Commander Gavens."

"Bré, I don't doubt your work, but for safety measures we will keep guns on the robots until we are sure their programming holds." Gavens didn't wait for Bré to answer, *"First, get your men in place. Efviari come with me."* Gavens and Efviari quickly ascended to the comdat board. *"Efviari, would you like to have the honors?"*

A smile as huge as Eftiam itself crossed Efviari's face. Walking to the switch board he looked back to make sure all were prepared; he flipped the switch. At first it seemed nothing occurred, but then lights flickered here and there and then started to come alive along the comdat walls along with a humming sound. Gavens and Efviari looked to see if the robots moved. They did not.

Seconds passed; then Primie hollered out, "Their eyes are turn'n red!"

Then two robots stepped forward, looked down at their weapons, dropped them, and then moved to a warrior. Holding out its hand, one said, "Hello, my name Peter,"

The warrior shocked, moved his laser aside, taking the robots hand, he shook it, "My ... my name's Fred." The other warriors followed in the same manner. Now all robots did the same over and over refusing to shut up. Laughter broke out everywhere.

"Well, I do believe we have a lot of re-programming to do. Please notify Dr. Chambers, Bré so he can help you with the programming. We need to have Eftiamrs working with him and you, so we can make sure the robots have useful jobs to perform. You have an interesting job ahead."

"Yes, Commander Gavens."

"Neil, we need you to come immediately to Eftiar's chamber. He's fully awake and very weak. He wants to speak with you and his children, and then he'll address his people"

"On our way Jean; is everyone waking now? Wow, you can telepath to me way out here?"

"Yes, and yes, most all are coming around and scared more than anything and get this they're claiming to have spoken with the Imo Macos while unconscious."

"I'm not surprised. There is so much for us to go over; it's hard to know where to begin."

"Eftiar keeps mentioning a person named Efviari; says he must speak with him."

"Let him know Efviari is with me and he'll be there."

Efviari overhearing this turned toward the back wall of the ship comdat area. He held something in his hand. Holding out his hand to the wall, an opening appeared in the wall itself. Efviari stepped toward the opening...

"Why're you running out, I thought you are the great savior for your people?"

"I ... I do not know if they're ready for the change, or I guess if I am ready for change. I know I should avi with Eftiar, Efiari and Efiar."

Neil never got to say a word ... *"Efviari, the time is now,"* All Imo Macos spoke and all in the 'Preamble' overheard and unbeknownst also to those in the sig city. *"Tia* (Time) *now is short; you must take responsibility with Efiar."* This shook Efviari up. He headed for the nearest seating which was an old office chair. Sweat broke out across his brow. Plopping into the chair ... *"What if she will not have me, Neil?"*

"I gather you are speaking of Efiar? You heard what I've heard; all the people are saying the Imo Macos' spoke to all of them, and just now, so I'm sure they know what is possibly to be and what is not. So Efiar undoubtedly knows too. Efiar believes in the Imo Macos more than anyone on this planet, I believe. She will not doubt what they have projected. Give it time; get to know each other and I'm sure things'll turn out fine. Now let's go see them and get started on this new way of living for Eftiam. Bré and First, along with the others will make sure things are in working order around here. If they need us, they'll call."

Chapter 21

Eftiar, Efiari and Efiar were seated together, looking quite out of place next to Jean, Dr. Chambers and a few other crew members offering food and drink. *"I know this is a lot for you to accept Eftiar, but from what we just heard and what you and your children heard while in coma, Efiar and Efviari are to guide your ites together. They are to be united as a couple."* Jean avi explained.

"I do not understand how he is to guide with her when he has not been seen, heard of or... Do not speak as if I am not present. I will not ef with someone who is chosen for me," Trying to rise, finding she was still too weak, she fell back into her chair, Chambers reached out to assist her; otherwise, she would have fallen to the floor. Recouping, *"I do not know this Efviari and he has not spoken through my havis. How can they be so cruel as to say I will ef with this ... this ... ite Juni? How do I know if he is the right coloring?"*

"Since when does coloring have anything to do with it?" Jean avi asked.

"Well, it has not been spoken just accepted that we have to be of a certain shade to guide. Although Eftiar says my Eftiara was the first of tio (two) shades to guide."

"What color is tio, Bré Two?" Chambers queried, careful not to use telepathy. He felt sure this would upset the Guides way too much.

"The number two, Doctor Chambers, Sir."

"Thank you," Chambers responded.

"Who is this Bré you speak to in the air?" Efiari questioned.

"Oh, things have changed so much since you were in coma. Trust me for now that it is just your compus (computer), now called Bré Two. We will explain it all to you when Commander Gavens and Efviari get here." Chambers offered.

"It seems to me if the Imo Macos are linking you and Efviari, then it doesn't matter what shading he is, does it?" Jean projected to Efiar, not letting anything deter her.

124

"Also remember Efiar, this Juni saved your life in the upu," Efiari stated.

"What is this he's minding?" Jean queried.

The slide wall opened allowing Efviari and Commander Gavens to enter. *This young ite fuai carried Gavens to my sig.* Eftiar saw him drop Commander Gavens to the floor. *Can he fuai with speed? I must admit I've never tried. Well ... I've never had the need to. I do want so for Efiar not to be resistant to the Imo Macos wishes. She knows they are right. Are her hormones making her behave in such manner? Oh Eftiara, please come to me and help me guide these changes in the right way. The Imo Macos say it is time for me to aspid* (death) *join you. I long to be with you forever; our offspring's must do well when they guide, our Eftiam depends on it. I hurt so bodily all over; it is time for me to lie down again.*

Without thinking of the consequences Gavens crossed the room like lightening and scooped up his friend Eftiar in his arms in the biggest bear hug! Eftiar's body jolted like a spastic dysfunctional child, his arms flailing and legs straddling Gavens' body, not sure where all should go.

"My friend, I'm happy to see you once again ... awake ... ah you know what I mean."

Watching from across the room, Chambers took in Eftiar's eyes. They looked like cats-eye marbles and his legs and arms flailing made him think of a palsied child. He couldn't help but laugh out loud causing the rest around him to laugh outwardly.

Now Eftiar also smiled trying to compose his lu (lavender) upudo, down around his bony limbs, *"It is also good to be back with you my friend Commander Gavens."* Even though he was minding Neil, his awareness took in Efviari.

Acknowledging this, Efviari bowed his head in deference to his head Guide. Exchanging a few more moments with Neil, Eftiar now gave his full attention to Efviari, *"Thank you for saving my Efiar's life in the upu. I will never be able to repay you properly."*

"You are welcome, Eftiar and Efiar. There is much for us to discuss since our Sig City went into comatose state. From what we hear from the Earth/Sigmets, we all minded with the Imo Macos of what is to come here on Eftiam." Efviari showed his unrest by shifting from one foot to the other and now began pacing in front of Efiar as Gavens always seemed to do.

This indeed made Eftiar and Efiari laugh, *"You Earth/Sigmet back and forth land walk as does Gavens are you aware?"*

In the middle of his pace, he stopped, looked down, and then smiled, "No, I was not aware, but we are related you know."

"Yes, but…"

"No, I mean, Neil and I are distant relation."

"Sir Efviari, you will address Commander Gavens with dignity given his station!"

"EFTIAR, EFIAR, he… he has a bland streak the same as… as … you, Efiar…" Efiari avid unbeknownst to all.

"Wow, so he does. Efviari this is the first I've noticed that. I guess I just thought you always had a streak, with your being a relative to Eftiar's family. That's probably why I didn't realize you awoke from coma with it."

Without realizing it Efviari placed his hand to his hair in question. Neil didn't wait for an answer, turning again to Eftiar, *"Hold on, hold your horses Eftiar, Efviari and I are on a first name basis. He knows to address me with my title in front of my crew members only and or in forum with your people …ah ites."* Eftiar's frustration showed dramatically. *"We have much to avi, Eftiar. You also owe this man the lives of all on Eftiam. If it wasn't for him; you'd probably still be in coma. Shall we go into the din- sig, where all can enjoy drink and foods and get all facts together? Much has happened in this time; we need to update you and your kids."*

As if they had pre-knowledge, robots streamed in offering help to those who could not stand well? Eftiar, Efiari and Efiar fell into their enveloping chairs, mouths open wide enough to allow flies to enter, shaking silently with fear. The Earth/Sigmets and Efviari all smiled. Efviari avid, *"Don't fear them; they've been re-programmed for all the service jobs in the city and above."*

The robots stopped in front of the three Guides, "My name is Eric Juni, please allow me to assist you into the din- sig Guide Eftiar." The Juni reached down lifted Eftiar into his arms. The other two robots followed suit with Efiari and Efiar, cradling them as they walked to the din- sig.

The others followed in a similar state of disbelief. Jean, Chambers, Efviari and Neil enjoyed taking in this picture.

"Do I really have a bland streak, Neil?"

"Yes, you do, haven't you always?"

"No"

"So much has happened in a short period of time; we do have many things to discuss, my brain is spinning."

"Efiar has remained silent. Do you think she disproves of me for an ef?"

"Ah ... my man, women are so hard to decipher, maybe Jean can help with this later on. Oh, and you best let them know you are a telepath."

Chapter 22

Settling into the din- sig, ready for talk, "Commander Gavens, there is a problem."

"Yes, Bré ... ah Two." There seems a slight difference in their voices.

"The entire city wants to hear the mind talk. May I suggest you move all to the guest orientation imo-mirror sig?"

Eftiar and Efviari looking to one another gestured knowingly without comment. They both simply raised and floated out the door together as the robot Eric hurried to catch Eftiar if he fell. Robots came and received Efiar and Efiari into their arms, fuai land walking them into the guest orientation imo-mirror sig. The others followed both gliding air and or land walking.

Before they arrived, chairs were fuaing into place as the robots placed them for comfort and assisted many who were still weak. Earth/Sigmets were also still giving aid to LP's. The buffet of fruits and drinks were brought from the dining sig by robots. It was most perplexing for Eftiamrs to watch the mechanical ites perform these tasks once performed by human Junis; soon they did soften and began to enjoy the prospect. The imo-mirror -screen descended among the plants of various purples hanging from the ceiling. The first to appear on the imo-mirror screen was Eftiar. He did not rise from his chair, as the movement from one room had exhausted him.

Tears dripped his cheeks into his upudo collar, *"Ites of Eftiam, this long awaited dai has come in such an unusual parallel, with our new friends from Earth/Sigmet."* Smiles and giggles drifted throughout the sig. *"In our comatose state, we all spoke in different levels with the Imo Macos. For those of you, who may not yet know, some of our Earth/Sigmet friends too have avid with the Imo Macos and I expect they will from now on."* Sudden alarm was voiced throughout. Eftiar upheld his hand, it quieted, *"I do not know just how much involvement there is, but we do owe them a debt of gratitude for helping to care for us and help save our lives."*

"No Eftiar that is not quite right." All turned to see who was speaking, and then quickly the imo-mirror screen showed Commander Gavens for all to see. He was not in his usual clean uniform, he was unshaven with disheveled hair, but his fierce look commanded their attention. Neil looked down at himself, *"Excuse my appearance, ites of Eftiam, but we have been busy while you slept away the long dais* (days) *and nights."*

How did I know such word? Neil gestured around at his Earth/Sigmet crew. They too looked very tired and unkempt. Again, laughter was sprinkled throughout the sig and Neil grinned broadly, *"As you see I'm te (*one*) who's blessed with your wonderful art of telepath... er ... avi here on Eftiam. Some of the others of my crew have also, but we'll get into that later on. Right now, I want to let it be known there is a great man amongst you who saved your lives."* Small whispers could be heard throughout the hall. *"The Imo Macos chose him to do their bidding and awoke him from coma earlier than the rest of you. He helped us unlock the secrets of the black box, which gives us the story of Eftiam and how you came to be here and what had to happen for you all to survive. We didn't believe the box could be dangerous when we pulled it from the comdat ... ah I mean compus* (computer) *on the dark side of Eftiam; that's when everything and everyone stopped and or went into a comatose state. I must admit he gave us quite the chase, and I've yet to find out how he achieved some of it."* This time Neil chuckled out loud to himself before going on, as he did this he looked peripherally into his audience and saw a few smiling as if they too knew this secret. "Eftiar, Efiari, Efiar ites (people) of Eftiam, may I introduce Efviari, the man responsible."

The entire sig screamed joyfully clapping their hands and webs, for those who just came from the life upu, as well as clapping and holding each other. The embarrassment showed on Efviari as he came up on screen. Hanging his head, he would not look out into the crowd.

"Efviari your ites await," Neil whisper avid only to him.

"Neil, I am not their Guide. I did only what the Imo Macos required of me."

"Right now, these ites only want to thank you for what you did. Enjoy this moment, and then we'll get down to explaining everything from the beginning to your ites; they deserve the truth. You've all been

through much, and I must say, so have mine. Really look at how tired and run down they all appear."

Fidgeting in frustration from foot to foot, *"Ah ... ah ... Ites of Eftiam, I only strived to obey our Imo Macos."*

The mechanical Junis started to speak out loud, 'Efviari is niet aving to us'... 'Niet aving?'... 'He is the chosen one'... 'Look he has a bland streak as Efiar'... 'They are to be ef'd!' After the last avi, the room was silent just long enough for shock to overcome.

"Is this not so, Eftiar?" A former Juni of Eftiar's asked from the congregation.

Eftiar began by explaining, *"Efiar went too far into the upu the dai we all went comatose. She almost did not survive."* The crowd now looked closely at Efiar. *"Efiar explained to us that Efviari here saved her life."*

The crowd now came to their feet; hands and webs, again clapping, many voices expressing the expectation of a complete efing of this couple and of their Guiding together for Eftiam.

Until now, nothing had been avid from Efiar. She quickly fuaid to her Eftiar's side, all wondering at her quickening strength, *"How dare you think you can pick my ef for me!"* This blast wiped the smiles from many faces, causing hurt to everyone's mind. *"He has never avid passed my havis!"*

"You are wrong Efiar!" Standing smugly, hands on his hips, one could not help but notice his muscular biceps, broad six pack chest, with narrow waist and muscular thighs, so unlike Junis of Eftiam; Efviari avi ripped through her havis and into the minds of all present. Efiar, taken aback, could not react further. This allowed him to pursue, *"The day in the sig tunnel after your fuai land walking run in the pu, it was I who avid you. You did hear me, you must admit, just as you do now. Remember, you looked around asking if it was Eftiar and or possibly your Juni calling from down the sig hall. You even wondered if it was the new Juni with the coloring close to Eftiar who avid beyond your havis. Also, the dai (day) leaving the dining sig to go with Eftiar and Efiari to the main havis sig, you avid to your Eftiar about the handsome new Juni. He was going to have Linti check your havis."* Efiar went faint; Efviari and Eftiar together caught her fall.

"Please, give Efiar time to grasp all that has taken place. This is not to worry about now; we have other pressing business to finish here; right Efviari?" Eftiar avid with a smile like he never smiled before.

Gavens avid. *"Yes, we do have more pressing business at hand. Ah, I do think though Efiar should retire to her private sig."* Immediately robot Eric appeared before them, lifting her, and carrying her with utmost care off to her quarters. *"Er; I believe I have Bré Tio* (Two) *to thank for that."* Eftiar avid.

"You are welcome Eftiar."

Eftiar, seemed so perplexed. *How did she know to call ahead for the service?*

"Commander Gavens, I do believe we should begin from our decision to go into the dark side to encounter the mechanical ites. Please everyone, feel free to avi what you saw, heard, and experienced. This helps us get a full enough account of all that happened."

Gavens started describing the encounter on the dark side all joined hands without thinking; it seemed the most natural to do. Listening carefully, Eftiamrs and Earth/Sigmets slowly rose to their feet; even those who were weakest seemed to be given strength by others; webbing together or clasping hands and webs as was natural. All eyes now closed, with heads raised heavenward. Efiar was even escorted back into the meeting place still cradled by her robot. She too with eyes heavenward, but closed, stood clasped by Efviari and Efiari. Even the robots joined hands with all. In the quiet and into the minds of all, *"We the Imo Macos are here to help finalize this joining of Eftiam ites. It is time for those of you to enter the upu for your final Eftiam lessons. This will make all of Eftiam equals in complete respect."* Not one ite in the room land walked out of the sig … all fuaid still holding hands and webbing. This included every single person and mechanical person on the planet, *"Please proceed to upu life pools."*

Quietly all proceeded to the nearest pools. Without speaking those webbed getting into the pools, gills on their back now showing for upu breathing. They helped those without webbing and gills into the upu life pools. Upon entry, they automatically went through the door into the open upu. Not one human had life-surviving equipment for breathing or protection from the elements for their skin.

<>

Gavens knew he was entering the water; he could not stop himself. *A trance? Am I in a trance? I don't feel like I'm in one, but I can't stop moving into the water either. Who are you people that you can make me do this?*

"Jean? Can you hear me?"

"Yes, Neil. I can't stop moving into the water, but I have total trust in these Imo Macos. I have no fear, do you?"*

"No, I guess I don't."

"Then go with it and trust. The LP's who were Earth-ites did it before us and they came out fine, so yes, we will too. It's up to you to reassure all of us."

Neil tried to avi out to the rest of his crew, but it seemed that everyone was only able to communicate with those closest to them by sign language as they moved into the waters. He could also feel his warriors no longer felt like warring, they wanted only to know what lessons were going to be given them by the Imo Macos. The robots entered ahead of the others as though they had waited the longest of anyone on Eftiam; everyone entered without apprehension.

<>

Some had entered from above ground, some from other areas of sigs. Now those already webbed and gilled could only wait for their return. Some came quickly back to the surface, namely the robots first. They were not given webbing and gills, nor lesson. Some surfaced slowly after a twenty-nine-hour period. Those offering service help did not take apting in this waiting time, just stayed ready and alert helping them adjust to their new webbing and gills. A new kind of awareness spread without the need of words or mind talks, just a wonderful dawning of comprehension.

Chapter 23

The mon (month) that passed was busy with adding more sigs to the under city. The new knowledge gained by the new Eftiam ites seemed to increase their eagerness to accept this newfound lifestyle. Efiari, Efviari and Linti enjoyed working with those new ites to help them understand the ways of organic sig architecture.

Efiari liked his new family member-to-be. They seemed to understand te (one) another without aving, smiling as they proceeded in each new task.

Linti was more relaxed now that all ites were of Eftiam. He even took a few dais (days) to spend quietly with his family, trusting in Efiari and Efviari's lead. His welcome of knowledge that there would not be battle eased his mind as never before.

Eftiar and Commander Gavens led the work to get the main Bré designed into this new city under the sea.

Jean and Efiar worked together designing new organic furniture, lamps, hangers, and many other household items needed for the new additions. New farming areas were set up by Primie and his unit on land. They even experimented with different growing techniques on the dark side. Primie was the first to be ef'd with his new Eftiam wife.

What was most astounding being the robots were no longer moving or speaking as robots? The Imo Macos made them more real than anyone could imagine. Bré admitted she could not have engineered such an outstanding change. Even the eyes were no longer red.

With the last dai (day) their masterful structuring unfolding for Eftiar and Gavens, Neil noticed a change in Eftiar.

"Do you not feel well my friend?"

"I am very tired friend. I am not used to manual labor every dai (day) *as you. Please forgive me; I must go to my sig and rest."*

"Do not worry I can handle the finishing of this project. We did te (one) *fantastic job here, if I may avi myself."*

"That we did. I take leave now," Not waiting reply Eftiar fuaid from the havis sig.

Chapter 24

Efiar awoke lying on her bed, feeling great exhaustion from the strain of the severe manual labor of the dai (day) before, but forcing herself to rise, she fuai land walked within her private sig. *I cannot ef* (mate) *with this Juni. He does not fit within the normal mold. What is normal mold? He did penetrate my havis and now all know it. The ites of Eftiam expect us to ef without query.*

"*Eftiara are you there? Please come to me, I need so to avi with you*" No reply came ... "*Why when I really need you, you are not there? I wonder have you ever really been there?* As she paced ... *I know I'm acting like a spoiled child. This is definite not the way for a Guide to act. But I have never had the chance to do so and I will! So, what if he is of* tio (two) *shadings, it truly does not matter. ... Smiling ...And he is very handsome and so-o-o strong ... so positive... he excited me when he returned me from the upu, but I never let him know. How could I? I never saw him after that ... I would not have niet avid that secret anyway. We need to know each other before any efing* (mating) *takes place. Listen to me! Throwing her hands in the air, raising her head to the dome of her sig, yes, yes, I am considering efing with him. Though what about Neil? He is now of Eftiam. The Imo Macos made it happen. Why? Although he is ef'd with Jean, it would be wrong to ef with him. Besides Neil is a closer relative than Efviari, I believe. Why must it be a relative anyway? There is more to this than the Imo Macos are saying. They do not say a lot, but they sure make this complicated. Are we completely at their mercy or are we able to have our own free will? Look at what they managed yesterday. All this time I have believed the Imo Macos' are from here on Eftiam, but now I doubt that. Are others wondering this also? Eftiara is with the Imo Macos'; is she no longer part of Eftiam?*

<>

Neil and Jean lay in their newly constructed sig-bed within their newly constructed sig. Jane had yet to add upu (water) plants, pu (jungle) plants lamps, pictures, etc. to make it more suitable to their needs. Her leg thrown over his flank, *"I feel so different now. I do not want to give any information to Earth or Sigmet. How do you feel about it?"*

134

"I am torn on this matter also. Our lives and home are of Eftiam now, so our loyalty lies here and frankly, I do not want to return to Earth or Sigmet; nor do I feel I owe a thing to either. After all the years of service, you would think I would. Also, not te (one) of our crew can now leave Eftiam. We require the upu (ocean) to survive. I did contact Berry discussing this and told him we no longer could leave Eftiam. I also suggested if they were to send any more ites (people) to Eftiam, they would likely experience as we, but it is more to ward them off from coming here. Eftiam is the Earth we once enjoyed, and I want to help keep it from the same fate as the Earth/Sigmets planets. Therefore, what I am saying is, I want to carry out the work my great-grandfather started. The Imo Macos chose him and his crew just as they chose us. Do you think I should take vote as to who wants to stay here on Eftiam or try to go off planet?"

"Neil, as you avid, we are of Eftiam now. So are the others. It is not an option for them. The only thing we could do is try and build an area on the 'Bramble' for a life upu pool, if they choose to leave; I truly doubt if any want to leave Eftiam."

"We still have many sigs to construct. With our newfound knowledge of using organic construction materials, we will accomplish this task in no time at all. It is so wonderful to experience, but I worry that we will not have enough to keep us occupied. Discontent could be our worst enemy. The way we were able to immediately switch Bré into the upu (ocean) and our area of sig city was remarkable. Eftiar's family suggested we name our own city and I be their Guide. I really do not feel this is needed. How do you feel? Again, I guess I am asking is this another vote decision?"

"Your niet is going tin (ten) thousand miles an hour. I think there is another more important matter for us right at present." No other minding was needed when he looked into her eyes. Neil and Jean held each other close. They knew they were going into the upu- life- pool (ocean). Again, they would ef (mate), with the knowledge of procreating.

Even though the Imo Macos advised for it, they both wanted this to come about for themselves, and the anticipation quickly overtakes their thought processes. Without speaking they rose and fuaid to the upu life pool. Entering the upu-life- pool they immediately dove to the door, hand in hand swimming out into open upu.

<>

Efiari sat before his compus (computer) devising new strategies. He was astounded at the ideas that were forming within him, and eager to implement newer and more adaptive ways for all on Eftiam to live. He niet avid all night to incorporate his ideas into the compus; now he waited for confirmation of their validity. He enjoyed this new Bré, making it easy to maneuver nieting (thinking) to fruition. Inside he knew they would be accepted, but it was hard to wait for reassurance. *Efiar is of no help these dais* (days). *Efviari will make a great ef* (mate) *for Efiar. Why is she being so obstinate about it? Can she not see how it is perfect? Women are exceedingly difficult to understand. Eftiar looks worn. I must speak with Efiar* (Sister) *about Eftiar* (Father). *Linti is incredibly pleased with all the sig cities we have built and so quickly. All the ites worked as te* (one) *unit making everything flow so much faster. These new Eftiam ites are good for Eftiam and to think I was so against them landing here. I do love the architectural side of things and the handling of the political battle games. Yes, the Imo Macos' were right; I am more adapted to this work than just sitting and doing everyday hum drum guiding for Eftiam. Efiar is not fully aware of what we have accomplished this past mon, she has been so tied up about efing, she cannot niet properly.*

Efiari, your ideas have been calculated and are most impressive. Would you like to start on them immediately?" Bré Two stated and questioned.

"*Not this min, but I will give avi when we are ready, thank you Bré Tio.*"

Relaxing his thoughts, he now wandered to the new Earth/Sigmet/Eftiam female ite he thought most beautiful.

<>

Fuai pacing in his sig room, Efviari could not come to grips with what happened that dai with all present. *Were the Imo Macos' wrong? Even without them aving, I knew I wanted her since age of tin mons* (ten months). *She is most frustrating. What am I to say to her now? She has not agreed to see me since that dai* (day) *before the entire assembly. Why? She has only seen Eftiar and Jean. I really do not understand. Neil advised me to speak with Jean. I will do this very thing minst* (first) *thing in the morn. Our language is changing rapidly now that the new Earth/Sigmet/Eftiam ites have joined us. All these new ... what was the word ... te ... tech ... oh yes ... technologies the new ites of Eftiam avid and mixing with our niet aving ... we now developed even more progressive production techniques. This is a great challenge I so want to share with Efiar. Probing ... someone niet* (mind) *probing me?* Efviari stopped his fuai pacing and stood very still, his upudo brushing to the floor. "Efiar?" … there was no answer to his call, but he knew the niet probing was still lingering … *"Efiar, this is enough. It has been te mon* (one month) *and you still refuse to avi with me, let alone see me. Why? We must try and work this out together! Please at least meet to avi and learn to become friends!"*

"I agree. We do need to be friends Efviari. And yes, I agree to see you in the morn." Efiar's avi was gone.

She truly has agreed to see me and avi with me and to be friends. Was she just trying to see if she could niet probe me? No, she admitted to aving with me in the morn. Where, when? No matter: I will be at her private sig door minst of the dai. May the Imo Macos be with me? Feeling exhilarated Efviari no longer fuai paced, but fuai danced airborne around his private sig.

<>

Lying prone, Eftiar tossed and turned. Apt (Sleep) was not to come as his niet (mind) kept re-living what the past few mons (months) had brought to Eftiam. There was no contact with the Imo Macos since the new Earth/Sigmet/Eftiam ites joined. The vast expansion of ites was more taxing than he expected; provisions of enough foods now a problem, lack of sigs, all needed to be under the upu; a matter of survival. The accomplishment of building the sigs was more than he could have imagined. Every ite (person) of Eftiam joined as te (one) to make all the new cities a reality in a shorter tia (time) than seemed possible. *Bré Tio* (two), *send my Juni, please."*

"Yes, Guide Eftiar."

Within minis (minutes) a mechanical Juni arrived. "You avid Guide Eftiar?"

For a long time Eftiar just stared, still taking in this most incredible fact this mechanical Juni before him, was only shortly before a device of battle. Now it was willing to be of great service to him and the entire Eftiam planet. *Quite an accomplishment Imo Macos, I applaud thee. Did they just take what Scientist Salinger built and add to or did they totally re-build the mechanical ites?*

"Guide Eftiar?" The mechanical Juni queried.

"Oh... a warm mint-cham spri (cham-mint-tea)*, please."*

"Yes, Guide Eftiar."

Now sitting on the edge of his bed his thoughts wondered to him and Eftiara meeting and efing (mating), the procreation of Efiari and Efiar, the death of Eftiara, the new Eftiam ites and so much more, now Eftiam history. This was somehow different; he was recalling the smallest of details from the beginning of his time until present day. And he kept re-living it repeatedly, not leaving out the smallest of detail.

The mechanical Juni returned, placing the mint-cham-spri beside Eftiar on the magnificent clear glass night table curved and twisted in a figure eight. "Will there be anything else Guide Eftiar?"

"No, thank you. Oh, do you have a given?"

"I am Brett Juni, Guide Eftiar," As he spoke, he bowed his head slightly, "I apologize, I assumed you knew."

"Maybe I did, but I guess I'm so tired it did not come to me. I need rest but seem unable to apt (sleep)*. I only hope this mint-cham spri will help me relax."*

"Yes, I hear you at different tias (times) of nigh. I sometimes feel you will call, and this nigh you did, Guide Eftiar."

"You wait for me to call? Do you not apt?"

Brett Juni smiled, "Guide Eftiar, I do not require apt as you humans."

"Really? What else do you not require?"

"Since I do not have a stomach, I do not require sustenance, my form of sustenance is to be re-energized, but since I have human skin, I do a form of bathing, but it is dry, in this way it does not interfere with my circuitry."

Eftiar was silent taking in this information and machinery before him.

"The Imo Macos made us so much more than we were, like now we can speak and we can learn too. They are truly the tes (ones)!"

"Learn?"

"Oh yes, I have read all the books in your library."

I can see he is proud of this; learning, that is phenomenal.

"Bré is now giving us learning information to make us even more responsible with our services for the ites of Eftiam, Guide Eftiar."

"What kinds of things is she teaching you?"

"Complete etiquette, such as how to hold a serving tray to make it easier for the ite to remove foods and or serving from a tray to a plate. Also setting a table, properly sliding doors ...

My goodness is this our next battle coping with mechanical ites as intelligent as we or more intelligent than we? Brett Juni did say he read every book in the library. Even I have not mastered this task. I must avi with Neil of this. And so I cannot even begin to compose this list. It is surely endless.

"Guide Eftiar?"

"You seem very happy with your newfound life. Do you remember any of your past?"

"The program is erased, so I have no knowledge anywhere in my memory banks, Guide Eftiar."

He avis this as if he has been trying to find the answer ... "You avid of the Imo Macos being the true tes, what do you mean?"

"Why the makers of us all, Guide Eftiar,"

Announced as if it should be obvious to me. Is this a secret we have yet to encounter and they already know?

Not waiting to be answered, "Will there be anything else, Guide Eftiar?"

"Ah, no, thank you. Brett Juni."

Eftiar grabbed his mint-cham-spri, fuaing to a chair. As he drank, his mind again, wondered to his past. Then back to the recent niet avi (thinking) with his present Juni. *Why does this avi bother me so much? What are the Imo Macos planning? Something just does not seem right. N*ow he found himself fuaing in a sitting position as he often did when his niet (mind) wandered to work out a puzzle. *If I were to place these niet avis into the compus then the main Bré would know. Tomorrow I will make sure to go land side with Neil and we will converse in that manner rather than chance aving here where the Brés' can see and avi. If he considers this a problem as I, we will then avi with the rest of our Guides to be. Yes, yes, it is* *most assuredly what I must do.* Finishing his mint-cham-spri, he felt more relaxed and felt sure he could now apt (sleep).

As he fuai arose from his chair Eftiara suddenly stood before Eftiar. The cup dropped to the floor shattering into a million pieces. *"Hello my love."*

Not once had Eftiara appeared before Eftiar in this manner. Always they joined niet avis only in the main havis sig. *"Eftiara, is it really you?"*

Without waiting for an answer, he reached out to touch her. *I am finally touching her physically! This is not a dream! But how is this possible?*

Reading his niet avi thoughts, *"The Imo Macos have given us this te* (one) *last tia* (time) *to physically touch, my darling. As she moved into his arms, "Is not this wonderful, they are giving us this te last tia together."*

"Last tia? What do you mean?"

"It is tia for you to aspid with me Eftiar. We are to let Efiar, Efiari and Efviari now Guide Eftiam. We will aspid together forever."

"But I must speak with Neil before ... Eftiara placed a finger to his lips hushing him and moved in to kiss her Eftiar...

Chapter 25

The added new fif (five) din- sigs and the old fif din- sigs of the city were enlarged to accommodate the entire new upu sig city and seemed to bustle with ites every hour of the day in varying numbers. The new mechanical Junis seemed delighted in the flow of their acceptance, chores of service.

Efiari awaited the presence of Jean and Neil. He had invited them this morn to let them view his new ideas and frankly for their company. He found himself missing his Efiar desperately. It seemed Eftiar (Father) and Efiar (sister) sought refuge in their private sigs as of late. *Why?* He did not know or understand, but when he saw them, he would avi (telepath) exactly how he felt.

"Good morn, Efiari, did we keep you waiting long?" Neil asked, entering the dining sig with Jean on his arm.

Not long my friend. I was about to niet avi Efiar and Eftiar to see if they would be arriving at table this morn. They have been neglectful of late. Jean, you are glowing this wonderful dai (day). Aving of glowing, there is someone I would like to niet avi with you about. She is of your sig city, and I wish to get to know her. Her hair is…

"Commander Gavens you are required immediately at the private sig of Eftiar." Bré Tio (two) announced. All present looked to one another in surprise.

"He did say he was tired last eve," Neil offered. Without further avis, they fuaid arm in arm toward Eftiar's private sig.

<>

Eftiar's mechanical Brett Juni allowed them entrance, "I am so sorry, he just would not wake this morn. I gave him mint-cham spri late last night; he could not apt (sleep). I also heard him aving aloud to himself."

As Brett Juni was explaining this happening, Jean walked to Eftiar, placed her hand over his forehead, and then slowly glided her hand to close Eftiar's eyes, *"Eftiar is aspid* (dead). *He aspid happily, I believe he was niet aving with Eftiara; she came for him."*

Efiari now fuaid before his Eftiar; disbelief written in his imo, *"Eftiar please awaken ... tia* (time) *to greet your guests Eftiar, please, please avi ... wake ... NOW! ... we need you ... hear me please, Efiar will not put up with this hoax you play..."* Now his body slumped to the floor causing his upudo to make him appear as a flower pulled from its branch and turned upside down. *"No, no Eftiar we so need you ...* tears flowed gently from his cheeks into his mouth, streaming down his chin into the collar of his upudo. He felt so helpless. *"Why isn't Efiar here? She would automatically know, we all should have felt his asping* (dying), *why did we not? Something is not right."*

"What do you mean?"

"It ... it is customary when te (one) *of us is asping, we the entire city feel the asping. I did not or I would have been checking to see who was asping. This is not the usual manner of asping here on Eftiam. You did not feel it either, so something ... is not right ... is not right ...* not finishing his avi, he fuaid into a sitting position, although it was difficult to tell with his upudo so spread and billowy around him appearing as a crestfallen flower. He rose in this same position from the floor fuaing from the sig room in deep thought, as in copy of Eftiar niet aving.

Looking to Efiari's back, Jean watched him leave, *"Now what do you make of that Neil?"*

"Plenty weird; I don't quite understand. He did say we would all feel the asping of te (one) *did he not? Bré why is it we would all feel the asping of te or of each other?"*

"Commander Gavens you are all of Eftiam; connected now and therefore you all feel each other in every niet aspect."

Neil looked to Jean with puzzlement, *"Ok ... now fuai pacing ... "If this is the case, then why did not LP's feel the mechanical ites on the dark side all this time?"* There was no response. Neil patiently waited ... silence ... *"Bré are you there?"*

"Yes Neil."

"You did not answer my question."

"I have no answer. My memory banks are working on how to give a solid answer to you."

"Thank you Bré." To Jean, *"I do not think she will figure that out. I know we best get to Efiar and let her know about her father. I'm not sure Efiari is on his way to tell her."* Turning they both fuaid from Eftiar's sig room, *"Do you know how they do funerals or how they bury, or do they cremate?"*

"I do not know; guess we will have to ask Efiar and Efiari or Linti."

◇

Efiar and Efviari turned to depart from her private sig entrance.

"What is the matter with Efiari?"

Looking where Efviari's eyes designed, she too saw Efiari fuai toward them in a sitting position, with his legs crossed no less. He was a funny sight to see. She smiled to herself, *so like Eftiar when his niet* (mind) *is working* ... and then realized something was very wrong, *"Efiari, what is the matter?" I have never used the word matter before ... those Earth/Sigmets' are incisively changing our language.* Efiari did not seem to hear a word avid to him; he fuaid into Efiar's private sig without announcing himself. Looking to one another Efiar and Efviari fuai followed Efiari further into her quarters.

Not looking up, he now fuai hovered in place, *"Efiar, I ... I ... I ... must ...* then he seemed to release everything within him from tears, to screams, to pain, spin fuaing; all in a pattern one right after the other, until he crashed hard in his seated position to the floor.

Efviari arrived first and helped to pick Efiari from the floor, *"What in the given of the Imos is wrong with you? Here sit on Efiar's bed."*

"AH ... seeming to come out of his trance ... *"What are you doing in Efiar's private sig?"* From Efviari's look of puzzlement, he realized he must look a sight. Tears still glistening Efiari's face, his upudo was completely disheveled and he was again crossing his legs as he sat on Efiar's bed.

"It is all right Efiari, we were outside my sig, when you fuaid so bluntly into my private domain. More to the point, what is wrong with you and to enter without announcing yourself?" Now arriving alongside Efviari, *"Just…"*

"Efiar, Efviari, Efiari" … Jean and Neil announced themselves before entering, but did not await an answer,

"We hope we aren't too late. Are we? A long pause, then all looked to Efiari. He shook his head negatively, then tried once again to avi, but he raised this tia (time) to stand before Efiar, *"Efiar… It's … It's … Eftiar (father) … he … has aspid (died)."*

The silence in the room became deafening, all eyes looking to the siblings.

"Tired, ill perhaps, but we would have felt his asping. Do not give out this kind of misinformation Efiari. Abruptly Efiar circle turned and fuaid to the sig entrance, not waiting to hear more, heading straight for Eftiar's private sig.

"Oh crap … Let's go?" Neil did not wait; he took off like a speeding bullet, and the others followed in hot fuai pursuit.

<>

Without announcing herself, she entered Eftiar's sig. His room was in neat order, he was not on his sig bed, *"Eftiar are you in your private upu pool life sig?"* No answer came, so she ventured further entry, to no avail. Turning to leave she spied his Brett Juni enter with a vase to be placed by Eftiar's bed. *"Brett Juni, where is my Eftiar?"*

"He is by now arriving at the infirmary for cremation," He placed the vase on the table and turned to leave, "Is there anything else you require Efiar?" By the time Brett Juni looked to her, she was on the floor fainted away. "Oh dear, oh dear … crossing the room, he bent to pick up Efiar in his arms, to place her on her Eftiar's sig bed, in a sitting position, dropping her head between her legs clear to the ankles. "Dear Efiar, did not anyone tell you of your Eftiar's asping?"

"Mmmmm…

"Efiar, are you alright?" Neil asked upon his screeching fuai approach.

"Mmmm … I"

The others arrived, all breathing heavily except for Efviari as he sped past Brett Juni and Neil to get to Efiar; seating himself beside her, he unconsciously began to rub her hand and kiss her hair.

"What happened here Brett Juni?" Jean queried.

"When I returned to Guide Eftiar's room sig, Efiar was here and queried of her Eftiar. I told her he should be arriving at the infirmary for cremation. She then fainted. Did not anyone avi her Guide Eftiar aspid?"

This brought Efiar's head up, realizing the full information being relayed. *"He could not have aspid, we did not feel him asping. We always feel one another aspid. It is the way of Eftiam. Something is wrong ... it's just not right."*

"This is why I was coming to see you. I agree something is just not right!" Efiari avi exclaimed.

"I did not feel his asp either; nor did any of the others that are new to Eftiam. So, I know the rest of our ites did not feel the asp. We must assemble the ites of Eftiam and give them the news."

"Brett Juni, did you say you sent Eftiar to the infirmary?"

"Yes, Commander Gavens, this is customary."

"Bré?"

"Yes, Commander Gavens?"

"Bré, have the ites hold up on cremation of Eftiar and have Doctor Simms and Doctor Chambers do an autopsy, and explain to them I will arrive shortly.

"Yes, Commander Gavens."

Jean was now helping Efiar, straighten out her upudo and hair. Tears seemed to flow gently from Efiar. Efviari also had tears glassing his eyes again. He blinked frequently to keep the tears from flowing. *"Neil, you think he was murdered?"*

"Well, when we have trio ites (three people) *here saying the entire planet would feel this asp, then yes, something is awry. We better make sure he aspid of natural causes."*

The room seemed to take on gloom and unrest, "Commander, are you accusing me of wrongdoing?"

"No, no Brett Juni, on Earth or Sigmet it would only be natural to do an autopsy before burial or cremation takes place. In this way, we can put the cause of asp on the asp certificate."

"This has never been a practice on Eftiam, for our Guides, why now?"

"I was not aware this is not practice. I'm sorry, I guess I assumed too much here." Neil looked quickly to Efviari for counsel in this matter.

"Brett Juni, in the past Junis of service on Eftiam, did autopsies always. Yes, it is not a practice for us to have autopsies for head Guides. However, with the fact that not te (one) *ite or mechanical ite felt Eftiar's asp, I do feel it would be best to have an autopsy done, do you not?"* Efviari avid in.

The Juni looked from one to other with sly speculation, "Well I would say this is for Efiar and Efiari to decide. If there is no further need of me, may I be excused?" Neither Efiar nor Efiari seemed to pay attention as to what was happening around them. The shock was still too immense.

"Of course; if we are in need, we will avi. Thank you," Gavens avid Brett Juni. Warily Brett Juni moved to leave, turning slightly, every few steps to eye all within the room. As Neil watched the Juni leave, *"Efviari I tried to avi Linti and I can't seem to get through to him. See if you can avi him to place a tail on Brett Juni."*

Efviari did get an avi to Linti. *"We are niet aving alike, Neil. There is something happening we must stay abreast of and take every precaution. Let us get together with Linti as soon as possible. I will give him the preliminaries of what we are niet aving so he can take extra measures if necessary. Efiari and Efiar are in no condition to think rationally at present."*

"Agreed, but right now I need to go niet avi with Doctor Simms and Doctor Chambers. Something more is coming about here. I cannot send avis beyond the present room. I am going to check and see if this is occurring with the others of telepath within my city area and would you please do the same in your city area? Jean, will you be staying with Efiar and Efiari?"

"Yes Neil, I am needed here at present. If you need me, please avi. Also, I will try to find out the full procedure of protocol for burial."

"Jean, I am unable to avi past this sig room. Later, try to do the same. Efviari is still able to accomplish this, he has contacted Linti. When I know more, we will all niet avi over this and other uncertainties. I am on my way to niet avi with Simms and Chambers,

not sure if they can find out anything, but at least we are trying." All this was being relayed as he fuaid to the door. He spun back, threw her a kiss, and was gone.

Chapter 26

The pu (jungle) seemed to be extra warm and humid this dai (day) as the sun slowly rose. All three gentlemen fuai land walked. Those that now mainly fuaid, felt strangely uneasy to make physical use of their legs, much as a sailor coming from the seas. *"I can see how muscle can atrophy easily. No wonder Efiar still does fuai land walk and run,"* Efviari avi mentioned.

"Neil, she has fuai land walked and run since she was tix (six). Seems she is most smart," Linti replied, *"But I don't niet (mind) telling you, there were so many dais (days) I did not enjoy this part of service to her."*

"Linti, we on Earth and Sigmet, did this for health reasons and it seems Efiar instinctively realized this to be necessary. My crew and I do this on a dai to dai basis, along with other physical exercises to keep fit for battle, but with so much going on, I have neglected to keep this dai exercise as needed. We all need to keep this in our routine." The animals seemed to accept them as part of the pu as they slowly toddled along. This was one advantage to telepath, keeping as quiet as possible as not to disturb.

"I cannot get Efiar from her private sig, or Efiari. It is like they are giving up. Do you have any suggestions?" Efviari confided to both.

Linti stopped in his tracks, looking down to the ground for the longest time, and then up to both, *"Yes, I believe I can help get them to become active once again. I will avi with both."* Leaving it at that without another avi, he proceeded to trod once more. Within a few minis (minutes) he stopped. Stepping back, he held up his hand in form of stop command. A panther was in their path. Linti slowly turned his head to look at Efviari who quickly niet avid (telepathed) with the panther, letting his tio (two) comrades hear the avi. The panther allowed them to proceed on; blinking as they passed by.

"This animal is beautiful and seems to be fine with us living on this planet, a true harmony with each other. I often wonder if this is what it was like on Earth in the beginning. I've still not heard from the Imo Macos as they

said I would. It feels vastly different now like they have stepped off Eftiam altogether. *"How in the hell did you manage that te* (one)*?"* Neil asked.

Efviari and Linti looked questioningly, *"What do you mean?"*

"Efviari, never have I seen anyone on Earth or Sigmet accomplish niet aving with a predator and have that predator walking away."

"Maybe you just did not know what we are able to accomplish with niet aving an animal. Animals are very telepathic."

"That is news to me."

"News? Hell? What is meaning of these niet avis?" Linti asked, *"Oh and Efviari is the only te besides Efiar, and asp Eftiar and Eftiara who can telepath with animals."*

Neil definitely smiled, *"Well news; let me see; have you ever read a newspaper?"* Both Eftiamrs looked at Neil still puzzled. *"I guess not. It is like when you read niet avis written on the computer. And hell; well, its slang language to some, but more to the point it is the home of the devil."* Now both looked even more confused. *"Forget it; we have more important matters to get to. Aving of certain ites who can send differently than others; I'm finding I can't send beyond a room now, where before I was able to send to all of you anywhere on Eftiam. Has anyone in your city been able to do this besides present company and Guides Linti?"*

"No, only those you mention and yourself. Maybe this was given you on temporary basis from the Imo Macos. You did fill in for Eftiar when necessary."

"You have a point there. I was also given message from the Imo Macos that I would niet avi with them, but as yet, this has not come about. It's driving me crazy for I have so many unanswered questions."

"Do not worry it will come from the Imo Macos. They have never gone back on niet avi." Efviari proclaimed.

"I pray this true. Linti what news of Brett Juni?"

"Brett Juni went straight from sig city, to the dark side into his old habitat. He walked around for a while, but we did not see anything out of the ordinary. He then returned to sig city. I still have a watch on him and all mechanical Junis. Brett Juni has been re-assigned service. I feel you do not trust this Juni."

"No, I don't and there is no foundation from autopsy that he played a key role in the asp of Eftiar and as far as Simms and Chambers can

tell Eftiar, aspid of natural causes. How long did Brett Juni stay at his old habitat? Did he act like he was looking for something?

"If anything, he seemed forlorn as though wanting the old ways to return for him. He stayed no more than sixt minis (sixty minutes). *I saved the tapes if you would like to take a closer look."*

"I have not avid with the Imo Macos since before the asp of Eftiar. And Linti, I too have reservation about Brett Juni. Something about the way he spoke with us just does not seem to equal the other Junis. Also, he seems to set on aiming to please. Like he over does it," Efviari avid.

"Well then, maybe we ought to look at the tape separately, then together. We each may be able to find a connection." Both comrades shook their heads in agreement without paying much attention to the areas they were fuai land walking, Neil stopping to pick up a twig to hold, a niet avi came, *"Another matter, we still have unanswered is if we are all to feel each Other asp* (die), *then why is it you Eftiamrs before we joined, did not feel the mechanical ites on Eftiam? If anyone should have felt it you should have more than we new comers."*

"A very complex query, Neil; I too ponder on this," Efviari avid.

"I placed this question before Bré; I could feel she truly felt she should know this answer. She stated we are all connected as 'te'('one') here on Eftiam. Now she is fully baffled, especially with the changeover of us newcomers able to send and receive on this planet, except for the mechanical ites. But now only some of us can send and receive beyond a room, also it seems some of us no longer can accomplish beyond a room, and it seems some of us no longer can send and receive at all. There surely has to be a connection we are missing. Maybe Chambers can help with this problem."

As they were aving to one another and fuai land walking little did they realize the panther was closely watching as if crouching, awaiting to attack his prey? Abruptly Efviari came to a full stop; it was a few steps before the other two realized he had stopped. Turning Linti seemed ready to avi, but Efviari hand cued for complete silence and no movement. He closed his eyes as if to get a better grip of the surroundings, or possibly communicating beyond their point. Slowly he turned to look at his companions. *"I think it wise to leave this part of the pu* (jungle), *there is something very wrong. The animal life seems to be fully aroused or should I say on guard and for attack. It is almost like even though I can communicate with them, they do not want to hear anymore."* No sooner had he avid, the panther again showed himself. Neil and Linti could tell Efviari was frantically aving with the panther. Efviari, bowed to the almost black lu (royal purple) panther, now showing his teeth ready to pounce. Slowly he spread his arms out across his companions, now fuai backing all three away. *"It is wise we leave the pu into open area by the shore."*

At the shoreline, *"Efviari, could you no long niet avi with the panther?"*

"Linti, I could niet avi with him all right, but he was not in any mood to be reasoned with. He gave me insight to some of what is changing with the animal life here on Eftiam. He told me the Imo Macos took away most of his abilities and that he now craved our bodies for food."

"Whoa it's like Eftiam is now like Earth and Sigmet," Neil felt a chill run his spine, *"Remember Efiar stating that Eftiara niet avid tias (times) are changing; all will now be different on Eftiam. If this is true, it is all presently coming to fruition. Maybe this is why we have been brought here."* Neil shifted his position looking around carefully at the tree line.

He swore he saw many animals' semi hidden in wait. *"I think I will carry weapons starting this dai (day), here land side. Don't ask me why, but I feel it necessary for us to return at this moment to sig city."* This was said with such caution, Linti and Efviari too eyed the tree line as they backed away to their siout, even taking the precaution of having one keep lookout while the others proceeded into the siout. As their siout lifted off for the upu (ocean) they could not help but look back. What they saw amazed them. Coming out from the tree line were at least tvent (twenty) animals. *"Let us pray we won't have to carry weaponry within sig city."*

"I do not think we need to go that far," Linti avid.

"No, Neil is right. Things are changing rapidly. The Imo Macos are quiet for a reason. Possibly, they do not want us to rely on them in the same manner as before." As he avid, Efviari could see the panther standing at the edge in open watching; his message came through without telepathy causing Efviari to shiver. However, he knew this animal would be his best ally of the pu. Time and adjustment would

make this happen for him and the animals. He would begin this new work with this thought; accomplishment was just around the corner.

Neil too noticed the panther and felt the other carnivorous animals at the forest edge were in anticipation of a meal. He used his wrist communicator to ask warriors to come land side in readiness with weaponry ASAP. Within tin minis (ten minutes) battle warriors in tio (two) siouts arrived alongside their siout for escort.

<>

Going into the dark side of Eftiam pu (jungle), Neil felt a very strong presence. Efviari also seemed restless. *"Do you feel it Efviari?"*

"Yes, there is a heavy change to this side of Eftiam pu and it knows we are here. I have never encountered such a strong feeling of a presence before. Linti set our beams to search the surrounding areas before we go to the mechanical ites habitat."

"Yes Sir, Commander Gavens." Linti turned in his borrowed uniform with ease, giving orders for surveillance of the complete area of the dark side in order get a better feel of what was going on with Eftiam.

As they focused beams over the land below, a warrior shouted and pointed, "There!" Something is definitely moving down there." As all looked in the direction the warrior indicated, all that appeared to come to the naked eye was brush, leaves and trees moving, but the way they moved, all the battle-experienced warriors knew something was there … silence dominated for at least fif minis (five minutes), and then… "There it is again Sir." Everyone saw this time, "Wow, another robot. I thought we destroyed all the robots?"

Our language is changing back to when we first arrived, Will we lose a part of Eftiam. Will we lose telepathy ability? "Efviari do you also realize that warrior is speaking in Sigmet/Earth language again?" Gavens avid.

"Now that you avi it; yes," He continued to watch the beam pick up the mechanical ites movements.

"Sir one is over here and another … wait … oh gosh, I think there's at least fifty of 'em." Another warrior added.

"Linti let us circle back to the habitat."

"Yes, Commander Gavens."

Gavens found himself going from hatch window to hatch window trying to observe all areas for signs of mechanical ites. *It seems funny to hear the language of Earth/Sigmet. It sounds foreign. On my return to Sig City, I am going to sit down and review Grandfather's tapes again. Even though Bré gave me a wonderful bri*efing; maybe something will jump out at me.

Neil and Efviari looked at each other quizzically, as they watched and heard Linti; he was no longer aving. At first Linti did not notice until after giving the order. He quickly turned to Efviari and Neil, "What is happening; I no longer avi as before. We are returning to old Eftiam not the new as promised by the Imo Macos. Efviari, they have lied to us!"

"Do not be so hasty to doubt them Linti; perhaps it is something to do with this side. Maybe we will learn more on our return to Sig City."

Efviari was trying to give reassurance; but doubtful himself.

The pilot, "Sir, we are coming into the mechanical ites habitat."

Everyone tried to ogle out the closest hatch window of their siout, stepping on each other's toes in their efforts.

"It does look like new mechanical ites are being processed," Linti offered.

"Linti, did mechanical ite Brett Juni go near the compus when he was inside?" As he avid to Linti, Efviari turned from his place at a hatch to catch his expression.

"Not that any of us could tell. He just seemed to walk around, but he did touch things walking through, but it looked more as if he was reflecting rather than making a deliberate move. Now that I avi, mayhap he was making sure to not look like he had an action in niet (mind)."

"Agreed," Gavens and Efviari simultaneously avi projected.

"On our return, I will place mechanical ite Brett Juni under Eftiam solitude. Now for this matter in front of us, what are your orders, Sirs, since the absence of Eftiar?"

Efviari smiling, "I think since Commander Gavens is more experienced in battle, he should be the one to conduct this problem. Commander, what are your orders?"

"Thank you Efviari, I believe we should go in and take this habitat back. However, as you say we need to leave the black box in this compus. Therefore, after we have again dismantled the mechanical ites, then we will place a complete crew of battle warriors to guard this station. Bring the siouts alongside the entry door so we may unload our battle ites."

"Yes Sir, your orders will be carried out." Linti bowed his head in respect; turned, "Battle warriors, to the doors armed and battle ready. We will do as last time we came into this particular area, and again take back this habitat."

Without question, the warriors moved into position. Linti, Gavens and Efviari would stay on board this time for they had no armament. As the warriors moved to the door; the first four warriors got on one knee raising their weapons for battle; the second four behind stood and raised their weapons in turn.

"Warriors at the ready, we are coming alongside," Linti announced into both siouts. There was no laser fire coming from the habitat or mechanical ites.

"Efviari, do you notice the mechanical ites do not even realize we are here. Notice also their eyes are not red either. It seems a change is made to this particular model."

"Yes Commander, it seems these mechanical ites are designed for a different job and do not forget they did undergo change with the Imo Macos, as the rest of us. This mechanical ite Brett Juni is wiser than I anticipated."

"Well, I think he has plans for our Sig City and this planet. Do you now see what I feared is coming to fruition?" He did not await an answer from Efviari but went straight to Linti and grabbed two of the warriors from the line and pulled them together. *"Change of plans, I want you two men and a couple more if you need them to collect one of the mechanical ites for Doctor Chambers to study." Without thinking, I have switched to speaking in Earth/Sigmet and relying once again on those battle warriors to do the job. They are a peculiar type, indeed.*

"Aye Sir," The warriors stated as they bowed their heads in honor of their Commander. Backing away they rejoined formation at the ready.

"Linti, contact First and add another tio (two) *siouts here; we can make sure every mechanical ite is disassembled. After this is accomplished, we need to make a complete study of the compus* (computer) *here."*

"Neil, why did you not contact First yourself?" Efviari made sure only Neil heard his avi.

"I felt it necessary to give Linti a learning experience of Earth/Sigmets' operations in time of battle. We all can learn and teach even as we are in battle. I do not see this as a heavy battle we are embarking on. An inner feeling made me want to help Linti excel in his position."

"The minst siout is alongside the entry to the habitat; do you wish our battle ites to disembark?" Linti queried.

"Yes, by all means proceed." Commander Gavens avi ordered.

"I too have just learned something of your way of battle," Efviari avid.

The three in charge took station at the helm to watch on the imo-compus.

As the door slid ajar, the guns were scanning at the ready. The mechanical ites looked at the intruders, blinked their eyes then proceeded into the habitat without attacking. Proceed with caution warriors," Linti ordered.

The first of the battle ites entered the habitat along with mechanical ites. One of the mechanical ites turned to a warrior and offered his hand,

"Hello my name is Stacy Juni, what is your name and may I be of service?"

The warrior took a few seconds to react, resting his laser across his arm, and shook hands, "Ah … I'm Pete … what exactly is your specific job?"

"As yet I have no assignment, but I will soon, Sir."

"Uh, are you going to Sig City?" Pete asked cautiously. Many warriors were now standing within hearing distance.

"Oh yes, and some of us will be here setting up our home base."

"Home base, eh, would you like to show us around Stacy Juni?"

"Of course, within this area, we do repairs of our circuitry." It looked the same as before with wires hanging from the ceiling, tables for the robots to lie on and robots placing the wiring within other robots. He proceeded to lead them further into the habitat, down halls revealing rooms containing other mechanical ites in storage. "These Junis are awaiting programming." Then they came to beds and dispensary area. "These were definitely not in use."

"Stacy ... ah ... who uses this area?" Another warrior asked trying to make sure he sounded casually quizzical.

"We no longer use this area, maybe te (one) day we will, when we finally make our Juni ites more progressive."

"More progressive? Like how?" Pete questioned.

"Soon we will be able to be updated to the quality enabling us to make use of this area."

"Nicely phrased, not to give an answer," Gavens avid. *"I think they are trying to become human. How on earth did they get this far by themselves? Maybe they had some help."*

"What are you saying?" Efviari avid.

"I am not sure yet." Gavens started to fuai pace, head down, within the limited space of the siout, *"Bré, do you have access to this comdat?"*

"Yes, Commander Gavens."

"Has there been human access to this comdat besides Sig City personnel and of course, you?"

"No Commander Gavens."

"How about non-human?"

"Yes, Commander Gavens."

"Is the mechanical ite Brett Juni using this comdat?"

"Yes, Commander Gavens."

This stopped Neil in his fuai pacing, looking intently at his compadres, *"Explain."*

"His last entry was three days ago."

"What exactly did he do to the programming?"

"He assigned changes to the mechanical ite Junis per your request." The shock on Linti's and Efviari's faces avid many ramifications; neither avid, remaining still in their disbelieving.

"I see, thank you Bré." Fuai pacing again.

Efviari slowly fuaid to a chair, letting it enwrap him. *"This is not right. Things do not happen like this from mechanical ites, do they? How is this possible?"*

"He's a very advanced mechanical ite." Neil proffered. *"I learned a long while back on Earth and Sigmet to never doubt my feelings when it came to changes occurring that were unlikely. There is much still not known of science. I've learned to accept without question and solve the problems from just that."* For the first time in ages, Neil took a good hard look at Linti and Efviari and what surrounded him. Both now wore clothing made as of the old Earth/Sigmet rather than custom variation upudos. They had avid many tias to him their enjoyment of simplicity for movement and comfort. *Did I ignore what was in front of me? How long has it been since he had a quiet evening with Jean?* He knew he should be focusing on the dilemma before him but could not bring himself to do so. He seemed to hear words from far off in a distance. *Silver... silver ...cord ... silver cord. What has that to do with now? I remember something or someone telling of a silver cord, but who or what, or where? Why think of this now? I've got to get back to now ...* Neil seemed to float literally off the floor of the siout. He started to spin in midair, slowly ... now faster, he knew instinctively that he was not functioning of his own will. Seeing without really seeing he knew Efviari and Linti were trying to catch him, to bring him back to the siout floor, but just as they neared, he would move off again spinning, each time faster than the first until he no longer could make sense of where he was ... his eyes were closed, but he was seeing everything taking place, through his closed lids he could see a hue of lavender softening and relaxing him... *"Who are you? What do you want of me?"*

"We are the Imo Macos."

"Finally, you've come. Why now, why not before? I have so many queries for you. Why can't I see you?"

"Right now, there is too much fear within you, so you cannot see us. Calm yourself... Eftiar is here to speak with you first."

Slowly a presence came into view, *"Hello, my friend. I miss the physical State with you. No, no do not try to avi, just allow the niet aving. Since joining the Imo Macos much has been clarified for me, but I too am still learning Neil. You are going to speak with the Imo Macos for many hours now, and you will come to see you are needed here on*

Eftiam. This will be your home until your asp (death) *and you too will be joining with the Imo Macos. It is part of your destiny. Before I leave you Eftiara and I ask that you help Efiar and Efiari to become Guides of Eftiam as they were born to."*

"*I miss you Eftiar, but I know you are glad to be with Eftiara. I am only sorry I didn't get to meet Eftiara.*" As if Neil projected her, Eftiara floated in from the background beside Eftiar. She was the coloring of Efiar with a large white streak as Efiar. Her eyes glowed with the nature of super intelligence beyond what Neil had ever seen. It was almost like seeing God there and not Eftiara, or God himself in her form. She did not speak, but stood next to Eftiar letting his arm enwrap her waist. *How can this be? It's as if they're right here.* Neil found himself trying to reach out and touch them, but he could not. *No don't go friend, we have so much to avi ...* they faded into the distant lae (lilac) fog. *Something moving, what? It's silver ... oh yes ... silver cord ...* he found himself moving along this cord like a road, he traveled many times before. The light was bright once again ... *They ... they are so beautiful, it seems hundreds ... no thousands of them ...* tears were welling within him, he felt so overcome with love.

Chapter 27

On his return Linti went straight away to Efiar's private quarters. Rather than wait to be announced, Linti burst into her sitting area. "Efiar are you here?"

Entering from her bed sig, looking quite disheveled, *"Linti, what brings you so hastily into my sig room?"*

"I am sorry for the intrusion, but we must avi. I too long have allowed you and Efiari tia (time) to grieve, but your ites need to see and hear from you. They need guidance and as you are head Guide, I insist you leave your sigs this dai (day). Your Eftiar would not approve this behavior," he avid in harsh manner, but with great concern as a father to his child.

Rather than be upset, Efiar fuai land walked to Linti and hugged and Simid (kissed) him on the cheek. *"I so have missed you and our fuai land runs and Eftiar not being there in my life dai to dai to boss me around."*

This caused Linti to burst out laughing returning the hug and he return simis (kisses) her cheek. "Maybe I should spank you too."

"I have not been just grieving, but I have been with the Imo Macos off and on. The lessons are of the changes for Eftiam. I know that Neil is now comatose getting lesson."

Startled at her avi, "Yes … yes, he is in coma and I do not think it will be a short one either. Oh, and Efviari wants to see you of course." With this statement, she blushed. "Aha … I see you grow fond of him, does this mean you will ef (mate) with Efviari and make me the happiest of all Eftiam?"

Still growing her lu (lavender) blush stronger to almost la (royal purple), *"Yes, I truly know we are to be ef'd* (mated). Changing the subject, *"I was about to fuai to Jean and Neil's sig quarters, would you like to come along?"*

"No, I should see Efiari and scold him and then go to my family a few minis (minutes). I am to meet Efviari at Neil and Jean's private

159

quarters, so most likely I will see you there. I am glad you are ready to be with us again." He simid her forehead and was off.

<>

Sitting on the edge of their bed, she looked at this man; she so desperately Loved in such a short period of tia (time). Jean could not imagine herself ever being without Neil. *Good looking with his sandy curly hair and broad stature, eyes, those dark pools, with a circle hint of blue grabbing, pinning me so that I never wanted to turn away and oh all that muscle. But he has had to stay in good physical shape for space travel. Since they brought him in from topside and the dark side no less in a total comatose state, just like the LP's went into all at once.* Yes, she knew it had to do with the Imo Macos, *but in the heat of battle? Why?* None of it made sense to her or anyone else for that matter. Now she was expecting their child. *It is only a week*, but she knew without anyone telling her. The changes felt within her were remarkable, but then nothing seemed normal since coming to Eftiam. Everything was felt in such a larger and more emotional yet intellectual dimension. Her telepathic powers were stronger here on Eftiam. She related always with Efiar, Efiari and Efviari daily, but she noticed Neil no longer was able to send past the room he was in. *Why is this, when the Imo Macos gave him this power when we became part of Eftiam? Many of the people of Eftiam also now lost this ability.*

"How is he?" Efiar avid, entering the room without first getting an acknowledgment.

Jean jumped off the bed, stunned to see Efiar, enter, *"What are you doing here? It's been so long, what made you leave your quarters? Oh, Efiar, I am so worried. Can I really make you understand how I feel?"* Tears flowed down Jean's cheeks at such a quick rate; they abruptly dampened the collar of her uniform.

Efiar, fuaid to her side and grabbed Jean by the shoulders, *"Jean you must be strong for Neil. Yes, I do understand how you feel, I've grown to feel deeply for Efviari and know he is my true ef. The Imo Macos are with Neil. I know, for I too have been with them an exceedingly long period, right along with Efiari. All of you thought we were hiding out because of our Eftiar, but this is not the case. We too have been getting lessons. There is much for us all to avi over and plan for and rebuild. The Imo Macos will be leaving this planet for another. They avi explained that this is part of the process. They stayed with Eftiam longer than most to get it started, since it was an incredibly young planet and needed much attention, with Earth ites landing here and not born of Eftiam until a new generation was born to Eftiam. So, we will have to rely on each other from now on. Eventually they will return.*" In this tia (time) of aving to Jean, Efiar kneeled beside Jean causing her upudo to billow out like an open flower. The tio (two) women hugged each other in pure pleasure of friendship and confidence.

Jean's head lay on Efiar's shoulder, *"Efiar, why then are we here? Why is this happening to all of us in such weird ways? Oh, I'm sorry I'm bombarding you with questions and not asking how you and Efiari are feeling."*

"All I can avi right now is to be just a little more patient. We must wait for Neil to come around. I'm sure Efviari and Linti avid of the new Juni Mechanical- ites. The battle warriors have disconnected every new Mechanical- ite on the dark side."

"My Jean, that is good news to my niet (mind).*"*

A mumbling of sorts came from behind Jean. Looking around her, *"Neil, you're awake. Oh, this is wonderful."* Jean turned bending as she avi exclaimed hugging and kissing him, *"Please, don't try to rise; you've been out for tvent dais* (twenty days)*, dear."*

"Really? Well then, I have a lot of catching up to do. It is good to see you Efiar."

Jean noticed how Efiar and Neil looked upon each other with a newer Clarity as if they both knew everything expected of the ites of Eftiam. *Does Neil have some gray streaks in his hair?* She would inspect that further when they were together more intimately.

"We must go before our ites within fif dais (five days)*, do you think you can be ready?"*

"I feel good enough now." Neil did try to move out of the bed.

"Don't you even think about it!" Jean avid loud enough for the entire Sig City to hear and all mechanical ite Junis in the area came running to aid.

"Is this what it's like to be ef'd (mated)*? My woman gets to nag?"*

"When you need it yes and don't try to tell me you won't nag at me," Jean Avi bantered with a large smile, reaching over to hug him till his neck cramped.

"Well, I can see you tio (two) do not need any of us here," Efiar avid.

Juni Grey, would you please bring in some broth for Commander Gavens?"

"Yes, Guide Efiar."

"Wait just a darn min; I want real food, not broth."

"Well, that is too bad, you are not getting anything heavy, you have not had sustenance on your stomach for tvent dais (twenty days)," Efiar avid in.

"Now I have tio nagging at me."

"Oh, you do need help my friend," came from Efviari and Efiari, hovering in the doorway.

"Looks as if we got here just in the nick of tia (time)," Efiari avid, *"But we are most happy to see you back with us."*

"Help men, they're trying to feed me broth instead of real food."

Efiari and Efviari glanced at each other... *"I think we will leave that to our nurses to decide. We have more pressing matters to avi of, like the mechanical ites we dismantled and what is going on on the dark side,"* Efviari avid.

"Yes, fill me in please, since you do not care to really give me nourishment to a starving relative either."

Smiling Efviari avid, *"As te (one) we did not understand what was happening with you. It is the te tia Linti and I ever saw someone do the antics like yours going into coma."*

"Well, I felt so hot and sweaty and I could not focus on anything around me. Plus, my language was again changing back to Earth/Sigmet and some of the warriors were starting to speak rather than avi. It was like everything was getting to be too much for me to take in at te tia. I was aware you and Linti were trying to catch me and bring me back to the floor of the siout."

"Catch you, Neil?" Jean avid, eyes wide.

"Yes, Neil was spinning in the air and every tia we reached out to grab him he moved off and spun even faster until he was going so fast, he crashed to the siout floor," Efviari avid. *"We had to leave him there*

unconscious, because we had to get things under control within the habitat. We knew when First arrived he could take over, so we could then get you back here.

When First did arrive, we found he brought tio (two) technical ites to work on their compus and with tio Brés help we figured we could get things solved. Already they determined that Brett Juni downloaded new equations into the compus to make the newer mechanical Juni ites. We did think that this Juni was acting alone, but we found he has the niet (brain) of Doctor Salinger ... Realizing Neil was not quite with him, he held his hand up and went on, *"You see the Doctor placed his niet into the compus when he realized he was starting to asp (die), he left an equation for the niet to be placed into Brett Juni."*

"Are you serious?" Neil avid.

"Quite. When Efiari arrived with First, they took over for us on the so-called battle process, so that Linti and I could bring you back here to Sig City."

"Let us face it, it was not much of a battle, it was just a matter of dismantling," Efiari avid with a great smile. All the men joined in laughter understanding the comic side of their experience. Efiar standing beside Jean seemed to watch only Efviari, noticing his movements and flow of body and muscle as he avid. His concentration was heavy, but he knew she was staring at him. He did not dare look at her. It had been so long since he was near enough to touch her, as he so longed to do.

*"There really hasn't been much to deal with in the way of battle here on Eftiam, Nei*l avid, still chuckling. *"That was quite an achievement for Doctor Salinger to carry out. Bet Doctor Chambers loved that. He has more than enough to place in his journal for years to come. Doctor Simms, also."*

"He's having a great time with the niet of Doctor Salinger and being able to avi to Brett Juni through him; remarkable to avi the least. We think his niet will give much information over time. He says he cannot wait to give you the ... what is the word ... oh ... skinny on it," Efiari smiled at himself for remembering the odd avi word. *"Did you also know the Imo Macos decided to let you use your messed-up language in order to give a sense of more words to our vocabulary here on Eftiam? But they referred to it as co-mingling of vocabulary."*

"It seems all of us have been given different lessons and to some degree The same in lessons, so tomorrow after you have rested Neil, we should sit and confer to ready ourselves to deliver the message of the changes and possibilities to come," Efiar avid.

With this, they avid their farewells, and quietly fuaid the room, leaving Jean and Neil to enjoy the tia together and catch up.

<>

All Sig city ites assembled in the large imo-mirror guest hall. Tor (four) newly assembled throne chairs were placed at the front of the hall. All ites were quietly avi gossiping amongst themselves about this new wonder as they took seats. From the sliding side wall entrance fuaid Efiar, Efiari, Efviari and being carried by a mechanical Juni ite was Commander Neil Gavens. Now the muttering amongst the assembly grew louder. All took their chairs except for Efiar, wearing the upudo Eftiar had made for the minst dai (first day) of her bland streak showing her ites their new Guide-to-be. Now she wore this upudo in tribute to her Eftiar and Efiari with glowing pride. Efiar stood erect awaiting the assembly to settle. Slowly they placed full attention on her, *"Ites of Eftiam, we have had many mons* (months) *of change, but now we know and understand those changes and want to relay them also to you. You see we now have tio* (two) *chairs added before this sig guest hall. This means you now have tio more Guides."* ... It was silent for several minis (minutes), but then the response slowly ruptured within sig hall....

Jean did not know of this that morn when Neil left early to meet with the others. He did not request her presence, but she was as surprised at this change as the assembly of ites around her. Neil never avid te (one) word to her that he was to be a Guide on Eftiam. He spoke against it, why the change, what was going on. *It is not right. He never told me.* Her anger showed everywhere within her and in her outer body language also. *"Neil, you didn't want to Guide, what is going on here?"*

"I was so exhausted last eve, my dear. Please don't be angry with me. The Imo Macos have made this so. I seem to have no say so concerning this matter."

Before Jean could answer Neil, Efiar held up her hands again requiring silence, *"We will get to the Guide assignments in the matter of business this dai, and you will understand that we here on Eftiam will all realize fulfillment as a unit. We all gained the niet avi ability and then some of us slowly seemed to have it dissipate in different manner. Well, we think we now have answer to this, and that many other queries you all may have answered before you leave this dai."*

Linti entered from the slide door with Doctor Chambers, Doctor Simms and Brett Juni. They carried something within a jar. All cranked their necks trying to see, as they watched them place this jar on a clear glass table, similar to the chair thrones' design. No one had taken notice of this table until now. All also noticed the change of Linti's clothing to more Earth/Sigmet worn design.

"Linti, why do you not wear your upudo?" A shout came from the audience.

Linti turned toward the assembled ites, "Since working with the new Eftiamrs, I find their clothing much more comfortable and very adaptable for battle ites. I would like to make sure this becomes new design, and if any of you may adapt an even better design for our battle ites…"

As he proceeded to ask the ites to think on an even newer design uniform for Eftiam, Jean's mind wandered back to Neil and why he did not confer with her. At the same time, she unconsciously watched the faces of the ites and how they accepted the new concept and found it to be compatible.

Coming to this planet brought her and Neil together. *So much has happened since our arrival.* Last eve Neil spent sleeping, but she was content to be with him and him with her. She seemed to be counseling and nursing everyone taking no time for herself; *this I must change. Balance is not as it should be.* She too felt exhausted. Coming back to reality, she realized Chambers and Linti had given their presentation on the brain of Doctor Henry Salinger, which was now out of Brett Juni, but they wanted to show them his brain for better understanding of its patterning. She wanted to hear more on this, but she would take time later with Doctor Chambers and Doctor Simms to go over the analysis in a one on one to really get to the meat of the matter. Also, they had included Efviari, for he too was standing and finishing his presentation of the non-battle on the dark side and the happenings with all the battle ites involved. Still looking on the platform she could not help but wonder since re-programming Brett Juni seemed to be acting super normal. Perhaps something else was done to keep him from taking off on his own. But this she was not sure about.

Efiar now stood, *"Efiari now will be our Guide Political Representative and work with Linti and Efviari on Eftiam battle matters and Eftiam counsels. We will now hear from Efiari."*

Efiari came to his Efiar's side. He held her with him. *"Efiar and I want to avi with you about our Eftiar and his asp* (death). *We know all thought we were totally absorbed in mourning of our Eftiar; this was not completely true. We each were mind aving with the Imo Macos as well as Commander Gavens. Here on Eftiam we always knew of an asp until now; Imo Macos say this no longer will be."*

Some of the ites stood with all aving unanimously their uncertainty about this new reality. Webs flying airborne around with great exertion. Earth-ites could not decipher their telepathy so it looked quite comic, but dared not laugh.

"Yes, there are many new ways we need to accept from here on. Doctor Jean Spencer has dedicated herself to Eftiam in so many ways and she revealed a new way for mourning of an asp to us. Doctor Spencer, could you give an avi on this?"

Startled, Jean touched her hair, her uniform she adjusted, and then slowly stood, *"Well on Earth/Sigmet, we come together in a great hall such as we are joined now and we either have a coffin with the body of the aspid person or the cremation remains within a jar. This sits in the front of the assembly. Usually before the service everyone takes tia to give their sympathies to the family and or loved tes* (ones). *Then a minister or Guide gives a small avi about the ite who has aspid. After, any other ite may avi something special about their aspid ite; they too can avi to the assembly. It helps with our grieving. Does this help explain a mourning of asp, Efiari?"*

"Very much so; since we were not about the city after Eftiar's asping, we would like to have such a service. Guide Commander Gavens, would you be willing to conduct such an assembly?"

Surprise written on Neil's face, *"I ... I ... would be most honored."* Efiar and Efiari still holding hands looked away from Commander Gavens back to their ites.

"Efiari and I are most happy to represent you as Guides for our Eftiam. Efviari will also be council liaison Guide of the pu (jungle) *and upu* (ocean) *mammals. The best avi yet, I'm happy to announce he and Efiar will Ef within the mon* (month*). "* The crowd stood clapping and yelling jubilant praises which could be heard in the surrounding ocean and land side by the forest menagerie. It took a good te min (one minute) for Efiari to get the ites to settle and retake their seats. *"This too will be a new way of celebration avid to us by Doctor Spencer and Guide Commander Gavens. We have decided to keep this as a surprise for the occasion. Perhaps Eftiar's service and celebration efing with Efiar and Efviari can become a tradition here on Eftiam."*

Efiar now took over, *"Commander Gavens has had to make a great adjustment coming here to Eftiam with his entire crew, and do not deny this newest assignment he has been given by the Imo Macos.* A small rumbling a gain broke out within the ites. *"I am not sure how to explain this, but here goes ... Not te* (one) *original Eftiam ite will be aving with the Imo Macos ever again."* At first one could have heard a pin drop, for the impact was far greater than any ite of Eftiam could have ever imagined.

Queries from the congregation; 'Did you chase them away?' 'What did you do wrong?' 'Are they leaving us; if so, why?' And many more questions before the crowd quieted.

"The Imo Macos are on their way to another system and the making of a new planet. Yes, we of Eftiam are a very new planet, and the Imo Macos made it so we could live and learn in a manner that most planets do not get a chance to enjoy. Now that we are a thriving planet, we no longer need their full attention, so they are now offering to others and will return later to niet avi *to see how we are surviving."* Rumblings were beginning again, Efiar raised her hand, *and "We will still have niet avi available to us. Guide Commander Gavens is the only ite able now to communicate with the Imo Macos at any time."*

Audience anger broke out, 'That is outrageous!' 'Why him?' 'He has not lived on Eftiam since birth, he has no right.'

Before Efiar or Efiari could avi, an avi came from the fourth chair keeping the assembly of ites from uprising, *"Everything you avi is true. I had more avis queries for the Imo Macos than you have raised here. I felt the very same way you do until I listened to the Imo Macos advice. My Great-Grandfather was sent to this planet by the Imo Macos. You see his sioutous was taken under an unknown force, which I found out later was the doing of the Imo Macos. They placed his sioutous on a new course for this planet. Therefore, he and his crew founded Eftiam through the Imo Macos. As his descendant I am bound to Eftiam, as are many of my own crew members, I later came to find out. We were not thrown off course as I thought, when looking for new planets for habitation. I've been advised by the Imo Macos this was not by chance; they again made sure we came to Eftiam to be re-located. Our Bré, now the main comdat or compus whichever you prefer to call it, was conceived and designed by Doctor Justine Harper and Doctor Henry Salinger, both crew members of the original crew from the 'Preamble' that landed here on Eftiam. Now yes, you ites are descendants also of that original crew landing here on Eftiam centuries ago.*

The silence was overwhelming. He had their complete attention and then some.

Getting back to Bré, the Imo Macos designed her further to handle the new complete changes made here on Eftiam. It would take too much tia (time) here this dai to go into all the history of Eftiam to present dai, but Bré and I are working to make a history documentation com-mov for all to avi and see when completed. The Imo Macos are a marvelous entity to behold and I regard this assignment as a Liaison Guide here on Eftiam in the highest respect with which it was given me. I believe ... no, no I know they chose me for this, because I and my crew have been through much more on Earth and Sigmet and can be of great help to those of you who have lived on Eftiam since birth. We may be encountering new challenges in the future and so they felt I was best suited for the job. If you the ites of Eftiam wish to change this assignment, I really don't know how it's possible for they say now I am the only te (one) who can and will avi confer with them from here on and as long as Eftiam exists or until I asp (die). At the tia of my asp one of my offspring will be gifted with the assignment, whenever that may be. *I will try and carry out my duty to the best of my ability from here to eternity. Thank you."*

The silence was complete, no one moved. Then one person stood and started clapping. All looked around to see Doctor Spencer with tears sparkling on her cheeks. Slowly more and more rose and clapped.

"I love you, Neil Gavens."

Chapter 28

"Catch me Daddy," Neiliara yelled. With that contagious smile showing, what father or anyone could resist.

Now bald headed, with deep la (royal purple) skin he came to the end of the slide to catch his Neiliara. Without waiting she came down in semi-sliding fashion stopping herself every few feet with her hands. Fear was still a factor for this child of three years. *"Let go and slide without your arms. Hold them in your lap Neiliara; Daddy will catch you."*

"I'm afraid."

"Do not cut your words, you know better."

She let go, he was there as always at the end of the slide to catch her. He set her down to the ground. Her beautiful wavy lae (lilac) hair fell toward the sand floor; as she stared at her feet, *"Yes Daddy but when I avi to others they think I should avi that way not with proper avi. It's embarrassing and hard to do both."*

Per usual Neil could not be angry with his daughter. He crouched to her level, *"Why have you not avid this to me before?"*

Hugging her father around his neck, and aving into his ear, *"You have enough to avi about at this time. I did not wish to burden you with menial avis,"* Pulling away taking in her father, *"Look you have lost your hair with so much work with the Imo Macos. Mommy loved your wavy hair, you know. She misses running her hands through your hair."*

"Neiliara, have you been aving your mother's thoughts?" She pulled away and again her eyes darted to her feet. She hated that her father could catch her up so easily. Neil took his thumb and index fingers, raising her chin to look into her eyes, but she struggled to keep them to the ground.

"You know that is wrong of you. Yes, I know it's hard to stay out of ites niets (peoples' minds), *but it's something we try very hard to keep from doing. Please try ridiculously hard not to do this, it can harm you te dai* (one day). *"*

"Will I ever learn right Father?" Now looking back into his la (royal purple) eyes.

"Yes, it will get much easier. I know you worry about all ites close to you and yes when I've aspid (died) *you will most likely then be keeper of the Imo Macos. They will let us know when you are to begin lesson with them."*

"But not until I'm much bigger. Daddy, why does Admiral Berry want to retire here on Eftiam? He has never been off Earth. Why now?"

"I believe he wants to live a quieter life. His family is aspid (dead) *and we are the only family he has left."* His daughter looked at him with heavy skepticism. *"What is it; you are not sure of him are you?"*

"No, something is not right. There is more he is not telling us." Maybe when I see him in the present, I can give you more information. We best go, Mother has lunch ready," Reading her mother's niet.

<>

Admiral Berry did not watch as the ship descended the landing pad. He was too seasick to care; he forgot how much he hated flying in outer space and he was land footed for over fifty years now. Why did he now take to choose such punishment? Simple enough; for him, it is all he could think about.

Finally hearing the engines shut down he unbuckled, heading straight for the can to emit anything left in his stomach, which now was mainly bowel. Not once did a patch help, even doubling them up, that's why he took the injections and that didn't help. Coming from the bathroom, before him, "Welcome to Eftiam, Admiral Berry, my name is Rupert Juni your personal mechanical ite." Speaking as he held out his hand.

"Ah, thank you … wouldn't happen to have something for sea sickness, would you? I don't fly well." Berry could not get over how human the robot felt to the touch and how characteristic his actions. He remembered Gavens told him Salinger and Harper out did themselves, but he was pleasantly surprised seeing it for himself.

"Yes, Admiral Berry, I will return with an antidote." Off the robot sauntered.

"Welcome Admiral Berry," The female voice aired.

"Well Hello Bré, it's been ages since we conversed, good to hear your voice."

"Yes, Admiral Berry, there is a siout awaiting your presence at the docking station. Your belongings will be brought to your quarters."

"Thank you Bré."

"Mechanical ite Rupert returned with his concoction, "Here you are Admiral Berry, down the hatch and you will be back on track once again."

Berry did as request; just wanting to get the nausea gone, "I think I lost tons of weight in the three years flight here. Not that I couldn't lose a few."

"Are you ready to go Admiral? I will escort you." without waiting Rupert Juni turned and headed for the door. Admiral Berry set the glass down and picked up a quick pace to keep up with the robot. As he walked with the robot Rupert Juni, he could not get over how quickly the antidote took effect, he felt like nothing had happened and he didn't have sea legs either. Already he saw many new things, could also hear, and see new things on this planet. The excitement built even though there was a cloud hanging heavy on him. Pushing this cloud aside, he enjoyed his eagerness now taking over; more so looking upon this revolutionary machine the siout!

<>

Stepping from the siout Wayne touched the wall one last time. He saw Neil and waved.

"Wayne, welcome to my home planet," Neil avid.

"Neil it's so good to see you, my God you really got purple, didn't you?"

Now hugging with his arm around Neil's back and still holding their handshake to his chest. Berry could not help but to take in everything around him, and especially the siouts. He left Neil's handshake to go over and feel the siout wall again, "Whew, I … I can feel it living, it's fascinating. This is quite a landing pad you've built too. It's phenomenal, turning in a circle. You know the idea of a planet being purple sounds awful and even though you sent many com-mov of this planet, one can't really appreciate the beauty of it until one can see with one's own eyes. Absolutely gorgeous! If this is any indication of what I'm about to take in, I won't be able to ever sit still, just with all the learning to behold!"

"Rupert Juni, I think he likes the place," Neil avid.

"Oh yes, Commander Gavens, he really does. The antidote worked well, are we ready to get going?" Rupert Juni placed his arm in front of himself a jester of service, indicating the loading area and another smaller siout. Berry jumped aboard eager to see the inside of this small organic craft.

Inside Admiral Berry took in everything within; the two purple-shaded people before him at the helm smiled, "Please Admiral Berry take a seat and buckle in." Berry could not do that he went straight over to the Pilot taking in the complete comdat console. The Pilot was polite and let him look over the compus console. *"He's wearing an implant com-mov Neil."* Efviari avid.

Sighing resignedly, *"I figured as much."*

Another avi came through, *"Daddy, Mommy, Auntie Efiar and I are together. Admiral Berry is not here to decide only about his retirement. His trip was not his own to take, more a helpful way to get here."*

"Admiral Berry I would like you to meet Guide Efviari our pilot, my dear relative and friend and husband of Efiar."

"I am more Liaison Guide my friend. Excuse me if I do not shake your hand, my right hand is rather busy at the moment." Efviari gestured to his arm in the control slot of the siout panel...

"It's my pleasure. I've heard so much good of you and your entire planet."

Efviari nodded his head, but made no further comment, going back to his controls.

"So, Wayne what brings you to Eftiam?" Neil made sure the avi went through the entire ship, and Efviari could further send it on to the other Guides.

"Why Neil, as I explained before I came, I want to retire here on Eftiam if you will have me."

"This is a true statement, but I believe whoever placed the implant has other ideas for him," Efviari avid to all concerned, *"Please take your seat, we are ready for lift off."*

Of course, the second Admiral Berry took his seat it reached out to grab him, scaring him badly enough to jump up and away running into Efviari. Efviari partially turned, *"Please do not be afraid. The chair will adjust to your form and make the ride much more comfortable."* This made Neil smile in reflection of the minst tia (first time) he sat in the chair upon meeting his aspid (dead) friend Eftiar. Berry cautiously took his seat again, this time giving credence to the chair accepting his body. Getting over his shock, he watched from the window, "We're flying out over the ocean, aren't we?"

"Yes, right now we are." Efviari knew this was a sign for him to do a little sightseeing of the jungle, then Neil would get the Admiral talking and the view could veil how they would be getting into Sig City.

Flying over the jungle Admiral Berry took in the sights of the similarity of animals, plants and trees as on Earth/Sigmet, although everything was different shades of purple. "God, sure made the colors so blended and yet so gorgeous. I really can't describe it any better. One could never tire of this."

"Wayne is there another reason you are here besides your desire to retire here?" This brought the Admirals head around almost like a spinning top. The fear in his eyes told Neil something was unusually wrong. He took a little time to adjust to the query.

He gave Commander Gavens hand signals. These came from low in his lap as they used years ago in a classroom to communicate, "No, Neil, I don't know what more I can say other than you are my only friend left, and I too haven't family, so I want to be here with you in retirement, that is if you will have me and I've missed space travel."

Wayne was telling Neil about his implant, placed in his left eye. His code indicated it was sending sights and sound back to Sigmet and from there to Earth. This is being done by the Council, Neil who feels you are hiding something from them. The Earth/Sigmet Councils apparently still wanted to take over Eftiam. Another clue he gave Neil was he missed space travel, when he never flew after his first flight due to sea sickness and the meds never helping.

"Well, as I told you before, I want you here, but it is up to the Guides of Eftiam to decide who stays not me. I however will put a good word in for you. When were you planning to make the change?"

174

"The complete transfer six months after my return. You know three-year travel, six months and then another three-year travel back. I must finish out my term on the Council, although I really haven't anything but voting power and liaison now. Man, I'm really having a hard time with you using telepath instead of using your mouth, it just doesn't seem natural and the loss of hair and the purple skin and eyes. It's really weird."

"It took me ages to get used to everything, but its second nature to me now. I best warn you; the entire crew is the same way."

"Ah … yeah that is what perplexed the Council and many others of both our planets, that not one of your crew members elected to return to Earth or Sigmet."

Laughing heartily, *"Well you're in awe just looking and feeling things right now. The ites … I mean people here make it so wonderful, it's a blessing to want to stay on a planet such as this."*

"Gentleman, we have arrived," Robot Rupert Juni offered.

"Wow, I didn't even feel that ride and or the landing. It was like sitting in a chair just enjoying simple conversation. I can see we are in a different place;" as the door slid open.

Efiari stepped forward to welcome them, *"Hello Admiral Berry, I trust your flight was a good te* (one) *I'm Efiari, Personal Relations for Eftiam. Normally I would have welcomed you, but we thought Commander Gavens would be the most appropriate."*

"Hello, Efiari, you have a beautiful planet here. I'm looking forward to seeing much more. Aren't you one of the Guides here for Eftiam?"

"Why yes, I am. Admiral I would like you to meet Linti, our Head Battle Guide for Eftiam."

Admiral Berry automatically gave protocol and saluted Linti. Linti saluted back, as Neil had showed him to do. Neil was giving Wayne the courtesy of being the first arrival on Eftiam, since his crew. "I look forward to speaking with you on your military set up here on Eftiam, Linti."

Linti standing at attention, "Yes Sir the pleasure will be mine as well."

"I am sure you are ready for some rest and relaxation and want to freshen up before meeting the rest of our Guide members, friends and

crew members. Please follow us, not abating Efiari fuaing, Linti, and mechanical ite Rupert Juni fuai land walking, they preceded. Neil and Wayne fell in behind. Neil purposely fuai land walking to accommodate and to leave some things unrevealed.

Upon reaching one of the four tunnel paths, Rupert Juni stopped, "Admiral Berry this way please." Efiari and Linti went through another lane without turning. Admiral Berry could not help but crane his neck to take in the back view of Efiari fuaing.

"Rupert Juni will bring you in for lunch Wayne, so get some rest and freshen up. Your belongings should be in your personal sig about now."

Chapter 29

*"A*dmiral Berry is definitely here to see about retiring, but yes, you all were right about the fact there is another motive. The implant is in his left eye. So, he and I developed hand signals; another way of making a language. He used these signals this dai* (day) *about his implant and it is the Council eye. When we were at academy together, communication was forbidden. Who sent him to us in this manner? Gavens queried. They feel I am hiding something from them about Eftiam, which is true I have done just that. He is truly my friend and does want to be here, but not under these circumstances. What we must figure out is how to help him out of this situation and discourage the Earth/Sigmet Council from suspicion and to keep them from coming here. So, any ideas you may have would be helpful."* Aving this, nearing the end of his summation, he could not help but look to Jean.

"Oh Neil, I am so sorry this happened for you," Jean responded. Neil gave a regretted smile.

Neiliara seemed to hang back, still speculating. Neil knew his daughter would wait to avi until meeting Wayne. *"Admiral Berry is due here for lunch with us any min. Bré is the rest of our party on their way?"*

"Yes, Commander Gavens, all are in tunnels now." Bré announced, "Commander, you asked to be notified of a change."

"Yes?"

"There are tvent (twenty) Earth/Sigmet war ships three years out."

"Do you feel they are coming in our direction?"

"Affirmative, Commander Gavens

"Thank you Bré, place this as a priority and keep me posted of major changes." Focusing his sight to his family, Neil crossed to them placing his arm around his wife and drawing Neiliara to his side, placing his hand to her head of hair, *"The Imo Macos warned me of this from Earth/Sigmet ages ago, but not Admiral Berry's involvement. We will have our first battle here on Eftiam, not something I look forward to."*

Before they had a chance to discuss the approaching situation further, Efiar, Efiari, Efviari and Linti fuaid into the dining sig. Efiar and Jean hugged as if both women had not seen each other in days instead of a couple hours before. As both women turned to the others to avi their 'hello' they resembled kangaroos with enlarged pouches expecting the offspring to pop up any minute now. *"We are very worried Neil, with Admiral Berry here on Eftiam. He is here under false pretenses. We should not have let him come," Efiar avid.*

"I agree with you that he should not be here under false pretenses. I know he wants to be here as an ite of Eftiam in good standing. He has made this noticeably clear to me; I was just explaining this to Jean and Neiliara. Maybe we should look at this more objectively; like Admiral Berry's presence could help us advantageously."

Jean spied Rupert Juni first, Berry behind as they were about to enter the din-sig. Crossing the sig quickly, fuai land walking, "Admiral Berry, it is so good to see you, welcome to Eftiam."

"Jean, you look marvelous, why I didn't know you were with child; congratulations."

Neil crossed the floor to greet his guest, *"I saved the surprise for your arrival. Rupert Juni, thank you for showing Admiral Berry here, we will call you when he is returning to his private sig."*

"Yes, Commander Gavens." Rupert Juni departed the din- sig.

"Efiar, you and Efviari are to be the only tes (ones) *to fuai,"* Neil spoke to all of Eftiam leaving out Wayne of course, as he crossed the room fuai land walking, guiding him to the others. *"Wayne, I would like you to meet Guide Efiar, and the rest of our party you already know."* Efiar nodded her head…

"Father!"

"Oh my, how could I forget you my dear child. Wayne, this is our beautiful daughter Neiliara."

Admiral Berry stooped to her level, "You're as beautiful as your mother and you have her gorgeous auburn … I mean lilac hair. It's a pleasure to meet you."

Neiliara was hoping he would take her hand as she offered it to shake. He did. "The pleasure is mine."

"Father" … has … She fainted away to the floor.

Neil was the first to reach her; quickly, he raised her feet above her head. As he held them, he became aware his daughter did not pass out. *"Neiliara, what are you doing?"*

"Dad tell him I am a weak child and cannot ever leave Eftiam. They are here to take myself and Efiar to Earth for further study." Neiliara made sure to give this information to all the Eftiamrs. Neil could hardly control himself, he started to shake. *"No Dad, you cannot let him know. As soon as I touched him everything came to me of their plans."*

Jean now stood beside as well as the rest, congregating around to where Neiliara lied and Neil seated on the floor still holding her feet above her head. *"Oh goodness of all tias* (times) *I can't get on the floor."* This time being heard by all present.

"It's ok Jean, she fainted. You know how it is for her. Neiliara has just had an awfully hard and anticipating dai. It just got to be too much for her. Bré, please ask for a Juni for a concoction after fainting and to take Neiliara to her private sig. Daughter I must show you how to faint. This was a poor example," his last few avis privately spoken

"Well, I really only read about it in te (one) *of your Earth novels, I guess I need more practice."* This made Neil smile down into his daughter's precious face, looking so demure.

I must watch out for your faking incidents I assume?"

"I would not have had to simulate this, if you had not brought him here. This will cause war, for ites of Eftiam. We will not let Auntie be taken. But we do have an advantage and yes, he wants to help us." This child does not realize they will not allow her to be taken either.

"I will go with her," Jean avid. No one argued.

"Was it something I said?" Admiral Berry inquired.

"Oh no Wayne, Neiliara is very frail. She tires quickly. She's been this way since birth. We very much do not believe she will ever be able to leave Eftiam. Jean and I so looked forward to showing her Earth and Sigmet, so she would understand her heritage better; but that seems out of the question. We worry for all those of Eftiam leaving planet, that they would have the same problem." All watched the Juni, Neiliara and Jean leaving the din- sig.

This made Admiral Berry smile widely; one could not help but hear what proffered from his mouth, "Oh Neil, I am sorry to hear this. Is this true of most people who live here on Eftiam?" Berry's eyes were now taking in the sights of this din- sig as he queried.

"We are not positive, but we believe it could be a problematic situation and needs more investigation."

"The splendor of this room is awe inspiring! How on earth did you get those chairs such a clear beauty with such artistic curves?" Berry asked as his hands glided over the structure as if it was pure gold.

"Eftiam is made up of exceptionally talented ites. Also, I do not know if you are aware, they are organic," Efiar avid with pride, *"Everything on Eftiam is organic Admiral Berry."*

"Please call me Wayne."

"I will do so in private company as you wish, but not in assembly. Protocol is te of the binders of Eftiam." Efiar's body showed rigidity letting him know she would not be told how to avi her wishes, *"Shall we take our seats."*

<><>

Halfway into the meal Jean did return. *"Admiral Berry sorry I missed most   of the meal conversation, but Neiliara can be quite demanding,"* Jean avid taking her seat.

"Please Jean, call me Wayne. You don't need to tell me about kids. I can probably advise you more. I did have five but must admit my wife was the real care giver for them … the subject spoken as his head resumed taking in the grand tour. And tell me, when did you start speaking with your mind as Neil does?"

Jean's head spun to Efiar and Neil, wordlessly apologizing for an automatic avi which too caught her by surprise. She also noticed how Berry's hands were pounding his chest to Neil while doing his best to keep his implant from seeing. *There has to be a way that Simms and Chambers can take care to fully remove the implant, but let the Council still believe they were getting information.* She would talk with the Doctors the next morn. *"I … really cannot remember exactly when,"* she stammered. She was not about to tell him when this all came about, *"Gosh Wayne, I am so sorry for your losses, your wife also?"*

"Yes, with all pollutions of mans' greed and different types of war fare on Earth it's desperate for all. The Council is working extremely hard to try and change this, but I must tell you it's happening on Sigmet now also. Man, just can't seem to give up pollutant luxuries and they're willing to accept younger deaths; my young ones included. My wife another story, I lost her to the big 'C'."

"We did not realize Earth was in that dire of straights," Efiari avid. *"Of course, this is why you so desperately hunt for another planet to inhabit and start the same process over again."*

The room became quiet for a good min while they waited for Berry's response.

Finally, Wayne spoke, "Yes Earth and Sigmet are looking for planetary habitat but this time the Councils have vowed to keep the new planet clean and free. It will be part of the conditions of agreeing to go to another planet to live."

An almost, whisper avi came from Neil, yet heard by all, including the camera for Councils, *"They vowed to do this when leaving Earth for Sigmet."*

Efiar avid, *"This is a serious problem for you Wayne and we realize our planet is in your Councils' sights, but this is not the tia* (time) *to discuss how to go about handling this subject. After all you have just arrived. Did you know that we now do memorial services and efing celebrations here on Eftiam?"*

"Ah ... Ah ... No ... I didn't know that." Berry now showed signs of insurmountable thanks for Efiar's subject change. "What does the word efing mean?"

"It means mating in your language. We never had a larg (large) *celebration, but that has all changed since Jean explained this to us. We do enjoy it more. Bré, would you please show Eftiar's asping* (dying) *service and the double efing here on Eftiam for Admiral Berry,"* Efiar Avi requested.

"Yes, Guide Efiar."

Berry looked over the room to spy if a screen would come from a wall or ceiling. This did not happen. Instead in front of him at the table a hydro- gram-mov projection of light appeared and the complete showing began at the same time. His mouth gaped, "You don't have to use a wall screen? Damn this is like a sci-fi mov of teleportation."

"Actually, this is not new technology Wayne. We got it from old scientific files of Earth. We just made sure to use organic materials and

not something that would pollute our planet," Efviari avid, *"Maybe we could collaborate to help out Earth/Sigmets' making changes to both planets and just maybe you would not have to leave your planets."*

Wayne fought his head moving to locate Efviari. He so wanted to see the hydro-gram-mov, but Councils had other ideas, so the camera took over.

"Bré, please stop the hydro-gram- mov," Efiar avid, agitated with Efviari, letting him know just with her look.

"Yes, Guide Efiar"

It blinked out of sight, and Wayne was looking to see if there were after affects. "Ah … oh yes, this would be wonderful if you could help save our planets, but I do have doubts because of the existing problems." Berry stated.

"We know you tried to clean up your Earth a long time ago, but even with this start it was too late, the damage was done. Neil's great-grandfather's crew tried hard to make the Council see long before they left Earth. Your main problem on both planets is your governments wait until your ites complain and are asping en masse. Just take the instance of when you used cars and traffic lights. A light was not put into place until at least fif asps (five deaths) *occurred from accidents with vehicles. We have advanced technology and are willing to help. However, we have a condition for our help. You will not come here to inhabit Eftiam,"* Efiari again avid with assurance, looking straight in Wayne's eyes to make sure his implant was getting this information. *"Since I am Guide Public Representative here, please let me explain Admiral Berry and Councils of both your planets. We are aware of your implant Admiral Berry!"* Efiari gave this a few moments to sink in, knowing the distance and the sioutous having to relay it on to their respective planets. Admiral Berry was quiet, but his smile was filling the room for the forwardness shown by this group before him. *"Therefore, Council, we are going to remove the implant from Admiral Berry's eye. In addition, we will check for any other type of spy object you may have given him and or placed within his sioutous and siout. So, with this avid, could we escort you now to our hos-sig, Wayne, to have your implant removed?"* Efiari and the rest of the male party rose.

"Most assuredly, please lead the way," Wayne stated rising still filling the din- sig with his huge smile, as they left.

Chapter 30

Neil's mind was racing with all Wayne disclosed to him; all this time the Council felt Neil was taking over Eftiam for himself. This was hard for him to fathom. *It's hard for me to believe Wayne did not know about the war sioutous' on their way here. The Imo Macos confirmed they would come here. Apparently, Wayne had fully been kept from receiving information.* He had Linti, Efviari and Efiari all compiling data with Bré to assess battle operations. Pacing his room … W*hy do they want Neiliara and Efiar? Yes, they are telepaths, but Efiar lost her ability to avi with the Imo Macos when I became liaison for Eftiam. But they know not of this; therefore, reasonable they want her as well. Efiar wants to bring him before our ites. I feel it too soon and the others agree with me. I do not understand this reasoning. I should discuss this with her. I purposely have not counseled with Wayne alone and I know he wants to, but I cannot chance any queries from him, that I would refuse to avi. Also, it would not be fair to the rest of our Guides. This is a tia* (time) *for strict protocol. We are a very new planet of ites, and trust is most important. What was it the Imos avid?... Oh yes, 'you are a planet of deference, a planet of change, do not avi in the old way. I know the answer, but strategy is important for all ites of Efti*am. *Jean will give me a hard tia of this, for I must use Neiliara. Why is Jean so obstinate about Neiliara of late? Is it because she is with child and that extra protective Mothering? She knew we would not have normal children when I became Liaison.* His problems were complex, but not insurmountable. *Efviari will help me convince Jean.*

All were meeting within Doctor Chambers' office sig. His office was very open aired with many shades of purple, making it inviting and easy to the eye for any patient and also for the Doctor of Science to work. The air plants were everywhere hanging from the ceiling, and a water wall was part of the decor giving peace and tranquility. Always Admiral Berry seemed to be the last to sit a chair, as if he expected the chair to never let him go, instead of adjusting with the forming to his body. It made the entire party smile, "Do you think you will ever adjust to the ways of Eftiam?" Linti consulted.

"It's such a queer feeling to have the chairs grab and then form to me. I'll adjust; I so want to be here with y'all. It's been two weeks now and I feel so apart of Eftiam already," His Texas drawl letting one know he still spoke Earthen.

The usual party was present, with Simms added in case of a medical problem. *"Are you aware of why we are counseling here in Chambers office, Wayne? We still have you being monitored for devices even though we believe all removal has been carried out."* Efiar avi inquired.

"I can only assume you aren't sure you got all the implants."

"Yes, if anything should happen while we avi, we want to be on top of it. We will help protect you at all costs, but we must request your story of how this all came about."

"Wayne, it does not matter that you and I spoke of your coming to Eftiam, or that I have informed the Council, they do need to hear it from you," Neil offered.

"Thank you, my friend. I realize you haven't been able to speak to me privately but knowing how ethically you carry yourself as this old man advised you for many years is good for my heart. That is what prompted me to think of retiring you know. Well diagnosed, my heart isn't the same as it used to be. So, realizing you were the only family I had left and you weren't calling me as much anymore; I definitely knew I was coming to be near you one way or the other. The real kicker; one day you and I were transmitting, and I watched you play with Neiliara, I knew completely having adoptive grandchildren to play with and help raise, made it even more inviting.

When I put in the paperwork for retirement, I put in a request for a ship to Sigmet and then one here to Eftiam. Everyone started questioning me. They could not understand my wanting to come to such a foreign land and at my age and also with the medial chance I was taking. I knew how the Councils felt about you, so I was bound and determined to be here to help.

The night of my retirement party, they drugged my drink, placed the implant and then told me they had done so, because I would not be able to interfere with it, as you saw the day you removed it Dr. Simms, for which I am extremely grateful. I figured why not let them send me at their expense and not mine. Once here I knew we could do our sign language, hoping you remembered our secret of conversing. I was sure you could remove the damn thing. I didn't care if it killed me then or not, I was going to be here with you and your family."

Jean was sitting next to Wayne; she reached over placing her hand on his and leaned in to kiss his cheek. He grabbed her and gave her a hearty hug. This seemed to break the ice. "The rest you know, oh and of course when you stopped giving information to the Councils, they got even more suspicious."

"I quit telling so much because this is my ... excuse me ... our home now!"

Neil avid looking only to his wife, *"The Councils still had the intention of coming here and I felt we could not have that happen to Eftiam."*

"Well son it did just the opposite, it made them more suspicious."

Efiar, Efviari, Efiari and Linti had trouble taking this; a different way of understanding. They were not used to this sort of thinking; this was new to them and they had to accept and learn quickly. *Thank you, Imo Macos for, giving us Neil Gavens and his crew; I see now, we would not have made it without their help, Efiar avid out as if in praying.*

"You are most welcome Efiar," Came from the Imo Macos in far off, sounding as if from across many ages, as though many solar systems away they could still hear her.

"Oh!" Avi from Efiar, overcome with surprise from her niet outburst.

All looked her way, *"Are you alright Efiar, it is not our baby, is it?"*

Efviari avid with utmost concern.

Efiar looked to Jean smiling, *"Are they like this when a baby is coming?"*

"Most assuredly. But only with the minst, after that it is considered old hat."

"What is 'old hat'?" The original Eftiamrs, avid curiously.

"Like once it has been seen or done, then you are used to it, so it is no longer new or unknown," Jean avi explained.

Efiar smiled at Efviari, *"No dear, but I did hear from the Imo Macos a trio mini* (three minutes) *ago. I thanked them for something, and they returned an avi, so they are with us right now during this*

council. *It startled me, for I have not been able to avi with them for
such a long tia.*"

"Really, I would love to meet them, where exactly are they?"
Wayne asked.

This brought raucous laughter to the table, Neil offered an avi,
"That is not as easy as te (one) *may think Wayne; you will have to wait
to possibly meet the Imo Macos. It is too deep for me to go into at this
tia. Maybe once you are truly settled here on Eftiam, then it may
happen."*

Wayne had a very perplexed look, but decided not to push it, so he
went on, "Efiari the ships haven't turned, back, have they?"

"No Wayne they have not, but how did you know?" Efiari avid
troubled.

Is he already feeling aving?

"I've served too many years on the Council to not know the
thinking. So, I would advise Linti to set for war!" Wayne took time to
take in every face at the table, "Linti I would like to offer my help."

"Thank you, Admiral Berry, I would appreciate your help along
with the rest of our ites."

*"Daddy, I know you are going to correct me for listening in, but I
cannot sit here and do my studies when Eftiam is in crisis! Grandpa
Wayne is sincere and does want to stay with us for the rest of his tia*
(time)*, which is not long. If he had tried to make the trip back to Earth
before Doctor Simms repaired his heart with our technology, he would
not have survived the voyage. His condition was way beyond any Earth
technology. Truthfully, I do not want or feel he should try to make the
trip back to Earth."* Neiliara avid.

*"Whoa, what is this calling him Grandpa already? Since you are so
adamant come ahead and join us...."*

Never getting to finish his sentence avi, a door slid from an
adjoining room and in fuaid Neiliara with great speed. She did not look
to anyone except her newfound Grandfather Wayne. Stopping at his
side, she quirked her finger for him to bend to her, Wayne did so,
"Grandpa Wayne welcome home!" Then bluntly abrupt she flung her
arms around his neck and simid (kissed) him on his left cheek.
Bouncing her dear self into his lap, jarring him to the point he had to
grab hold of the table for fear they would fall. Laughter broke out

watching this scene, as well as avis'… *'Look at that'*… *'She foresaw more than the rest of us'*…

"Well, Neiliara you have spoken have you not?" Efiar avi queried.

"I know you felt it also Auntie, can we keep my new Grandpa?"

"You know we have to take a complete Sig City vote before that may be answered."

"Yes, Ma'am, but you will place a good avi for him will you not?"

Grandpa Wayne just smiled a broader smile than the dai they had taken the implant from his eye.

"Yes, I have been after the Guides to let me place Wayne before our ites for a vote."

"Oh?" In her naivete, *"Why have they not agreed?"* As she avid, she looked around the table to the Guide Council.

"Sometimes Neiliara things are not as easily decided as you may think. Not everyone has insight," Efviari avid.

"Well Uncle, he is more than fine and I really do not feel he should go back to Earth, even though Doctor Simms took care of his heart, too many complications could arise and I want my grandfather with me for a long tia, after all I just got him!" Smugly, she crossed her arms looking around the table once again. Then she coyly leaned back into Wayne's chest and looked up into his eyes, *"By the way Grandpa, tia— means time in your language."*

"Took care of my heart? You fixed it? I was told it was unfixable."

"On your Earth, then yes it was unable to be repaired, but here on Eftiam we have the means; therefore, we repaired your heart," Dr. Simms answered.

Berry could not help noticing the phrasing of 'your Earth' when Simms himself was born on Earth. "I'm beholding to you, Doctor Simms, and you Doctor Chambers, in more ways than one. Thank you for giving me extra life. It's too bad the people of Earth and Sigmet will not be able to enjoy the wonderful things here of Eftiam and its people, but then again maybe it's not meant. Both haven't done well by their planets and to destroy more is wrong. I too for a long time was a part of it in my short sightedness, when waking I tried to fight back, but it was too late to get many to see my side. No, I am afraid there isn't hope for Earth or Sigmet."

"Wayne, please excuse my daughter for talking about you as if you were not in the room. Sometimes she reacts before thinking of the consequences," Jean avid.

"Oh, it's ok, she's just a child, I fully understand."

The entire table smiled and some even laughed abruptly to this comment, *"No Wayne you do not understand. Never treat our Neiliara as a child, she does not think as a child. She is not the norm you would find on Earth or Sigmet, considering her age. As a matter of fact, not any child here on Eftiam, but I must tell you Neiliara is also further ahead in many respects to the other children of Eftiam. You have been warned."*

"What on earth do you mean?"

"Don't you dare avi a word Neiliara!" Neil avid to her alone, *"Give it time Wayne you will understand."* Instead, Neiliara quietly stayed in her Grandfather's lap with a Cheshire cat smile, while her grandfather looked perplexed...

Chapter 31

It was hard for Wayne to realize that yes; it had been a full year here on Eftiam. In his time, here there was one major change: the building of new siouts and sioutous for war. Every day it was his job to oversee the building of these crafts. He marveled at the technology upon arrival and the new-found technology since. It seemed someone was always able to develop new methods organically and appropriate for a given situation. No one paid for food or lodging or anything else one would need. It was given without argument. At first, he thought they were giving him everything out of citreous until he requested to pay his way. Instead, it was avid to him by Efiari that he was overseer that all ites have a position of standing on Eftiam, and therefore all is given in return. Everyone was able to choose the profession they wanted to engage in and delve into other areas as well to see if they could develop more for their people. The knowledge and foresight of these people made him embarrassed for Earth and Sigmet. The people of Eftiam and Earth/Sigmet/Eftiamrs freely intermarried; he himself was dating a cousin of Efiar and Efiari's family. The only exception for Wayne was that he was the first of Eftiam not to require the ocean for life support or initiation that was given only by the Imo Macos for those to have telepathic ability and those born on Eftiam.

Preparing for his morning trek to the assembly bay, while reflecting, he smiled wryly; who would have thought he would get so purple. It just made him recall one of the Council members on his trans-talks, commenting he looked ill and suggesting that he come back to Earth; also asking if he would stay purple if he did come back. Heck he didn't know if he would stay purple or not, no one considered leaving Eftiam not even him. He too was intentionally not handing information back to Earth because Neil had asked him not to. He didn't know why, but Neil would reveal it in time that he was sure of. But the planning of this war was now beyond communication. He tried to advise Neil about this, but carefully refrained from discussion.

He found his granddaughter astounding in her telepathic skills and her new brother Jeniari also on the same path of telepathy; as well as already fuaing from one parent to another of his own whim. Thinking of this he shook his head thoughtfully.

Neil was not telling him everything, which sometimes hurt. He was so used to being on the inside of everything, but then again near his time of leaving Earth for his suggested retirement, he knew then he was being kept out of the complete loop. Nothing beyond normal for retirement time, but it was ridiculously hard to accept. His growing old sucked until now being here on Eftiam. Hell, he did not care if his coloring was purple; he felt better than ever and had a beautiful family to call his own and a wonderful woman to spend his last days with. He loved going landside with his e-ray, totally different from the l-ray he carried on Earth and feeling as if he was on safari. After all Neil is on Guide Council and in communication with these Imo Macos. Wayne still wondered if he would ever see or speak with them himself. Probably not, because the Guide Council kept telling him, they had left their planet and were making a new planet in another solar system. Yet they could still communicate telepathically with them? This he found hard to place in proper perspective, but not one person on this planet doubted them, so he could not. Plus, he probably would not live long enough for them to return. Satisfied with his appearance he set out for his day to check the assembly of their crafts; it was such a pleasant morning.

Chapter 32

"Do you think anyone suspects?" Efiar avid to Neil and Neiliara, as she towels dry her wet hair from the life pool; this meeting was conducted in utmost secrecy, it was imperative that it took place in such privacy no ite would suspect, even those closest to them.

"No Auntie I am not receiving any avis in such manner. They have accepted what they see and hear. It was a grand avi."

"Yes, it really was, but let us niet avi. Hopefully, it can last long enough for us to finish preparation," Neil avi conveyed.

"How many siouts are completed, Neil?"

"Only a hunth (one hundred), but they are the most inspiring crafts I have seen with my own eyes. Even though we have built such a craft, I just hope we do not have to use them for long or to ki (kill)."

Neiliara read the empathy on her father's face. She knew this was causing more fracture on his body than he was letting on. He will asp not long after this encounter. She did not want her father to see, her avi or feel her emotion, so her body stayed most rigid as she bit back tears.

"Doctor Simms is training tio (two) new Assistants. There are so many newborn ites coming into our world. I am so pleased to see the new life on Eftiam," Efiar avi reflected as she looked upon her sleeping son, but also avid the anguish her Neiliara was going through. They were so tightly connected almost as if they were twins, they felt and avid everything of the other.

"Did you find it odd Efiar, that you and Jean gave birth at the exact same min and dai? I do believe the Imo Macos have something in avi for Efenavi and Jeniari."

"No doubt they do Neil. They sure can eat, can't they? I feel sometimes that is all I am doing is feeding Efenavi, but I would not change a thing. Efviari and I are so happy, and I know you and Jean are very glad for your newest addition."

With this avi, Efenavi brought attention to himself, letting them know he heard every avi. They all smiled, while Neiliara raised fuaing to the side of his crib. "Ok, you want me to hold you I take it?" Without waiting for another declaration Neiliara bent over and removed Efenavi from his crib, *"You always seem to know the min I come to Auntie's sig."* Cooing his contentment while Neiliara fuaid with him in her arms, *I believe we have another matter at avi."*

Neil perplexed waited for an avi from one of these tio (two) powerful ites, who together asking for a meeting but outfoxed him on matters most every time. Efiar stopped blotting her hair looking to Neil, *"This is not my avi, but Neiliara; she asked me to avi the matter."*

"Then undoubted my avi will be a complete 'no', so why even try to win me over?" Looking to his daughter, she did not seem to look his way, but took the transparent excuse to continue playing with Efenavi.

"Yes, we gave this great avi, but it also concerns me too and for ites of Eftiam. For instance, if we do not get enough siouts built in time to do battle, then we must have a backup plan. Neil, you are a man of war, that is partly why you were brought to Eftiam, this I have no doubt. But I ... no ...we feel you are thinking in physical sense of battle only and we of Eftiam have much more to offer for battle."

"The Imo Macos are not here to help, so there is no other way but to do physical battle and we also have an unlimited amount of mechanical ites, thanks to Chambers and his ability to design the mechanical ites to do our will completely. He has expanded the brains on his uncle's work to beyond brilliant; we are ready to go when we set them alive for battle. I feel most assured we will do well in battle here on Eftiam; it will just be the rebuilding that may take tia. You realize the Earth/Sigmets will leave their sioutous in orbit and come in on the small siouts to battle. They are not prepared for the type of siouts we have designed for battle; it will be a disadvantage to them."

"Neil, wouldn't it be to our advantage to also take out the orbit sioutous?"

"It would be great to do so yes, but it takes years to manufacture a te (one) system sioutous, which we are working to make ready in dais along with producing more siouts. Once they see what our siouts can accomplish, they will not tarry here," Neil feeling quite satisfied with his comeback.

"They would eventually return, Father, and we cannot allow it to happen. Therefore, we need a more substantial plan." Neiliara looked straight into her father's eyes.

"It sounds like a plan I would not consider, especially if you are involved, Neiliara. You are not old enough to …"

"Father, may I remind you, my physical appearance may appear that of a child, but my brain is of an adult and beyond normal. I speak with everyone mentally and that includes the Imo Macos," Realizing she was shaking by his insult, she handed Efenavi to his mother and fuaid speedily back and forth in a pattern identical to her fathers, when troubled.

Neil also raised fuaing in the same manner, but opposite to her. It was a very comical sight for Efiar. Even though, *my plants and furniture! So many of our family seem to almost knock over or knock over when avis of concern occur here in this private sig.* "Auntie, I will not hurt your plants and furniture, I cannot avi for my father."

"So, you are still a child when you listen in to private thoughts."

"It only happens when I am upset, which is rare. I will keep working on controlling this weakness."

Neil's patience was wearing thin now, especially when it came to his Neiliara. Still fuai pacing, *I know she is going to tell me the utmost I do not care to hear. Jean will think I am putting her up to her plan. How do I know it is her plan? Efiar did avi, it was hers. They are scheming,* "It is not that I am not in acceptance of your niet *(brain) which is far beyond most of us here on Eftiam, and I just want you to have some sort of a childhood to enjoy before taking on the pressures of adulthood. Yours will not be an easy one. And since when have you been niet aving with the Imo Macos, Neiliara?"*

Neiliara knew her Father was biding her for tia (time), *"Every dai since Grandfather Berry came to Eftiam. I am not sure, but I do believe they helped devise this plan."*

Stopping his fuai pacing, hovering and with a stern look, *"Let me hear of this plan, then I will speak with the Imo Macos before I make a decision."*

"Auntie I cannot tell him we do not need his acceptance. Even if he disagrees, we will go ahead with this decision, will we not?" Still fuai pacing.

"Yes, we will go ahead with or without his consent," Looking to her

193

child as if she was not aving her Neiliara, then slowly taking her eyes from her son *"Shall we sit and discuss this plan, Efenavi will need feeding soon."*

Chapter 33

*"C*an you believe Penny developed the technology for the new gamma-hydro-gun system?"* Efiari asked.

"Why do you find it so hard to believe Earth-ites are capable of accomplishing major technical breakthroughs, especially when she is your ef (mate)*?"* Efviari avi queried back.

Suddenly Efiari's la (royal purple) skin took on a deeper glow of embarrassment, *"Yes, in many ways I do find it hard to accept, but in other ways I have adjusted to Earth/Sigmet-ite ways. Penny fascinates me, but I felt for so long we were the only ites and I am still catching up to the fact we are not. Does that make sense?"*

"Not hardly, but it does take some of us longer to catch on to the real facts of life." Efviari avi jested, with a huge smile.

"It is good you understand me, Efviari. I would not avi these kinds of feelings to anyone else."

"Well brother you best get with the changes. Penny is bringing into this world any dai now and you are Guide Public Relations. No one should feel this way knowingly in such an out- front position."

"You are right, and I am trying to work on this matter. I see First and his ef just gave birth. We sure are having an enormous number of babies on Eftiam. They are our future. We must make sure our battle siouts are constructed exceptionally well."

"And they will be! No matter of fact they are!" Linti and Wayne offered simultaneously from behind the tio (two) Eftiamrs still half in and half out of the engine of a siout with parts scattered vicariously.

"Morn you tio, we do know they are minst (first) rate, but te (one) *can't help but to wonder about the enemy siouts coming into battle."* Efviari avi conveyed.

"Well, I can assure you there is nothing like our siouts on Earth or Sigmet. Remember, I was not long ago on both planets and part of council. In this way, we have a jump on them"

"Wayne, even though you are here on Eftiam only a short tia (time), *it feels as though you have been te* (one) *of us forever,"* Efiari avid with feeling.

"Thank you Efiari, I do feel te of you; such a comforting feeling. I was thinking of that this morn when readying myself for siout (small aircraft) survey."

"He is even beginning to sound like one of us," Linti said, grinning from ear to ear and patting his friend on the back. Linti loved having a companion now, a mentor who understood battle.

"Would you like to come with us to check out siouts this morn?" Wayne inquired.

The two Eftiamrs looked to one another, and then turned smiling, aving simultaneously, *"Yes Wayne we would like that very much, thank you for asking."* They spent two full hours checking out siouts and giving advice. They even got their hands into the projects as well. As they were coursing along to the large orbit sioutous (spaceship), Jean appeared with Jeniari on her back-papoose style.

"Good morn Jean, what a wonderful way to escort Jeniari. I will have to avi Penny of this."

"Efiari, she already knows. We have carried our children this way on Earth/Sigmet for many centuries. Have you seen my husband and daughter by any chance?"

"No, we have not; we have been here with the siouts and are now on our way to check the orbit sioutous. If we see them, we will avi them you would like to avi with them. Have you tried aving Neiliara?"

"Many tias (times) *and she is ignoring me, so I know she is with her father and does not want anyone else included. She can be most unapproachable when wanting her father's attention."*

"I have noticed this happening with Efenavi when he wants full attention from us," Efviari avid. *"Sometimes it is not a blessing to have your children-ites so far advanced from other children-ites."* Jean could not help but smile broadly at his use of Eftiam/Earth languages.

Wayne asked, "Have you tried the main-havis- sig?"

Jean, Efviari and Linti smiled wryly, but Efiari's mouth gaped. His avi came fast, *"How could you know of the main -havis- sig?"*

Wayne did not get upset by his avi, "Well I wouldn't be a very good Admiral if I did not make sure I knew the ins and outs of everything around me, now, would I?" Smiling with equanimity, "You are definitely learning much in a short period Efiari. Someone else also has to help care for all our folks on Eftiam."

Again, Efiari's face and ears beamed an almost black la (royal purple) instead his usual la, *"I truly am Wayne, and I truly am."* Now catching up, his inner poise now taking over, *"Oh, what does 'folks' mean?"*

"It means people or ites, just another Earth term."

"But Linti, I closed the main-havis- sig off, since we were not using this room. When was it re-opened?"

"Efiar, asked me to re-open it. All the havis were removed, and it is now more of a room more for meditation or when complete privacy is needed."

"Oh." Efiari did not seem satisfied with this, but avid no more of the matter. *"I must return now, are you coming Efviari?"*

"Yes, we do have Council this afternoon and there are many things to make ready for. If we see Neil or Neiliara we will send them to you straight away."

"Thank you. "Wayne, how did you find out about the havis sig?" Jean avi queried

"Jean, it does not matter how I found out, but the fact that I did; if we were at war right now, it would matter in a huge way if someone came in under cover into Sig City. Linti and I have discussed this at great length."

"You know Jean; I am blessed to have Wayne to help. He presents huge challenges for me and helps me overcome them. He has taught much in such a short time. I do think we will be extra ready for battle when the tia comes." Jean watched Wayne and Linti closely, believing they were being cautious in this critical tia, but she would not hesitate to mention it to Neil.

Before leaving both men took the time to coo at the baby, then fuai proceeded to their destination.

Chapter 34

Neil sat with his legs dangling into the upu life pool. He and Jean had taken a swim earlier, but he was tempted to go into the life pool once again, but since Efiar nearly drowned, a new buddy system was being enforced. *I so want to share this new plan with Jean. It's hard keeping anything away from her. The Imo Macos have not answered my query. Why? I fully understand the plan, which is excellent, but the use of Efiar and Neiliara in such a manner, I do not agree with.* There has got to be another way. Neil ran his fingers over his hairless head.

"What troubles you, my husband?" Jean queried moving to sit down beside her mate.

"Did I wake you? I just couldn't sleep, and I was thinking of another swim, but I listened to my inner ruling.

"Good, I do not think you need a swim at this hor (hour), *and I cannot go, for your son is soon going to awaken for his meal. Is there something I can help with?"* Moving close to her man, she could not help but simi (kiss) his bald head.

This made Neil reflect, *"Neiliara tells me you miss my wavy hair. Is this true?"*

"That child of ours has got to learn not to get into others' private thoughts. She says she only does it when she is emotionally upset, but I do not buy it. She seems to enjoy snooping. She is just too smart for her own good; says Jeniari is just as smart also. The Imo Macos had to give them all the extras. Yes, you gave up telepathy beyond a room for Neiliara and I wonder what we had to give for Jeniari? But these are every dai things you are not worried about. If you like I will sit quietly with you. Where were you this morn? I know you were with Neiliara, for she would not return avi, because she wanted to hog you all to herself!"

"Jean ... tears swelled his eyes ... he pulled her to him ... *I love you so!"*

"You know me better than anyone on Eftiam, Earth or Sigmet my love. As of now, no I cannot share with you. But this I can share ... ah ... Neiliara is aving with the Imo Macos."

She allowed Neil to hug her, but then pulled back enough to look into his eyes. *"What is it, Neil? There is much you are not telling me. I know you want to share, but at this tia you cannot, and you do not like what it is you will eventually be sharing."*

"You know me better than anyone on Eftiam, Earth or Sigmet, my love. As of now no I cannot share with you. But this I can share ... ah ... Neiliara is aving with the Imo Macs."

Jean sat straight up hugging her legs, *"God Neil, she is too young to start with them now. She is still a child."*

"No, Neiliara was never a child, not even inside the womb. You and I both know that; we are giving this child and maybe Jeniari to Eftiam as Guides to keep this planet in the wonderful state; we wish all other planets could enjoy. I too wish it were not now, but we are not the tes (ones) *who are making the decisions."*

"Then will the Imo Macos retire you? They said there would only be te aving with them before they left?"

Neil, now in a sitting position, wrapped his arms around his wife, *"After breakfast I will enter the main- havis- sig with Neiliara. We will try and communicate with them to see what is to come."*

His body language told her not to request more, *"Oh, I ran into Wayne, Linti, Efviari and Efiari this morn. They were all in siout* (small spacecraft) *manufacturing. Wayne let something out, which he knew without any of us on Council knowing. He said, 'maybe I should look for you in the main-havis -sig.'"*

Neil smiled reflectively, and then giggling, *"He's a great investigator; you can say that for him. I wonder how long he's known."*

"His avi; 'only a week or so after getting here.' No one asked if he knew what it was for. Efiari got very emotionally upset over his knowing, but he did speak frankly in front of him. They all know Wayne is here honestly, not as a spy." No more was said for Jeniari gave a cry of hunger to his mother...

Chapter 35

Efiar and Efviari lay wrapped in each other's arms, lying alongside their upu life pool, just after finishing their swim into the larger upu life pool. *"Should we check on Efenavi?"*

"No, I left mechanical ite Clarice Juni with him, he is fine, we both would know if not."

"Efiar, I did not go into your private thoughts out in the major upu life pool, but I sensed you were speaking with the Kamich and Dolifa. Is there something I should know?"

Efiar became restless pulling away, not looking into his eyes, *"I ... I ... do not want to keep avis from you Efviari, but I have made commitment to others not to avi this matter until the right tia (time). It will involve every living entity here on Eftiam.*

Efviari sat and turned her toward him, now looking down into the eyes of his ef (mate), *"Efiar, you are head Guide. I am aware there is much that you are not able to explain to me, but when I can be of help, only then may it be you should tell me."*

"Since it concerns others requesting my silence, I cannot avi. You will have to trust me my truest ef." No more was avid other than the true meaning of efing...

Chapter 36

"**O**K, my hubby what is bothering you?" Penny requested.

"Oh Penny, I do not know what is happening around me but there is something about to be changed or is changing. I do not like this absence of full control of my niet avis. I guess it comes with the position, but it just drives me crazy."

"Efiari, you worry too much," Now she tried changing the subject to distract him away from his worries. "Efiar says we will see Efriana in tio dais tia (two days' time). Who do you think she will look like? I believe Efriana should have the characteristics of both of us, you know, like she will not have the straight hair that you do. It will be curly like mine. Her pigment will be a blend of both of ours rather than just the pigments of Eftiam. And her eye pigment maybe will be one of each. Intuitively she just knew this could settle her husband's mind."

"Why you of course; you are the beautiful te (one), *therefore she will look like her Penny."*

This made her giggle; she too still had a time of it when it came to the way Efiari avi spoke. However, she loved this man without question.

"You know, I am taking lesson from Jean to telepathically speak. I so want to be able to communicate in the same manner as you."

"When did you start trying to niet avi? It does not matter to me. I think we communicate very well." As he snuggled closer to his ef, he felt the movement of his soon to be baby girl in his arms as he mentally connected with his child. This bothered Penny the most. He could already speak with their child and she could not. She felt very jealous and this was not wise, he could not help himself. He was lost in avi conversation with his Efriana and she was left out…

<>

This night every adult of Sig City seemed to be awake, not really knowing why, while the children of the city slumbered without a care.

Neiliara lay deep in heavy fitful slumber but with a furrowed brow of adulthood while she projected the plan to the children of Eftiam, leaving adults unaware. Why? What did the Imo Macos have in mind for these children? Preparation -for -battle? Children –in- battle?

Chapter 37

"*T*oday is another new beginning for Eftiam. Never before have we had such pressing responsibility placed before us in such manner.

The fruits of this labor are now evident over the past tvelt mons (twelve months), *long and hard labor with many changes and you the ites of Eftiam make me proud as we ready ourselves to proceed on our next journey together. The arrival of new ites to Eftiam, siouts* (*small spacecrafts) and sioutous* (spaceship) *and te* (one) *half ...*" the assembly laughs... "*the new mechanical Juni ites now ready for battle, new technologies, new battle equipment, avi teachings, the asping of Eftiar, new efings and our new infant ites ...* again clapping of hands and webbing, and much cheering, ... "*Building of our city, all that we have learned from the Imo Macos has made us strong. We are ready and set for battle!*" The crowd before Efiar stood and cheered a good fif mini (five minutes).

Holding up her hands they again sat while she avid, "*It has come to our attention this morn that the Earth/Sigmet sioutous' have entered our atmosphere.*" A raucous aving broke out; again, she held her hand high for quiet, "*From here on ites of Eftiam in Commander Gavens' or Admiral Berry's avi terms 'the awaiting game begins.' It is tia to set battle stations to be on watch for an attack, but at the same tia we do not stop the assemblage of our te half sioutous or new siouts and battle weaponry. You will be called upon perhaps for more grueling tias than ever before. Please make sure to check your schedules with your advisors before leaving this dai. Keep your children with a guardian at all tias and or with the playground guardian. I will not go into your different positions, there are so many, but I know every one of us will do the best to his or her abilities. Commander Gavens, do you have an avi?*"

Gavens rose from his guide throne, coming alongside Efiar, "*They most likely will attack at night, thinking we will be the least ready. They are not aware we are good and ready for battle.*" Cheers arose; then quieted!

"In your private sigs please always have your mechanical- ite-Junis on guard as a precaution." This brought small grumblings from the audience, *"Linti, do you have any avis to give?"*

Linti stepped from the side of the platform taking position alongside the others, looking out to the ites he'd known since childhood and their children, "I have grown on Eftiam alongside ites of Eftiam, and now we bring new life for Eftiam. I am proud of the accomplishments we have strived for and made, and I am especially proud to be a part of all of you." standing ovation with voices united ... 'Linti our battle leader'... 'Our brother'... 'Our friend'... 'Battle leader'... now sang over and over again. Finally, his hands went up to calm the crowd. When all quieted, "I am overwhelmed, but we have yet to win this battle set before us, let us not celebrate until we are once again here all together. Admiral Berry joined us tix mons (six months) now. In that tia he has helped me more than I can express. He has shown us true brotherhood and is my dear friend and mentor. Thank you, Admiral Berry."

Admiral Berry waved from his position alongside Jean and the children.

"Aren't you going to say something Wayne?" Jean avi whispered.

"No dear, I am retired now, remember?"

"Right Grandfather," Neiliara avid with a smirk, and rolling her eyes, as she rested her head into him. He and Jean noticed how she clung to him these last tré dais (three days); even following him to his private sig. Jean and Wayne attributed it to fear of the upcoming battle.

Efiari came forward, *"Doctor Jean Gavens and her assistants will be setting up office in this main meeting sig for those of you who may need counsel. All medical staff is ready, for any need that may arise. Of course, we will try reason minst with the battle ites from Earth/Sigmet, but we feel this will not be a fruitful endeavor. Commander Gavens assures us the Imo Macos are watching from afar and have given some advice, but we ites of Eftiam are still on a learning curve."* A small grumbling came from the group ... *"I know you will do your best and I am so proud to be a part of Eftiam!"*

Efiar turned to her ef (mate); he knew this was his sign to come forward and avi to his ites. Reluctantly he arose, *"I really have no avi to give other than ... GIVE 'EM HELL!!* Somehow this did not excite the crowd, then it dawned on him … laughing loudly … *"I have too long been speaking with Eftiam Earth/Sigmet ites in their language I am forgetting my own!"* Now the audience began to stir, *"Eftiam ites you will do well in BATTLE! THIS, I AM SURE!!"* This tia no one tried to stop the clapping, yelling, slapping of backs, and general comradely feeling.

"MAY THE IMO MACOS BE WITH US!" Efiar avid, as the assembly broke; leaning into her ef, *"Oh Efviari, I could not bring myself to mention the Earth/Sigmets are already trying to probe our Brés, nor go into the fact we already covered the entire Sig City. It will not keep them from coming but might cause some delay."*

"You did what you felt was right my lovely ef. I must get to my group now and re-check our gaml-hand devices at least te (one) *more tia."*

"Oh, did you avi with the pu (jungle) *animals of Eftiam?"*

"Yes, Efiar, they are ready and waiting for when they are needed to help. I also avid the mammals of our upu (ocean).*"* With that as his final avi, he simid (kissed) her forehead and fuaid quickly to his group.

Efiar looked around the sig meeting room, realizing she had no further task to address. She wanted to do something but what? *"Auntie, are you forgetting the responsibility, we have to plan for?"*

Efiar about jumped out of her skin. She turned around thinking Neiliara was right behind her, but she was not. Scouring the room, she realized Neiliara was sitting per usual on her grandfather's lap, the tio (two) enjoying each other to the fullest, *"Neiliara why do you listen to my thoughts?"*

"It is not that I want to, but I believe the Imo Macos have made it so our niets (minds) *are as te* (one) *for this battle, and I hear every avi of yours as well as my own, and it seems almost every te* (one) *else. I am feeling tired from the strain. Grandfather gives me such a ecure feeling more than anyone else. I cannot separate from him for long,"* now wrapping both her arms around her grandfathers' neck.

"Oh? Every te (one)*?"*

"Yes, why?"

"Does it not make you angry to hear every avi when you want rest?"

"No, I am comfortable with it, knowing my function within this battle. But yes, I do not want it to last past the battle. Do go and rest now Auntie, for we will be needed soon."

Efiar was ready to give a harsh rebuttal but thought better of it and fuaid quickly from the sig meeting room. *My Efenavi! I need tia with my Efenavi.*

<>

After three weeks in Earth/Sigmet tia everything was functioning normally on Eftiam and all the Earth/Sigmet siouts and sioutous were now in a circling orbit of their planet, "Why do they not set forth battle Wayne?" Linti avi asked.

Wayne looked at his friends in the main tech-station, "Frankly I can't figure it out. Maybe they just want to study us minst before they attack. Are they still trying to probe the Brés, Neil?"

"Yes, I believe they are because of this inertia, they do not attack. Bré?"

"Yes, Commander Gavens?"

"What exactly do the Earth/Sigmets seem to be probing in your banks and the tio (two) other Brés'?"

"The Earth/Sigmet sioutous' want as much information about Efiar and Neiliara as our memory banks hold. Also, they are trying to gain full control of my main memory and want to change the processes."

With an eyebrow raised, Neil looked around to the other council ites, *"Do you believe they are able to accomplish this?"*

"Absolutely not Commander Gavens."

"Then how have you kept their probing at bay?"

"Simple term; which Bré is the real Bré?"

"I applaud you, Bré!"

"Thank you, Commander Gavens." Any ite could hear her smile.

"I know of only tio (two) Earth/Sigmet ites interested in Efiar and Neiliara, and I feel this also made you aware. So, this is why they are trying so hard to get information from the Brés before proceeding with an attack. They are afraid of what our tio females can accomplish together and rightly so. We need to figure which is the main sioutous that will try and capture Efiar and Neiliara. I think the other sioutous' are only along for protection in case we do attack while they are trying to acquire Efiar and Neiliara." Admiral Berry offered.

Efviari was now fuai pacing the tech-station, *"This is why they are not proceeding with battle? So, maybe we need to interrupt the process with battle contact to try and turn them around."*

"Even though I explained to our ites we would try and deter with avi, I truly do not believe they will agree to turn around. Look Commander, you and your crew never left, but landed," Efiari avid.

"Truer avis were never avid!" Commander Gavens avi smiled. Before any other ite could express an avi, Neil held his hand to quiet them, *"Bré?"*

"Yes, Commander Gavens."

"In a calculation analysis would it be wise for us to attack first or await the enemy?"

"They are waiting for you to attack. At present their assigned mission is to remove Efiar and Neiliara from Eftiam."

"Why do they want to do that?"

"Earth/Sigmet Councils feel once they are removed, then they could easily format a conquest plan to overtake Eftiam."

"Do you know which sioutous will be the main te to remove Efiar and Neiliara from Eftiam?" Efviari avi inquired.

"Yes, Guide Efviari."

"Please project it to the imo-mirror."

"Thank you Bré," the image showed the sioutous narrowed the furthest distance out within the line of sioutous'. Gavens avid, *"Well that explains everything. I do not believe they will sit on this much longer. That is, waiting for us to make the minst move. We should raise the watch to code te* (one) *level."* It was a unanimous agreement of avis.

Chapter 38

"Father, they are readying to launch." During this avi, Neiliara made her way to her mother and brother. *"Auntie, are you coming to our sig or, do you want us to come there?"*

"Yes, Neiliara, I am already in the tech-station sending and receiving avis to everyone. We must ready to launch our siouts' with the mechanical ites. We will use them before we use human ites. Neil, Linti, Wayne, and Efviari are here with me," Efiar avid. *"I will be in your sig in a matter of minis; also, I am bringing my mechanical Juni ite sitter for our Efenavi. It will not hurt to have tio (two) mechanical Juni sitter with Jeniari and Efenavi,"* Efiar avid fuaing from her private sig.

<>

"Bré an update in compus writing, please, and please absolutely the shortest but sweetest explanations."

"Yes, Commander Gavens to both statements."

"Wayne, do you think they will launch just a few as normal?"

"Yes, they'll want to get a feel of it all before placing the heavy artillery. Linti, have we a count of scoutbots they've launched."

"A hunth (hundred)."

"Well, that's a small amount. I think they're very unsure, so they're proceeding cautiously. How many of our siouts have you launched?"

"The same amount Admiral Berry. They are now te mini (one minute) from encounter Sir!" All eyes not on comdats turned to the imo- mirror screen. Tio (two) of the siouts were blasted out of the atmosphere.

"There was not even tia to set up for us to shoot. The Earth/Sigmets must be using new technology." Neil could feel it, but he could not put this niet into an avi of explanation. *"Bré what new scoutbot technologies have they?"*

"Commander Gavens, a new type of gamma for detecting locations before the other party is aware."

208

"Can we do better with it than they are in anyway?"

"It will take only triot minis (thirty minutes) to re-figure, but yes."

"Get on it!" Neil started to pace, so everyone knew he was nervous of the situation.

"Yes, Commander Gavens."

"Triot minis (fifty minutes) *can be an extremely long tia* (time). *We could lose many siouts and mechanical ites,"* Efviari avid. *"Efiari is on his way, he had problems with some of the ites and mechanical Juni ites. They are beginning to panic. They also saw what took place on the imo- mirror screen."*

"Tell him to stay where he is, he can do better with the ites to keep them calm. Avi him to have all ites go to the main imo-mirror meeting sig, so they can be together. Plus, Jean, Chambers, Simms, Efiar, and others will be there. It will keep them much calmer."

"Commander, if you do not niet, I will leave you and assemble my ites."

Neil stopped his pacing, but one could see he was totally distraught, *"No, Efviari ... ah ... who will speak beyond the sigs for me? You cannot go!"*

"Commander, Neiliara is already relaying messages as well as Efiari and Efiar. Do not panic, it will be all right." Efviari could see something had upset Neil more than it should have.

Tell you what, I will send Efiari here, you will be more comfortable with his physical presence." Efviari avid all this as he fuai exited the tech-station with such speed his last words came from the sig tunnel, *"He is on his way."*

"Commander, we have lost fifth (fifty) of our siouts, we should send up more at this tia." Linti avid, "Also our sioutous is in place on the other side of Eftiam."

"Bré, your analysis and have you got that re-calibration completed?" Neil avi queried.

"Yes, the re-configuration is complete. They seemed to have tried to slip into my memory banks by a side door. They are getting smarter."

"Commander Gavens, where this new technology is coming from is beyond me. It must have been developed since my leaving Earth." Admiral Berry tried desperately to reassure him of his loyalty to Eftiam.

209

"*This is not a tia to place doubt with te another Admiral. Please take over here. Give Linti complete assistance in any way possible,*" Neil avid on his way fuaing out the door.

"*Yes Sir, but w*here the hell are you going?*"*

Turning hovering in midair in the doorway, "*I am a commander of sioutous. I am going where I belong. I will be out in orbit relaying from there. I am taking Efiari with me. If we need to project by telepathy, he will do this for me.*"

Commander Gavens I cannot allow you to take Efiari. He is te of our head Guides. He cannot leave Eftiam. His life will be in jeopardy!"

"*Linti his life is in jeopardy along with everyone else right now. Something is not right here. This technology is too new for Earth or Sigmet to be using. There is someone else or something else involved. We must find the source. We have an entire planet to protect. The cost of te or tio Guides versus many is nil.*"

"He's right." Admiral Berry affirmed.

Efiari suddenly in the doorway, fuaing to a screeching halt as Gavens reached out to catch him in mid fuai. This jolted Efiari as he flailed arms and legs relying on Gavens to keep him from falling to the floor.

"*Wh ... what is going on? I'm ... here.*"

"*You are with me; I'll explain on the way.*" Still holding Efiari by his newly designed part-upudo and part-Earth uniform, they both fuaid into the tunnel sig toward the docking station.

<>

Efiari relayed what was happening in the outer limits to Efiar, Efviari, and Neiliara. Jean was able to get some, but not all; enough to know Neil was out in the sioutous with Efiari. Penny was sitting next to Jean and saw her newly purple- acquired skin go quite pale.

"What is it, Jean? You know something, please tell me." Penny could not help but think how odd it was to see someone blush purple realizing how naive te could be when only just introduced to new experiences on another world during this time of crisis. There was so much new that needed to be recorded for history. She could not help but consider this might be her means of giving back to humanity by recording the small incidents te doesn't think of on a dai to dai basis.

"Neil and Efiari are on the sioutous."

"What the heck for? What can they do up there? Didn't they train people to do that work, so they wouldn't have to go up and stay in the tech-station where they are needed? I really don't understand, I really don't," speaking as she shifted Efriana to a better position in her backpack.

"Neil would not have ordered this had it not been necessary. Something is amiss; just look how fast the Earth/Sigmets took out our new siouts. How could they detect the siouts so fast? No something is wrong, but what? Te can only surmise. As much as I do not like them up there, I know right now it is the only and best way to protect Eftiam."

"You are right Mother. Father is there because he is a Commander of sioutous, and he knows it best. Also, he is there to find the perplexing problem about the technology that allowed their scoutbots to detect our siouts before we had a chance to set for strike."

Jean looked around for her daughter. There she was playing with the tio (two) boys and tio girl babies along with her aunt, acting as if there was not a care in the world. Jean could not help but just smile and shake her head, *"Neiliara you are a wonder. The Imo Macos blessed you far beyond te can conceive."*

"Thank you, Mother, for not scolding me. I do have myself open to all, in I may report or help where necessary. Uncle Efiari says it is a most spectacular view looking down on Eftiam."

"He is right daughter; I remember the tias I looked upon Earth and Sigmet and our planet. It is indeed a spectacular view. Do you have anything more to inform me on the happenings from above?"

"Not at this tia, but there is something I must avi with you about involving Auntie and myself. I have been meaning to explain, but the tia (time) was just never right."

Suddenly Jean froze as she stared at her daughter, with the dread of knowing her secret suspicions to be reality. Here it was now in front of her; she might never physically see or touch her daughter again after this dai finished.

<>

Entering the com deck of the sioutous, all froze at the sight of Guide Efiari and Commander Gavens. The first te to snap into sequence was Sendra, "Attention; Commander Gavens and Guide Efiari on the bridge."

First turned to see his Commander and Efiari, "Welcome Commander Liaison Guide Gavens and Guide Efiari, what do I owe the pleasure?"

"Commander First we are here in the capacity to offer help. Are you aware of what is happening with our siouts?"

"Yes, Commander, we have been in contact with Linti and Admiral Berry. No one seems to know how Earth/Sigmets achieved getting a shot off before te of our siouts could. We are now able to take out a few, but not enough to make up for our loss. The outlooks grim. I requested we go in with the sioutous, but Admiral Berry thinks it would be pure suicide."

"May we avi in your office?" Efiari requested.

Without another avi they scurried into First's office. Neil began fuai pacing, *"This is my niet avi and Bré's; the signal is coming from an alien entity. It is completely in another system, so how we go about locating the signal, I have not yet been able to determine. Bré has been trying to locate the exact point and possibly we can deter it in some way. I felt coming here we could possibly put out a better signal from the sioutous to find the source, but the Earth/Sigmets would be able to pinpoint our location, which places your sioutous in jeopardy."*

"Commander Gavens, Efviari is encountering scoutbots landing and mechanical ites are fuai land walking to the mechanical sig, he is awaiting orders," Efviari suddenly avid. *"He knows he should use the animals' top side to take out the Earth/Sigmet fuai land walkers. He will also need to use his gaml-hand devices to get around Sig City.*

"Tell him to open his channels to all."

"The 'Brambas' has been trying to locate the signal for over tio (two) hours now Sir. Sendra our best engineer navigator feels it's coming from a system not a far-off," As First states while he walks to the compus to bring up the maps and systems.

Neil stopped fuai pacing to look to the map. *No, no this cannot be ... why would they do this to us? It has got to be a coincidence ... not likely ... a test? How am I to fight this? ... What can I do? All Eftiam ites are counting on me to know how to handle this. It must be someone else ...* "Have you tried deflecting the signal?"

"Yes, but to no avail. I've requested Brés input on the matter, but she's not given me a reply."

Fuai pacing once again, Neil's frustration shows, "Ah ... Efiari, is there some other covering, we can devise besides the usual shields to protect our siouts and sioutous ... er ... excuse me ... the 'Brambas'? Neil nodded his head and smiled, acknowledging the name similarity of his own sioutous. It was First's way of showing respect to Gavens and asking for his forgiveness forever doubting his Commander.

"Let me avi with the other Guides," Efiari moved to the other side of the office and looked out to his planet as if it would help him niet avi better with them, *"All Guides of Eftiam, we need to devise some sort of cloakingdevice for our siouts and our sioutous now named the 'Brambas'."*

<>

"What about the cloaking we use over our Sig City, Uncle?"

"Neiliara, we have placed that upon the siouts and the sioutous ... I mean 'Brambas' but we have been unable to use them with this signal coming from somewhere in our system. It like takes over everything to the point we cannot even get directional control over our siouts."

"Then before they leave Eftiam they should cloak them, not after they have left Eftiam." Efviari avid, "This should protect the siouts that are left."

"Eftiam is the main charging of ion-electrons for us in every need. Agreed ... First, place the devices on before the siouts leave Eftiam," Efiari avid finding himself explaining to the group in front of him. *Such a simple solution; why did I not niet avi this myself?*

First did not hesitate, he gave the command to all siouts. He also told those that had taken off to return to Eftiam, land and get re-fitted with new cloaking devices before returning to battle.

Commander Gavens was struggling with his inner turmoil. *I must avi contact with the Imo Macos, since I am needed here. I cannot achieve anything else at this tia. There must be some way to take care of both...*

<>

*S*tanding before her mother, furrowed brow and pheromones exhibited upon her upper lip, and now wetness beginning to come between her inner thighs, Neiliara reached out and grabbed her mother by the arm, *"It is tia for Auntie and me to go. Remember my love is with you always."*

Efiar came along side Jean and Neiliara, holding Efenavi firmly to her, not wanting to let go, the tré (three) women held each other tightly, *"Jean, if we do not return; I know you will care for my son as if he is your own and you will not let him forget me."* A mixture of tears and silence between them, they all hugged with Efenavi yelping his dislike of their smothering embrace. Tears glistened on eyes and cheeks as they looked to him, but he smiled up at them as if he was aware of the absurd avi conversation taking place, and as if he knew the outcome. Fact is he did! Jean took hold of Efenavi; Neiliara simid him on the forehead leaving a wet spot, and turning, both speedily fuaid away. Efenavi struggled from Jean's arms to be set on the floor. As soon as she was in route to place him with her son and Penny's daughter, she noticed all the babies clustering together in the middle of te room and connecting their webbings.

Instinctively she followed the infants' suit. Jean avid the entire room to join forces along with all the children to help avi protect all the ites of Eftiam. Penny looked to her quizzically moving uncertainly to Jean's side. For the first time on Eftiam, Jean was able to niet avi to all the ites of Eftiam as a true Guide. She explained all that was happening above. In the midst of strong waves gushing over their Sig City the sea life schools reined themselves tight around the Sig City, also sending out avi help. Sig City itself was moving as if in earthquake, *"Neil, can you hear my avi?"*

"Jean?"

"Yes Neil, don't try to avi, just listen and receive."

Immediately, Gavens placed himself into a meditative state. Efiari also received the niet avi and life on Eftiam itself seemed to hum, and yes, all could see Efiar and Neiliara out in the blackest of night hovering in the non-breathable atmosphere above the siouts and their Eftiam. Astounded they pondered what looked like silver lae (lilac) cords. The cords also were webbed lying outstretched to all the

214

scoutbots assuredly Earth/Sigmet sioutous were kept at bay. The formidable spread made the largest of shields look small. Unquestionably a silver lae mist surrounded Efiar and Neiliara as well. Unbelievably these silvery lae cords could be seen by the Earth/Sigmet warriors causing them to ram their scoutbots right into this silvery lae shield, as if they were magnetized to do so. No matter how Neil tried to niet avi with Neiliara or Efiar, he could not reach them nor could he avi with any of the other Guides. The Imo Macos were still silent which unnerved Neil. He desperately tried to niet avi again with Jean, but nothing. He did find he could niet avi communicate with First. Te e (One) siout took out the fif (five) scoutbots that were between Eftiam and a shield, bursting into huge gamma flames, while others spiraled to Eftiam, then exploding into great flares. Signals came from the Earth/Sigmet sioutous to try again to take down the shield, meaning they would take down Efiar and Neiliara. Neil processed this immediately.

"First, move 'Brambas' into the open and show them we are ready to do serious battle. This will draw attention from the shield, Efiar, and Neiliara while I niet avi the other Guides. Hopefully they will niet avi me with their help."

"Yes, Commander Gavens." First avid, as the 'Brambas' was returning in a timely manner from Eftiam resetting the cloaking devices. Entering back into orbit the sioutous now became the special attention of battle. It was working so well they were able to take out scoutbots with little difficulty. The new gamma-hydro-gun worked magnificently as he knew it would. This filled him with pride to see their expectations deliver a bounty beyond belief of craftmanship.

Within his meditative state, Commander Gavens could see all ites of Eftiam, including babies, webbed together. The babes were helping Efiar and Neiliara with their niet avis holding the shield; their niet avis stronger than any other ites. *I now understand this is our future we give to our Eftiam. Our children of tomorrow are stronger than we can even hope to be.*

"Commander Gavens, we're placing Efiar and Neiliara in the line of fire. Moreover, if they cannot shoot through our shield neither then can we. So how do you plan to battle with the larger sioutous'?"

Commander First queried. Better yet Sir, why not try and telepath with your daughter and Efiar."

"I have tried and cannot avi with them, our Guides or the Imo Macos. I believe the webbing and the signal that emits from it is blocking the path of communication." Neil did not realize during this avi conversation, Efiari was niet aving all this communication back to the others. *"First can you possibly hydro-gram me to the main com-center?"*

"Of course, I can." First avid.

<>

Signals were arriving again, from the Earth/Sigmet main sioutous for the taking down of shields, meaning Efiar and Neiliara included. Neil processed this immediately.

"No Commander Gavens, if anyone should go, it should be me. That is what they expect. Remember they sent me here to bring back Efiar and Neiliara." Admiral Berry butted in.

"Efiari?"

"Yes, Commander Gavens, I am aving to all. Please continue." The avi relays were so readily transmitted at mind-boggling speed. Even without niet avis, Efiari could feel the gratitude from his Guide Commander; enhancing his feeling of brotherhood, while the lives of Efiar and Neiliara's lives were at stake. *"Admiral Berry what do you plan to do?* He avid for Guide Commander Gavens."

"Shit, the same thing your Commander is thinking of doing; wing it!"

Berry now chuckling.

"You tio remember my ef is suspended out there!" Efviari avid.

"My Daughter also!" Commander Gavens avid.

"And the mother of my godchild and granddaughter I'll have you know; now let me get to work here. Before I hydro-gram order to everyone; Neil I'd like to speak with you privately." Admiral Berry avid.

"Some privacy with Efiari doing the avi communicating for us."

Chapter 39

Commander Hinkle, there's one of those hydro-tele-grams coming in from the 'Brambas'. The comdat announced; "Admiral Berry," from the Communication Engineer.

Hinkle chuckled, "So that's what they're calling their ship, eh. Bet I know who gave her that name? It's about time he sent something. I was beginning to think Berry was not on our side anymore. Open up the line."

First came a lavender fog, then it seemed to clear and in full view was Admiral Berry, "Commander Hinkle?"

"Beginning to think I wasn't going to hear from you. What is with this shield and that woman and child in front of us? Is this some kind of com-mov (movie) the Purples are projecting to throw us off? Is this similar as to what you keep telling us about? And why haven't you contacted us sooner?"

"It's been years since I've been out in the field. It's taken quite some time for me to get them to trust me and no they aren't a com-mov, they're real." Admiral Berry stated.

Commander Hinkle jumped up from his seat, "Are these the two we came for?"

"Yes, but even I can't seem to get my hands on them. They've outfoxed me every step of the way. Now you can see what I've been up against in trying to capture them to bring them back to Sigmet or Earth. In addition, I'm too old to go out there in a scoutbot and try to bring them aboard. They don't answer anyone here on Eftiam either. It seems they're out there on their own. I wouldn't suggest firing at their shield; you might damage the merchandise we are to take back with us. Have you any ideas of how we can capture them, because I sure as hell don't!"

"It seems we sent the wrong person to this planet. Gavens was supposed to send in his warriors and he didn't follow orders. Now he's a fugitive. Are you sure you aren't in cahoots with him, after all he was your pride and joy boy?" Hinkle heckled.

"How dare you be so downright insubordinate? When we are back on Earth, I'm bringing you up on charges. You seem to forget whom you're talking to." Berry shot back.

"I beg your pardon Admiral, please forgive my doubting you, but it has been a very long time and you haven't been heard from," Hinkle blustered, "I will put on my thinking cap. Are you where I can reach you?"

"No, no I am in different locals trying to stay scarce, so I will get back with you in about ten minutes or so, if all goes well." With that, the hydro-gram fizzled out as fast as it had arrived.

<>

"Wayne, how did you know I could not avi with Efiar or Neiliara?"

"Neil, I see from this com-mov screen, it's written all over your face. Remember I've taught you when in battle not to lie, just fudge a little to hold them off a little longer. No doubt they'll contact Sigmet to find out how they want to maneuver the situation. You bet your bottom dollar every Council Member from Earth is on Sigmet. So, the relay message won't take as long."

"I am surprised Hinkle is the te crusading this battle. He is still just te to carry out orders not thinking for himself. How he made it all these years commanding a ship boggles the mind."

"Yeah, he is a jerk, isn't he? Too bad, I won't be pressing those charges Now let's get together with the others to discuss how we're going to handle things from here. Your mind hasn't exactly been at its best for battle with Neiliara out there."

<>

"Commander Hinkle, the Admiral is on hydro-tele-gram again." The Navigation Engineer announced.

Off to their left lavender fog of light and in its light, was Admiral Berry, "Do you think I can get through the shield? You better tell me the truth, because if you think I'm bluffing, I best cut this communication now."

"NO! Wait … yes, I was testing you. I had to see if you're legit. Now, I know we can't get through or take down the shield, which has completely blocked our signal. Hell, I told you I can't even capture these two females. By the way, Hinkle, where did you get that new ray to beam onto their scoutbots before they knew what was happening? I knew we were testing a new weapon, but I didn't realize it was operative so soon." Now Berry was fishing hugely.

"Ah, well … it ah … was placed in the ship before we boarded," Hinkle lied.

"That's weird man, because these Purples keep talking about the signal coming from some other system, but you sure faked them out, huh?"

"Yeah right; ya know Admiral I think we will just wait these two females out. They can't stay out there forever. Besides shouldn't they be solid ice by now?"

"That's just it; they have so many secrets I can't get to yet. I've been trying to earn more of their trust but they just won't let me in on everything. I will let you know the minute I know.

"Well then, I'll contact you when I see they're out of the sky, how's that?"

"Fine, talk with you then; over and out," Hinkle said.

<>

"We've dispelled them for now, but I really can't say for how long." Admiral Berry proffered, looking to Linti and then to Gavens on the com-screen.

"Efiari, have you brought the other Guides into you?"

"Yes, Commander Gavens, but I still cannot reach Efiar, or Neiliara. Linti and Admiral Berry. "Please close your eyes now and hold hands; you should be able to bring him along."

"We are only niet aving with the Guides are we not, Efiari?"

"Yes, Commander Gavens and Admiral Berry and Jean. But I do feel other entities also and I cannot deter them"

"Do not worry, it is the Imo Macos I believe, plus our babies and Efiar and Neiliara."

"Babies?" All avid in unison, except for Jean.

219

"*Yes, from what I have niet avid, they are helping the most,*" Neil avid.

"*Yes Neil, since I realized what they were doing, it made me bring all the rest of Sig City together and now I've been able to avi with all of you in every aspect on Eftiam and where you and Efiari are on the 'Brambas.*" Jean avid.

"*Bré?*"

"Yes, Commander Gavens?'

"*Is the Imo Macos keeping Efiar and Neiliara alive?*"

"Yes, Commander Gavens."

"*Are the Imo Macos controlling the signal that is coming from the far system?*" No reply came from Bré.

"Bré, are the Imo Macos controlling you?"

"*Bré, I expect an answer,*" Still no reply, "*Bré are the Imo Macos controlling you?*"

"Yes, Commander Gavens."

What a nice way to give me the answer. "*Thank you Bré. DAMN!*"

"*Now we know we are not in charge nor are the Earth/Sigmets',*" Efviari avid in. *Nor Neil. And Neil, you are not in any state to make confident decisions that is probably why they are not aving with us. I'm not to be dealt with rationally either. Efiari I am extremely proud of the way you are able to convey your aving.*"

"*Thank you I did not know myself, that I was capable. It may not last, but while it is with me, it is a blessing. Admiral Berry, I do feel you and Linti should be in sole command.*"

Agreed, came from all but Neil. *This is the minst (*first) *I have not been in command for many years. I know they are asking; the right decision.* "*I ... agree, but you must let us know every decision.*"

Whoa..., I sure wasn't expecting this to happen. It just doesn't make sense. I don't know enough about the planet and its people. I'm still on a learning curve. But let me see, ah ... First, I need to know if the people are able to keep helping to hold Efiar and Neiliara up there?

"*What you do not know is Linti is very capable, and you have Efviari, Efiari and to help. Wayne, we do not know that answer, because this has only happened for short intervals needed here on Eftiam,*" Neil avi conveyed, "*But I do feel we need to break meditation for our natural born Eftiam ites about tin* (ten) *at a time for apt* (sleep), *for safety precaution. The babies are in a very deep meditative state, so I do not believe we should break them. Do you agree with me Jean?"*

"Yes, Neil I d o."

"I must say I have never fought a battle close to anything like this, it's plain weird to me."

"You are not alone Wayne, none of us newcomers have either. This is all completely new." Gavens avi replied.

"Neil please avi First I approve his choice of name for our sioutous."

"I will do that Jean."

Linti avid, *"I think it tia we just let things apt for now and await the Imo Macos. Do you niet the Earth/Sigmets' are apting also?"*

Chapter 40

"**W**hat is going on? Why are they stopping? Don't these people realize they are at war? Their world is in jeopardy! God, this is so frustrating, unable to figure out your enemy," Hinkle was not speaking to anyone in particular, "At least they are giving us time to digest all that has taken place. I don't trust Berry. He wanted to come here to this planet to retire and be with his Gavens family. Maybe we can get through this shield. Bet he's just trying to throw us off." as Hinkle spoke, he relayed all this back to Sigmet and knowingly straight to the council. He so wanted to go ahead and take down this silvery lilac webbing he could see from his small portal. He really didn't believe it would hold them back. "You know I am sure those two females somehow fired shots from guns hidden to take down our scoutbots" You could tell by the way they burst into gases." somehow, he had to convince the council the webbing could not be damaged by their ships. Walking away from the com-screen, he hit the button on the box, "Is that analysis back from our main brain yet?"

"Not yet, but I expect it in about fifteen minutes or less, Commander.

"When you get it bring it straightway to my office."

"Yes Sir."

His confidence was so great he stuck out his chest sauntering to his nutrition station. After pushing many buttons, it processed smashed potatoes, T-bone steak, corn on the cob, salad, and a nice cabernet. A meal fit for a king. He sat at his dinette devouring and slobbering food to chin finishing every last savory morsel. Out here in this ship of ships he was a king and he now knew what Gavens had always had. Yes, it was what he too wanted, and he was bound to keep it, but he knew he had to take down Gavens first. "I will get you Gavens if it's my last breath."

Chapter 41

It had been a week and not one Guide had apt (sleep); meditate they did, but not full body apting. Tempers were short, and hairs, beards, and clothing in full disarray. The babies, mammals and land side animals were still in deep meditative apt. Of course, the only ones with full energy were the mechanical Juni ites

Without warning within this quiet solitude, waves began to jostle Sig City. The signal, *"Please report to your stations immediately,"* came from Efiari.

"What is it Jean asked?"

"The Earth/Sigmet sioutous' are trying to break the shield. Every sioutous is inching together, focusing on te (one) *point of our shield to disable it. We fear they may be successful."* Efiari avid.

Jean could not help herself; she went to the babies and touched each and every one of them, *"This is the moment you were destined for."* A synchronized smile returned to her from every babe. She too took her position within the webbing of Eftiam ites.

"Father, they have finally realized Grandfather is in tio (two) *places at the same tia* (time) *and no longer part of them. You must pull yourself together, we are out here protecting all ites, and it is our position of birthright to do so. Accept this now and please help us! You and the other Guides must be the niet avis at our backs; we are going to be too busy here to avi back and forth."* Before Neil could answer the avi was dropped. *My Imos, I forgot about Wayne's mechanical ite being on Earth. I am sure they have destroyed it by now.*

"Too late now, we must go on. "Earth/Sigmets' realize Admiral Berry is in tio places at the same tia," Efiari avid to the rest of the guides.

Linti broke in; "Te sioutous (One spaceship) is almost through … All siouts and mechanical ites into position … it's through, attack, attack …"

The sound of the siouts and gamma-hydro-guns avis roared throughout Sig City reverberating heavy sounds sending the city into tremors as they felt the many undulating waves over the city itself.

Even though this was taking place, a good many a hunth (hundred) or more miles above Eftiam, the reverberations frightened them beyond belief; especially the original Eftiamrs who had never experienced nor avid anything of the kind. The newest ites of Eftiam, called to them, explaining to them this battle they were experiencing would make them stronger. Fear was showing causing many to want to run, but there was no way they could break the webbings. It would harm their efforts. They had to stay strong.

The 'Brambas' took one shot with its huge gamma-hydro-gun; the Sigmet sioutous burst into flames, then burst again into a thousand pieces with explosive gases filtering amid the debris floating in all directions throughout the black, starless sky. The other sioutous slowed to almost a stall, waiting for orders as to whether to pursue further through the shield, which now had a large hole in it. All ites of Eftiam could see and feel Efiar and Neiliara were in the midst of repairing the hole; all focused their concentration to this area to offer their avi help, while the 'Brambas' made sure it placed every gamma-hydro-gun at ready.

Slowly one of the Earth sioutous inched closer to the damaged shield, a small red ray coming from underneath the sioutous. This red line sent shock waves into the shield, causing it to vibrate as if electric pulses went throughout the shield, emitting a fiery glow. Then it seemed to undulate in waves up and down, then back and forth, still the shield seemed to hold.

Linti avid tio ites (two people) in their siouts (small spacecraft), "If this Earth sioutous gets through our shield; aim for the area where the L-ray came from and take it down. This should be a vulnerable powerful point of the sioutous."

"Bré see if you can get into their main compus, namely Commander Hinkle's sioutous."

"Yes, Commander Gavens."

"First have every siout ready, even those on the ground."

"Already ordered up Sir; Linti, is doing a remarkable job. He has been taught well."

Gavens smiled recalling his experience with Berry, *"Yes, Admiral Berry is a fine educator."*

Efviari, avi announced, *"Some of their scoutbots are getting through the shield."*

Linti and Berry give orders for the siouts to attack. This time the count was far different. The siouts took out more scoutbots (Earth/Sigmet small spacecraft).

While this was going on the Earth/Sigmet sioutous were now moving in together to take down the damaged area of the shield. All ites were aware they would get this sioutous through.

"Commander Gavens, I am into their main compus (computer)."

"Great and fast Bré; now let us do some changing to their sioutous. Efiar and Neiliara could use the help." From that point on not te ite could hear the avis he sent Bré.

<>

Efviari and the land animals were defeating Earth/Sigmet warriors as the scoutbots worked to take out the mechanical ite Juni City. Efviari was grateful they had not figured out the location of the human Sig City. He knew this was the doing of Neil and Bré, getting into Hinkle's' sioutous compus. Yes, they were working on something more, but he could not tell from the avis what exactly. While the pu animals and Efviari found this mainly to be child's play, for they outnumbered the Earth/Sigmets. Larger animals took care of the Earth/Sigmet humans; the smaller animals protected Efviari and some carried supplies, so he and his battle ites could destroy the landed scoutbots.

Mammals of the upu (ocean), kings of this vast upu the Dolifa and Kamich assisted Efviari with all areas to help keep the Sig City protected. This then was relayed to Efiari and the rest of the Guides. They and other mammals made sure to take out the scoutbots that descended to the bottom of the upu, by swimming in strong rotational schools. They compressed themselves so close to the scoutbots that you could not differentiate the schools. They compressed the small mechanical ships, causing the scoutbots to burst from the inside out. Efviari extremely proud of their abilities; he would have a rich history to detail for the future children of Eftiam.

<>

Those webbed in Sig City, were aving the battle going on above them and around them. The week of waiting for the Earth/Sigmets to initiate battle helped by allowing these ites to take turns for apting, to replenish their strength. Their help was strong for Efiar and Neiliara. Mechanical Juni ites came along to wet the mouths and brow of human ites, each with upu (water) and special protein pu (jungle) juice plant added. However, Jean could feel some sort of undercurrent, which now started to drift into other ites. She tried to release herself from the web of aving, but to no avail despite her desperate avi of a need to know. She did not know who or what was holding her back, but something was, or someone was as she tried to fight her way free.

Babies still in meditative state un-webbed themselves from their parental arms, suddenly rose above all their heads in this great imo-mirror sig meeting hall. Parents webbed hands desperately tried to break free to grab for their children before they fell from mid-air, but like Jean they were solidly bound. Once all the babies were together, they turned on their backs and joined their heads into a circle and thus began to spin lightly, increasing their speed more and more, until they too were as the mammals moving at an indecipherable rate; te could not tell they were babes cradled within this circle. This motion stirred all ites below, lifting them from the floor into an automatic fuai, forming a pyramid of circles … never breaking their webbings. Fuai speed was increasing, it is causing the mechanical ites to perform to a greater degree than those already in formation, beyond what the Earth/Sigmets' knew as the 'speed of light'.

<>

Efiari and Gavens webbed, while the crew of the "Brambas' made sure every instrument was in good working order. Hearing a sound behind them, the crew turned to see Efiari and Commander Gavens webbed together hand and foot, spinning in clockwise rotation so fast the only way they knew it was them, was the newly designed shorter upudo of Efiari's uniform.

"Efiar and Neiliara are webbing in a standing position," Admiral Berry hydro-gram transmitted. This caused the crew to forget Efiari and Commander Gavens. Watching from their com-mov screens they realized the tio (two) females were now moving in a same rotational spin as the tio on their sioutous. All were spell bound, glued to the com-mov screen, not knowing what was to come next.

<>

The Earth/Sigmet sioutous acted as if they were on an auto pilot course, now on top of the damaged shield hole to make their way through. They were aware not all of them were going to make it through. But they also knew they could leave much damage for those left to take over the planet. Hinkle made a decision for one of their ships to pick up Efiar and Neiliara, while the others kept the battle going strong, hopefully those of the opposite side would realize too late and or be unaware of his plan. "Man, this is the weirdest battle I've ever encountered. This definitely is one for the history banks. I will be glorified of the tell." His overweight body straightening to some degree trying to produce frontal chest of pride along with his wry smile.

Same dai born babies stay their meditative state. Mechanical ites were not giving up reaching up and out to bring the babies from their airborne state. To no avail. Heads still aligned into a circle kept up their indecipherable rate of speed. This motion stirred, keeping all ites lifted from the floor into an automatic fuai array of pyramid of circles … never breaking their webbings. Fuai speed was increasing, it causing the mechanical ites to an even greater degree of speed than those already taking place, beyond the Earth/Sigmets' so called 'speed of light.'

<>

Everyone on the 'Brambas made sure to stay their positions. Guide Efiari and Guide Commander Gavens webbed together, caused all within range to keep them in their peripheral eye to help, if necessary, but unsure how if the call came about.

Efiar and Neiliara webbed tightly spinning as te, making the darkest of the atmosphere become lae (lilac), palest lae, and lu (lavender) kaleidoscope so bright that eyes had to be shaded from the glare. This glare kept growing until many human warriors had to turn away.

Humans with avi clarity witnessed every change. Suddenly Efiar was no longer with Neiliara; she descended like a bullet quickly to Eftiam, still in fuai rotating motion. Now it seemed her webbings grew into long, cord-like extensions of silvery lae, wrapping around Eftiam itself, picking up this planet and seeming to make it spin. She and it also began spiraling like a spool of thread, as new silver tentacles extended from all abstract angles of the planet. These glittering threads slivered out into the atmosphere until they located Neiliara attaching to her. Now Neiliara began to spin even faster than before, while all the silvery cords wrapped her in cocoon, until she no longer could be seen with naked eye. The mini (minutes) seemed like hunths (hundreds) in passing.

At the same interval, the Earth/Sigmet sioutous could maneuver, only one way, backwards until they were back to where they began alongside the main command sioutous. In retaliation, the Earth/Sigmet sioutous opened all bay doors in order to shoot the Neiliara cocoon from the sky.

Neil and Jean knew and could feel what was about to happen to their daughter, they having been in battle many tias (times) before. They held on to each other's avis more tightly, causing others within their webbings to scream, as Neil and Jean avid out their daughter's name to no avail; every Eftiamr trembled in anticipation of the outcome.

The youngest of land animals gathered in clusters, te(one) female and te male, of every breed. At the same tia, under the upu (ocean) the youngest of mammals gathered, te female and te male of each. Forming single lines, they proceeded toward the tentacles upon the ocean floor. Now the tentacles grew broader to allow the animals and mammals to glide upon this silvery road, as if on an escalator. Once leaving the planet and gliding into space, they began to disappear, leaving only a small fractional star that incorporated the cocoon.

<>

"Sir, we still cannot fire bay one L-ray and or any of the others," The Navigating Engineer said.

"What kind of engineers have I got? Aw, come on. They said there's nothing wrong with those guns!" Hinkle roared, "Check the comdat configurations again!"

"But Si…"

"Damn it … just try it again! Also have one of our crew go suit-up and get outside to check the guns. There may be something blocking them that we can't see." Hinkle had never ever been in a position like this; everything happening was new. No one on Earth or Sigmet would believe what was happening out here in this odd wilderness. He was so used to taking orders and giving them; go in attack with warriors and take over; now finally having to think left him uncontrollably strained. Hinkle's nerves were frazzled, uniform rumpled from the wetness under his arms, and dripping from his brow, the deepest furrow between his eyes increasing. Who would ever believe that two females held them off, or this silver cord thing which seemed to emanate from the eye mucosa and purple sky, with animals and fish riding this cord attaching them to the child in this cocoon? And I thought this was a child? They'd put him in the nuthouse for sure. But he did have his whole entire crew to verify all this too, so the Councils would have to believe him, wouldn't they? Also, everything was being recorded. His ships couldn't move backward or forward. Why? He had the main tech comdat going over every inch to see if there was a glitch in software. Also, the Captains of each ship were checking their comdats, over and over again. These two females couldn't have gotten into his comdats, could they? Hinkle processed the matter for two more hours and still had no answer to support the situation.

The comdat showed the food bank was getting near extreme for Sigmet re-stock. Funny, though, he would have sworn he had just received the read out five days ago on the food bank and it was in good shape. They could wait out here for a month to two months depending on how they rationed. Surely the two, woman and child could not hold out for that long and now this weird turn of events. If he returned now, this would show poor face to Gavens and Berry, and he just couldn't have that. Besides he had a personal score to settle with Gavens. But he did think of the fact he was risking the life of the crew. Running his hands through his hair…

"Commander Hinkle?" the box scratched.

"Yes…"

"The report from bay side is that the guns are clear and operating properly," again the croak came from the box.

"Over and out," Hinkle did not want to get into matters at this time, he needed rest and to think.

Chapter 42

Efiari lay motionless in his state aving every emotion and move his Efiar was making. He tried to bring himself back to be at her side, but the Imo Macos were not allowing this expectancy. His avis seemed to soar without energy. Efiar, he knew was not aving in real sense; she was just a tool of the Imo Macos as Neiliara. Intuition told him his niece would not return to Eftiam. She was no longer human, but of the essence of the Imo Macos or something completely new. He could feel Bré aving back and forth between the main Hinkle sioutous and Neil, but he could not differentiate the avis. Penny and his Efriana were safe within webbings, contributing their help with avis. Efviari was the only Guide not in meditative state. He could see him and his juni ites running with the animals, attacking the Earth/Sigmet ites. Not te was able to reach the Mechanical Ite City or Sig City. The sight was marvelous and he avid this to the rest of Sig City ites. He felt he was watching a com-mov on the imo-mirror instead of being the avi catalyst, but he also knew his niet (brain) was aving help in every aspect he possibly could.

<>

Jean and Neil's agony was severe. They felt their insides torn at the turmoil they felt coming from their beloved creation of themselves. Both wanted to hate the Imo Macos but could not … but recognizing the agony did not make it better. Suddenly the glare again appeared so strong to those without avi had to turn away, but those with avi saw Imo Macos appear. In many voices they spoke, "Do not fear or hate what is to be from the Highest of Power to come. You are aving the beginning of your replica Eftiam and its ites' beginnings going to another solar system. Our child ite with the oldest of souls chose to be used by the Higher Power for this new beginning; sitting alongside the Highest of Power indeed is rare. Be proud and full of love for what she and you have given." The glare died away leaving the kaleidoscope of Eftiam purples and silver throughout the sky.

No one avid, all were still absorbing the message given. All knew this to be truth, that they had been given gifts beyond those received by Earth/Sigmets and possibly all other human races. The Earth/Sigmet planets were trying to catch up, but unable to quite surpass them. Earth/Sigmet would go on as they are, making newer and far-reaching discoveries, just as they on Eftiam and other planets like theirs, just possibly seeing and acknowledging the gifts allotted by the Highest of Power.

<>

What had just happened? Not one person could logically explain the glare, which was now a brighter kaleidoscope of purples and silver throughout the formerly black sky.

"What just happened?" Hinkle asked still looking at his com-mov screen.

"Checking now Sir," a long silence held throughout the ship, "The comdat registers nothing, Sir," came from the Navigating Engineer.

Hinkle let out a huge sigh, totally unsure, "Let … let's try to move the ships once again.

"Yes Sir." All watched to see if the ships showed signs of life. The waiting seemed to lag on and on until … yes, one of the Sigmet ships inched forward. The crews within the ten ships shouted great cheers, all having envisioned being trapped in this orbital system unable to do anything forever: dying here in a stagnant unfathomable hell. The other ships started moving forward also. The gun bays were setting to fire their L-rays… just as they inched toward the cocoon, the ships made a short turn.

"What the hell…Sir?"

"Yes, I see! Did you try contacting the lead ship?" Hinkle asked.

"Yes Sir, they aren't answering." The Navigating Engineer responded.

Suddenly the Hinkle ship was thrown into movement. The crew on deck began to scamper back and forth throwing switches and hitting buttons, but the ship did not stop, it moved forward. Just before reaching the cocoon, it too made a sharp turn right. "My God, we are set to a new course … what is happening? I can't change a thing, nor can any other crew member!" Hinkle came alongside the Engineer, pitching her from her chair causing her to hit the floor. Now he was throwing buttons to no avail and kept on trying as his crew looked on scared and bewildered. Were they going to die? Where were they being taken? What was making this occur?

After a good fifteen minutes and thousands of miles from Eftiam, Hinkle gave up, speaking, "Notify Earth/Sigmet of what has taken place." He looked far beyond his years.

"Sir according to our records a signal was sent to them … and from our comdat, Sir. We are being navigated back to Sigmet. The other part of the message says we will never be given access again to this system."

"Denied! … I'll be go to hell … denied? … definitely, someone is into our comdats. How, I do not know. No one has access to this system; this is free space, so no one can be denied!" He would not let his crew know the inner defeat he was feeling and the desire for revenge, "I vow we will be back, and we will get Commander Gavens and Admiral Berry!"

Chapter 43

"Commander Gavens, the assignment is complete," Bré announced.

"Thank you, Bré." Neil had so many different emotions running through him. Anger was the first but displaced by the obligation he felt to Eftiam and its ites and the greater te (one) to Neiliara, the Imo Macos and his great-grandfather. He was unable to avi convey this, "Efiari, I turn it over to you to convey what took place here with the sioutous' from Earth and Sigmet."

"Commander it has all been avid to all ites the entire tia," as the sioutous' were set on a new course, those of Eftiam avi watched in a new wonder. They knew this was done either by Efiar and Neiliara, the Imo Macos or by Commander Gavens', but they avi knew that this query would remain unanswered.

Their niet avi (minds) felt Efiar descend to their planet to stand with her Ef, amongst the animals, entwining their webbings. All niet avis focused on the cocoon, awaiting the outcome.

Soon every ite received avi explanation from Efiari about the events above as the sioutous' of Earth/Sigmet were set to a new course away from their Eftiam and how Bré and you Commander Gavens played a role. There was no raucous glee, as all stayed webbed aving, their heads turned skyward, eyes closed and waiting.

Neil could only nod his head; there were no more avis to be given.

<>

On the morn of dai tré (day three), when it seemed they would never change this webbed position, eyes closed and still skyward, the vertical cocoon sprayed it's lae silvery tentacle cords outward with an avi all ites could read and or hear, *"I am ready."*

Stark lightning strikes hit every tentacle making it seem the largest of stars ever to be viewed. The beauty of the silver lae (lilac) kaleidoscope of color within slowly dissipated as the sky around it blackened once again, leaving this cocoon star glow glaring brightly from within. No te felt sadness or the welling of tears. They only felt complete joy in the evolution of this star and their Eftiam in the birthing of a new planet. Up and up the star cocoon rose, slowly slipping back out further into the darkness until it was nothing but a small speck, then a bursting flash it abruptly disappeared!

The first to un-web were Efiar, Efviari, and the pu animals and upu mammals, then Efiari and Neil. The babies descended back to their waiting parents, being cuddled again as parents un-webbed. All the other ites then emerged looking around, gesturing, smiling, hugging and only glad to be alive. Of course, the Eftiamrs made their way to their Sig quarters to apt, not knowing or caring how long their apting would be. All except te Admiral Berry, who was ravenous for food.

Chapter 44

Jean seemed in a fog, doing her wifely duties around their private sig. She had not seen Neil since that horrible dai (day), nor did she care. She did, but not right now at least. Jeniari seemed to sense her grief, so he seemed more bubbly than usual and wanted to play and be cuddled more. *At least I still have te* (one) *child. They are not getting this te. How dare they take her from me? Neiliara was never a child, Jeniari is. She never needed a lot of attention. But they say boys do require more. Neil has stayed cooped up in the main- havis- sig since that dai. Has he eaten? I should check on him, but I cannot yet. Neiliara, I am so blessed I was with you before you made your grand gesture for Eftiam and its ites. You are one special person. You will never be gone for Eftiam and its ites. I know we must have a memorial for you, but I so wanted tia for us before this took place.*

<>

Neil fuai paced within the sig cubicle. He had not showered, shaved, and had barely eaten since that dai … *Why have they not avid with me; I've tried and tried, but nothing. What am I to tell our ites? Why did they not take me? Why Neiliara? Why not Efiar?* … He knew the answer … tired, Neil took a seat in his lounge, looking fondly at the lounge beside him he had placed for Neiliara so she would not have to endure everyone else's avis constantly. *It would have been so peaceful for her.* The lounge had been moved into the sig a few weeks before the Earth/Sigmets came into their system. Reaching out he caressed the lounge as if she were sitting in it. He was getting ready to bring her to this sig and start her lessons with the Imo Macos, but to his surprise she was long in avi contact. They had asked for it to be done sooner, but he and Jean did want to keep her longer before she was to take on her duties. *I also wonder if I had brought her sooner as requested would they have eliminated my guidance for the Eftiam ites? Was I jealous?* Again, he got up from the lounge and fuai paced. His pacing was fast and furious, faster than what te would consider normal for thought.

This went on for over tio (two) hours and he fuai fell into his lounge. Not Te Eftiam ite could communicate with him in this sig, this he knew. Te of the main reasons he was here, but most of all he wanted communication with the Imo Macos. Too tired to think, Neil did apt tio hours.

"Neil my friend; you are not accomplishing a thing for Eftiam and our ites. We need you to wake and start the healing process for all," Eftiar avid.

Neil roused, eyes still closed, *"Eftiar, I've missed our conversations. Why have the Imo Macos taken Neiliara? Why will they not avi?"*

"The Imo Macos are with Neiliara and the pu animals and upu mammals beginning the new planet. I am here to reassure you they will be in niet avi with you soon. Neiliara chose this path to travel long before she was given to you and Jean. We only nurture, raise, love and send them into the future path they themselves have chosen to travel. It is the duty of the Imo Macos to help keep us on that path. Neil, you knew this the dai Neiliara was born. Do not take the path of anger Neil, as I did. It can only make matters worse for Eftiam and all of its ites," Eftiar fuaid into the background.

Into the foreground came Eftiara, he could still see Eftiar but fuzzily, *"Commander Gavens, I will be guiding Neiliara when the Imo Macos have completed their assignment by the Highest Power. Neiliara will now sit alongside our Highest Power. She is te most special. Now I demand you leave this main havis sig and go straight to your Jean. She needs your love and embrace. You have a wonderful Jeniari to love and soon you will be Father again. Efiar and Efiari will Guide as of now, Efviari will be Guide to the pu animals and upu mammals, and you will continue to avi liaison of our past lives and future to come as the Imo Macos see fit. This can change in tia but not the near future. The smallest of ites now born of same dai of Eftiam will be the new Guides of Eftiam future."* Eftiara and Eftiar dissipated.

Neil woke not groggily, but with determination, knowing where he must be and the path he must travel. Without hesitation, he plunged forward into a fast fuai pace out the sig door, fuai scurrying through tunnel after tunnel skidding to a halt hovering before his private sig door. *Will she see me? I will have to force her if not ... she is my true ef, this I know, there could never be another... we have a son to raise and love and send on, and now another on the way? Wow, I am going to be Father again, does she know? If not, I will act surprised for her sake. I had to for Neiliara and Jeniari. There is so much for us to discuss ... Should I knock? ...* Hesitating, Neil opened the door ... Jean was standing with her back to the door. She was humming to Jeniari, who lay in his crib lounge. Rather than avi, he stood and watched her, as she poured love into this child as she had Neiliara. *Jean has much love to give ... How could I have left her all this tia, she needed me and I her.* "*Jean?*"

Jean froze only for a second, not sure she heard her husband's avi. Quickly lifting Jeniari, turning she did not even answer, but fuai hurried straight across the room into Neil's arms, *"It's about tia you came home; we've missed you!"* looking down into Jeniari's eyes, wriggling complaint of being scrunched; but he smiled...

Chapter 45

The memorial for Neiliara and those that aspid (died) during their trying tia (time) of battle was a joyous occasion, te (one) of knowing they were on future paths.

"Ites of Eftiam, this is a joyous dai (day) *of memories, for ites of Eftiam giving of themselves so that we may go on in the safe harbor of our beautiful planet. Future Earth/Sigmet sioutous'* (spaceships) *will no longer be able to enter our system. In placing the shield over Eftiam, I did ask the Imo Macos to take me, but they avid a firm no and that Neiliara had already made the choice. Every ite has made a great sacrifice for Eftiam and we will never forget them. You will be able to niet vi with them through Liaison Guide Commander Gavens, but we will not be able to niet avi with Neiliara for a very long tia* (time). *Her position is such, she too as well as the Imo Macos will avi with her planet and help them progress into life." Efiar avid.*

From the side of the platform the sig wall slid open, showing a great new clear statue of the ites, upu mammals and pu animals that lost their lives and above in midair over them Neiliara hung suspended. The li (palest lilac), lu (lavender) and lae (lilac) were perfect for each individual and the silvery sheen covered them all like a veil. Everyone stood and clapped for the outstanding masterpiece shown to each of the ites of Eftiam. Neil and Jean could only show tears of joy in seeing the remarkable likeness of their daughter.

"Neil, it is such a perfect likeness of our Neiliara. Did you know of this?"

"No Wayne, we knew nothing of this. I wonder who did the sculpting."

"Efiari and I over saw the project. The sculptor requests anonymity." Efiar avi interrupted.

"Whoever it is, please thank them for us."

"I will be most happy to, Neil. I will see you later this dai, we have much to discuss," Efiar avid.

"Wayne, are you not tired of holding Jeniari?" Jean avid.

"A grandfather old I'm not yet, so leave us alone, huh kid, isn't that, right?" Wayne spoke and laughed heartily throwing Jeniari into the air,

"Soon this babe will avi and I will be giving him all the history I gave his Father and then more."

"The Imo Macos blessed us when they brought you to us," Jean avid.

"I too feel the same about me coming here. I only have te (one) regret, and that is I wasn't given privy to aving as the rest of you. You know like that tia in battle we all communicated with our niets (minds). It was te of the best things I've ever experienced." Wayne said.

"Do not doubt; the Imo Macos will return soon. I am sure they will honor your request. Te must be patient. Oh, and have you noticed you are starting to avi Eftiam language? Rather than wait for Wayne to avi reply, *"Come Let us all go to our din- sig, we have much to avi on. It has been a good while, since we enjoyed each other's company,"* Efiari avid. While in route of fuai to the din- sig, if one took tia to notice, the babes in arms all gave … catlike smiles ... aving amongst themselves,

"They are not aware." came from Efenavi, *"Do we want them to know?"*

"No, we have much to plan, besides this is fun," Jeniari gave avi commenting ... small giggles emanated from the babes throughout the tunnel.

"Tio ites land walk fuaing through the tunnel, ite te, "Did you avi that?"

"What?" avid ite tio … listens, "No?"

"I could have sworn I heard babies giggling here in the tunnel?"

"Sure …" ite tio laughs…

EFTIAM VOCABULARY

ASP(S): (Ā-SP) To death sleep. Aspid

APT(S): (Ā-PT) To sleep. Apting.

AVI(S): (Ā-VE) Wave messaging with the mind. Aving, Avid, Aviless.

BABUA: (BĀB-ŬĀ) Similar to a baboon animal of Earth.

CENTAR: (SÈṆT-ĀR) Miles.

COMPUS: (COM-PŪS) Computer.

DAI(S): (DA-I) Day(s).

DOLFIA(S): (DOL-F-E-AH) a fish of Eftiam similar to that of earth Dolphin.

EF(S): (Ĕ-F) Mate. Efing, Ef'd.

EVE DAI: (ĒVĒ DĀĒ) Evening.

EXP-AVING: (ĒXP-ĀV-ĬNG) Explain, Explaining.

FEVA: (FĔ-VAH) fever.

FIF: (F-Ĭ-F) the number five.

FIFTH(S): (F-Ĭ-F-TH) The number fifty.

FIFTHN: (F-Ĭ-F-THIN) The number fifteen.

FINITCH: (FĪN-Ĭ-CH) Fin of a fish, Tailfin.

FOR: (F-ŌR) The number four.

FUAI(S): (F-Ŭ-ĀI) Mobile by floating through the air. Fuaing, Fuaid.

FUNA/S: (FŬ-NAH/S) Funny, laugh or joke. Funaing.

GAML-LAV-GLOB-RAY: Laser gun more accurate. Worn inside clothing undetected.

GAML-HYDRO-GUN: (GĀM-Ā-HĪ-DRŌ) A form of plant organics and water made into a gun ray.

241

GAML-HAND: (GĀ-ML HĀ-ND) A device made of organics used to open walls to pass through.

GLOBA(S): (GLŌ-BĀH) Worlds.

HAVANA/S: Heaven/s.

HAVIS: (HA-VĬS) Clear head gear worn by Guide or Guides of Eftiam for protection.

HEILO: (HĒ-Ĭ-LŌ) Hello.

HOR(S): (H-ŌR) Hour.

HOS-SIG: (H-AW-S SĬG) A hospital domed room.

HUNTH: (HUN-TH) The number one hundred.

HYDRO-GRAM: (HĪ-DRO-GR-ĀM) A body transport by plant organic means and water, without the person being in the location of another.

HY-OXY-SIG: (HȲ-Ō-XȲ- S-ĬG) A protective bag with a mix of Eftiam oxygen and salt water to return the body to balance for survival.

HYDRO-PASSÈ: (HȲ-DRO PASS-È) vapor fumes left behind.

HYDRO-WEB-DEVICE: (HȲ-DRO-WÈB) Hand device hand held-pass through walls.

IMO(S): (Ĭ-MO) Image; such as a person.

IMO-GLAS: (ĬMŌ-GLAS) Mirror.

IMO MACO(S): (Ĭ-MO M-Ā-KO) Passed advising images.

IMO-MIRO: (Ĭ-MO MĬ-ROH) A video screen.

IMO-SHEAR: (ĭ-MO SH-ĒAR) Window.

ITE(S): (Ī-TE) Person or people.

JUNI(S): (J-ŬN-Ē) People of Eftiam, usually the working class of Eftiam.

KAMICH: (KĀ-MĬ-CH) Fish of Eftiam, similar to Earth Grouper.

KI: (K-Ē) To kill.

KNODG: (NĂ-D-G) Knowledge.

(LAH) The color of royal purple.

LAE: (LĀY) The color of lilac.

LARG: Large.

LI: (LĒĒ) The color of pale lavender.

LU: (LŎŎ) The color of lavender.

MACO(S): (MĀ-CO) Leader of Eftiam in death sleep.

METHO: (M-Ĕ-THO) Meditation, Information.

METHO- SIG: (M-Ĕ-THO – S-ĬG) The main meditation to speak with the Imo Macos.

MI: Minute.

MIN: (M-IN) One minute.

MINI(S): (MĬN-ĬS) Minutes.

MINST: MĬN-ST) First.

MINT-CHAM-SPRI: (MĬNT-KĀM-SPAH-RĒ) Mint Chamomile herb drink.

MON(S): (MŌ-N) Month.

MORN: (MŌR-N) Morning.

MORN DAI: (MŌR-N D-ĀĀ) Tomorrow morning.

NIET: (NĬ-ĔT) Mind.

NIET AVI AVI: (N-ĭ-ĔT Ā-VĔ Ă-VĔ) Communicate.

NIGH: (N-Ĭ-GH) Night.

NIGH-DAI: (N-ĭ-GH DĀĀ) Good night.

OPLATIC: (ŌP-LĀ-TĬC) Deepest purple diamond of Eftiam.

PASSÉ(S) DAI: (PĀSS-É DA-Ī) Yesterday.

PU: (PŬ) Jungle.

SIG: (S-ĬG) A dome room of an Eftiam home.

SIG-CARE: (S-ĬG-CĀ-RĒ) Mechanical ite serves responsibility of a house.

SIG-LAMPET: (SĬG-LĀM-PĔT) Bed lamp.

SIGMET: SĬG-MĔT) Second settled Earth planet.

SIMI: (SĬ-MĒ) Kiss; Simid.

SIOUT(S): (SĒ-AUT) Small aircraft of transport.

SIOUT-BUB: (SE-ĀUT-B-UB) A siout clear craft bubble nicknamed by the Earth/Sigmets.

SIOUTOUS: (SĒ -AUT-U/S) Large ship designed for space travel.

SIXT: (S-Ĭ-XT) The number sixty.

SPRI: (SP-RĒĒ) Drink.

SWIZ-YAH: (SW-Ĭ-Z-YĀH) Purple cheese, similar to swiss.

TE: (TĒ) The number one.

THANS: (THĂ -NZ) Thanks or thank you.

TIA(S): (TĬ-AH) Time.

TIA-DAI: Late.

TIN: (T-ĔĔ-N) The number ten.

TIO: (T-Ē-OH) The number two.

TIOD: (T-Ē-OHD) Second.

TIO-LETO: (TĬ-Ō-LĔ-TŌ) Twins.

TIX: (T-Ĭ-X) The number six.

TOR: (T-OR) The number four.

TRÈ: (TR-È) The number three.

TRE-PLETS: (TR-EE-PL-ĔTS) Triplets.

TRILI(S): (TR-Ĭ-LĪ) Century.

TRIAS: (TR-Ĭ-ĂS) Years.

TRĬ-OT(S): TRĬ-ĂT) The number thirty.

TVENT: (T-VĔNT) The number twenty.

TVELT: (T-VĔLT) The number twelve.

UN-APT(S): (ŬN-ĀPT) Awake(s).

UPU(S): (U-POO) Salt water, water, ocean.

UPUSUS: (U-POO-SŬ) Rains.

UPUDO(S): (U-POO-DŌH) Eftiam dress worn by Guides, tight fitting to waist, the blouses out like a flower tulip turned upside down.

UPU-HYDRO-GRAM(S): U-POO-HĪ-DRŌ-GRĀ-M) Visual telegram sent by the use of water and other organic matter.

VATOR: (VĀ-TOR) Elevator.

WEK/S: Week/s.

EARTH/SIGMET VOCABULARY

CAM-VIV: (CĀM-VĬV) Video Camera.

CAMO: (CĀM-Ŭ) Camouflage.

COMDAT(S): (COM-D-ĀT) Computer.

COM-MOV: (COM-MOOV) Movie.

COM-ROOM: (COM-ROOM) Main Deck.

COM-TECH: (COM-TĔ-K) Computer Science.

EFTIAMRS: (ĔF-T-M-RRS) Nickname for people of the Planet Eftiam.

SIGMET: (SĬG-MĔT) Founded planet by Earth, now part of Earth Planetary Habitats.

SCOUTBOT(S): (SK-ŌŬ-T-B-ŌT) Small craft, also referred to as a tender; holds a small number of People traveling from a large spacecraft to short destinations.

PLANET ORACE

HICTATAYA: (HĬK-TĀT-ĀY-Ā) Commander of ship.

PRIPA: (PRĒ-PĂH) Ship name.

www.ingramcontent.com/pod-product-compliance
Lightning Source LLC
Chambersburg PA
CBHW031121030726
47496CB00002BA/637